NEVER TOO LATE

MAXINE MORREY

NEVER TOO LATE

MAXINE MORREY

First published in Great Britain in 2025 by Boldwood Books Ltd.

Copyright © Maxine Morrey, 2025

Cover Design by Debbie Clement

Cover Images: Shutterstock

The moral right of Maxine Morrey to be identified as the author of this work has been asserted in accordance with the Copyright, Designs and Patents Act 1988.

All rights reserved. No part of this book may be reproduced in any form or by any electronic or mechanical means, including information storage and retrieval systems, without written permission from the author, except for the use of brief quotations in a book review. This book is a work of fiction and, except in the case of historical fact, any resemblance to actual persons, living or dead, is purely coincidental.

Every effort has been made to obtain the necessary permissions with reference to copyright material, both illustrative and quoted. We apologise for any omissions in this respect and will be pleased to make the appropriate acknowledgements in any future edition.

A CIP catalogue record for this book is available from the British Library.

Paperback ISBN 978-1-83751-148-8

Large Print ISBN 978-1-83751-149-5

Hardback ISBN 978-1-83751-147-1

Trade Paperback ISBN 978-1-80656-057-8

Ebook ISBN 978-1-83751-150-1

Kindle ISBN 978-1-83751-151-8

Audio CD ISBN 978-1-83751-142-6

MP3 CD ISBN 978-1-83751-143-3

Digital audio download ISBN 978-1-83751-145-7

This book is printed on certified sustainable paper. Boldwood Books is dedicated to putting sustainability at the heart of our business. For more information please visit https://www.boldwoodbooks.com/about-us/sustainability/

Boldwood Books Ltd, 23 Bowerdean Street, London, SW6 3TN

www.boldwoodbooks.com

To Rachel:
For Eric and everything else

To Raoul,
for life, and everything else.

1

Perspective is everything. When I was twenty, anyone aged fifty was old. Like, *really* old. I'm not being rude, but they were. That was how everyone our age saw them. Even when I hit thirty it still seemed like a world away.

Then one day, I woke up and there it was: FIFTY, in garish, flashing neon lights front and centre of my mind...

How the hell did that happen? Had I been in a coma? But nope, all the years were there. They'd just sped by at an unfathomable speed and although it felt like yesterday that I was holding a chubby, red-cheeked baby in my arms and wondering how on earth I was ever going to keep this tiny human alive – as well as will she *ever* stop crying – she was now a confident twenty-eight-year-old woman taking charge of the evening's activity, not to mention booking the entire five-star holiday to Goa.

There were various wrinkles, gravity wasn't always the kindest and the hormones had gone a bit rogue – although on that last point, what else is new? Haven't women been dealing with that particular joy in one form or another for most of our lives? Despite all this, I was, of course, grateful to have survived to see this age. Many, including some dear friends, hadn't, and so whingeing about it, when looked at from that perspective, was rather unseemly. Getting older is a privilege not bestowed on everyone so to receive that privilege was to be lucky. That said, I was still in some shock that this birthday had arrived a darn sight quicker than expected.

2

I slipped off my low-heeled sandals and took the young waitress's hand, doing my best not to crush it with a death grip, as I made my way down the steps into the warm water and gently sloshed towards the table. Wading through a hotel's ankle-deep water feature was certainly not where I'd thought I'd be having dinner on my fiftieth birthday. Then again, the past few decades had turned out very different from the plan I'd originally made for myself, so why should this be anything new?

'Isn't this great, Mum?' Sasha said, laughing as she followed me into the water, panning her camera around as she did so. Unlike me, my daughter didn't have a fistful of maxi dress in her hand. But unlike her, I didn't have young, toned and tanned legs, hence the maxi dress rather than the mini. Neither did I have her grace of a gazelle, or confidence of youth.

'Here we are, ma'am.' The young girl smiled and waited as we hopped up onto the bar chairs around our table. 'Is this fine?'

'Perfect, thanks.'

'Here are the drinks menus. I will be back shortly with the

food ones, or you can choose anything from the fresh grill here.' She indicated a space to our right where several open-air barbecues were being attended to by a number of white-hatted chefs.

Before the waitress could turn away, and without consulting the drinks menu, Sasha placed our order. 'We'll have a bottle of Veuve Cliquot, please. It's my mum's...' She wavered and caught my look. '...birthday!' she finished, wisely, without the addition of a specific number.

'Sasha,' I said quietly.

'You deserve it, Mum. No arguments.'

The waitress nodded with a wide smile and sloshed back off to fetch our order, the bottoms of her rolled-up uniform trousers catching the odd splash as she did so.

'Isn't this fun?' Sasha asked, moving her toes back and forth in the water.

'It's certainly different,' I replied.

When Sasha had seen the board earlier in the hotel advertising 'Dinner on the Water', she'd immediately said we had to do it. I would have been happy, and felt more at ease, with the hotel's actual restaurant but my daughter had always been one for trying new things, being spontaneous and doing her best to live life to the fullest. She reminded me of myself in that way. At least, a version of me that had once existed a long time ago but was now little more than a hazy and faded memory. These days, as demonstrated by my hesitancy in both the restaurant choice and the champagne, I erred more towards reservation and consideration in my decisions. Part of that came with becoming a mum – something, although unplanned at that particular point in time – that I wouldn't change for all the tea in Tesco's. The rest of it though? Who knew? But that other girl, the one who'd had all the plans, all the exciting adventures whizzing through her brain, the one who'd jump on the next train just to see where it went, she had faded into the distance when I'd boarded that plane home to England from Paris all those years ago.

3

'You OK, Mum?' Sasha's hand touched mine, jogging my thoughts back to the present.

'Oh! Yes, sorry. Miles away.'

'You sure you're OK? You looked...' She chewed her lip for a moment as she always did when she was thinking. 'Sad.'

'Oh, no, darling! I'm not sad at all. How could I be? I'm here, in this beautiful place with my favourite person in the whole world.'

With perfect timing, our food menus arrived along with two flutes and the bottle of champagne, deftly opened and poured by the waitress.

'Happy birthday, ma'am,' she said as she placed the bottle carefully in the crushed ice of the wine cooler another server had carried and positioned beside our table.

'Thank you.'

'To my gorgeous mum! Happy birthday!' Sash clinked my glass against hers.

'I'm not sure about that, but thank you. And I'd like to make another toast to having the best, most supportive, thoughtful, kind and beautiful daughter ever.'

'Being far less modest than you, I'll drink to that!'

She downed a good amount and I, a lot less used to drinking these days, took more sedate sips. It had taken me a lifetime to finally get to India and I was keen not to create a lasting memory of me flailing about in this water feature, rather than dining in it.

'I do know it's not ideal so soon after the divorce...' Sash began.

'Sasha, stop worrying. It might only be six months since it was all finalised but the marriage was over a long time before that. People get divorced all the time, sadly. At least your dad and me had an amicable split, which makes it easier, especially for your sake.'

'You're really OK with it? I mean...'

'Yes. To be honest, Tania, is that her name?'

Sasha nodded.

'Tania and he sound like they have a lot in common from what he's told me. We might be divorced but we're not enemies. I'm happy that he's happy.'

'I want you to be happy too, Mum.'

I leant forward and laid my hand on her cheek. 'I know you do, love. And I am.'

'I don't mean just right now. I mean...' She made a rolling motion with her hand. 'You know, going forward.'

'Everything is going to be fine, darling. Stop worrying. Now, what are you going to order?'

The locally caught fresh red snapper was cooked to perfection, as was the accompanying grilled tenderstem broccoli and hasselback potatoes. Sasha had gone for a 'dirty burger' which always failed to sound appetising to me but did, in fact, look delicious when it arrived along with fine-cut chips and a green salad. All of which my daughter demolished without breaking a sweat.

There were definitely things I missed about being her age – I've already mentioned the legs, but another had to be the excellent metabolism. It's hard not to see the unfairness of a woman's lot. Just when it feels like everything is going up the spout thanks to hormones, the powers that be also think it's a good jape to crank the metabolism speed dial down to 'slow'. So where once I could grab a morning croissant, sometimes two, a lunchtime meal with wine, and a not insubstantial supper without putting on a pound, now it seemed by merely looking at any of those, the calories superglued themselves to my waist by some weird menopausal osmosis. I'd thought about taking a look at that book, *French Women Don't Get Fat*, but in the end, I just cut out wine and chocolate and bread. I knew from my time in Paris that this wasn't what they did at all, but I'd done my best to avoid anything that reminded me of that part of my life and so, even though it was just a book, I didn't read it and kept to my strict, rather dull restrictions instead.

Sash was filming some B-roll for her vlog and I took the opportunity to soak in the atmosphere of this place I'd waited so long to see. The sun had long since sunk behind the horizon – I'd been amazed at how quickly it set in India, even though I'd read about it in my armchair travels. But there was some welcome warmth in the winter evening, so different from the dirty, chilly slush we'd left behind at Heathrow. I absentmindedly trailed my feet to and fro in the warm water beneath me as I people-watched – the chefs busy working away at the outdoor grills, the waiting staff moving about in an efficient but calm manner, and the laughter of other diners as they stepped down into the water and slowly sloshed over to their own tables.

'Another drink, Mum?' Sasha said, filming the empty bottle and glasses, already looking around for a server.

'That's enough for me, but you go ahead, darling.'

'Oh, come on, Mum. You have to. It's your birthday!'

'Many happy returns.' The voice was deep, educated and with that slight hint of Indian accent that I'd always found rather sexy.

'Oh!' I said, turning to acknowledge the expensively besuited man who'd spoken. 'Umm, thanks.' Thank God for the low lighting as I felt heat rush to my face.

He gave the smallest head tilt to the side in return as he smiled. 'I can't help noticing that your champagne glasses are empty.'

'We were just going to order some more,' Sasha informed him.

'Please. Allow me.' He glanced to his left and a waitress appeared as if from nowhere.

'Another bottle of champagne here, please.'

The girl nodded and hurried off.

'I hope you are enjoying your stay here in Goa?'

'Yes, very much so,' I replied when Sasha remained unusually quiet.

'You have been before?'

'No. No, I haven't.' Which is where I should have stopped. But I didn't. With a nervous jabber, I continued on. 'I've always wanted to visit India but my husband has a dicky tummy so never wanted to come.'

Inner Me was aghast. *Oh, God. What am I saying? And more to the point, why am I saying it? To a complete, and very handsome, stranger.*

'I see. That is a shame. I'm glad you have been able to come and visit now.'

'Thanks. Yes, never affected me. Stomach as strong as an ox.'

Shut up, Kitty!

I heard Sasha snigger and cough. I looked down at the water. Don't they say you can drown in two inches of water? This was at least a foot. Plenty surely and right now I was willing to try it rather than slowly dying of embarrassment.

'That's very good to hear,' the man continued.

I risked a look back up and saw the kind, open smile that extended to dark-brown eyes, framed by thick lashes. 'My name is Ashok.' He held out his hand and I shook it as I replied.

'Katherine. This is my daughter, Sasha.'

'Hi,' she said, shaking his hand much more confidently than I had. 'Are you eating alone?'

'I am. But it's not something I mind.'

'You should join us!'

'Sash...' Ashok looked about my age and I had no doubt what my daughter was up to.

'Do say you will! Mum's had a shit year and all she's got for company is me on her fiftieth birthday!'

I looked down at the water.

Make way! I'm going in!

'That's very kind, but you appear to have already eaten. Plus, I'm not sure your mother shares your enthusiasm.' Ashok spoke with easy humour, and no offence in his tone.

'Oh, no. Please don't think that. I just... I didn't want you to feel obligated.'

He appeared to study me for a moment. 'If you don't mind, then I think it would be very nice. But only if you are sure. The last thing I would want is to ruin your birthday dinner.'

'Great!' Sash replied, sliding off into the water. 'I'll grab another chair.'

'Let me do that,' Ashok said, turning and wading across to the table he was originally being led to. He lifted a chair and brought it back and Sasha and I scooted ours closer together so it was cosy but not unpleasant.

'I'm just going to find the waitress and ask to make it three glasses. Back in a sec!' With that, she scooted off through the water and disappeared round the corner.

'I—'

'I—'

We both started at the same time.

'Please, you go,' Ashok said, that easy smile loosening a few of the knots in my stomach.

Frankly, since Sasha had invited him to dine with us, it felt like a whole scout troop had started practising for their badges in there.

'No, it's fine. What were you going to say?'

'Please. You first, I insist.'

'Oh. Well, I was just going to apologise really. My daughter enjoys being spontaneous. I never know what she's going to do next.'

'She's a delight from what I've seen but if you would prefer it to be just her and you, I completely understand and we can say I had to take a call which lets us both off the hook without it affecting your daughter's generous offer.'

'Oh, no, please. It's not that.'

He did that head tilt again and the cordless light in the centre of the table highlighted the warmth in the deep brown eyes.

I dropped my head into my hands momentarily. 'I'm afraid I'm very much out of practice with socialising. The fact that I already gave you far more information than you could ever possibly have needed, or wanted, probably highlighted that rather well.'

'You and your husband do not socialise much?'

'*Ex*-husband,' Sasha filled in, a little too meaningfully, as she returned to the table.

'Ah. I am sorry.'

'Don't be,' I said truthfully. 'It's the best for everyone.'

'Dad's already got a new girlfriend.'

'Sasha. I'm sure Ashok isn't interested in any of that.'

I threw him an apologetic look and was saved by the appearance of the champagne.

'May I?' Ashok asked.

'Please.'

Having expertly filled our own glasses, he lifted his own for a toast.

'To Katherine, new adventures and new friends.'

I liked the sound of that. Admittedly, it also terrified me, but somewhere during the second bottle of champagne, I began to feel less inclined to worry about it all.

4

While Ashok ate his dinner, a paneer curry with rice that I made a mental note to order tomorrow, we ordered pudding. Sash requested the dark-chocolate bombe that melted under a cascade of hot caramel sauce the waiter poured with a theatrical hand and, for me, a yoghurt-based dessert called Shrikhand I'd discovered a taste for in the last couple of days. After that, we slid down from our chairs, Ashok gallantly assisting us both until we stepped back onto dry land, wiped our feet and put on our shoes.

'I'm going to order cocktails. You'll stay, won't you, Ashok?' Sasha asked, her hand on his arm.

'If you wish.'

'We do wish, don't we, Mum?'

Without waiting for an answer, she took off on her search for yet more alcohol, which wasn't a decision I was fully behind but with the whirlwind that was my daughter in charge, I did what I'd been doing ever since she'd planned the holiday – held on and hoped for the best. The world was already a little soft around the edges. It was a long time since I'd felt like that and it was really rather pleasant in the warmth of the still, Indian night. Pinpricks of stars shone in the sooty, velvet sky above and the tall, thin acacia trees in the landscaped garden stood elegantly at rest around us, their forms highlighted by strategically placed lights.

Ashok took a moment to roll down his trousers – impeccably cut, I'd noticed – which he'd managed to keep entirely dry. I, on the other hand, in my efforts to make sure that I didn't flash Ashok, or anyone else, too much thigh, had still managed to find a way to dip part of my hem in the water and was surreptitiously trying to wring it out without looking as unsophisticated as I felt.

'It's a wonderful idea, I think, the water dining, but it's not always the easiest to navigate, is it?'

Clearly, my actions weren't quite as surreptitious as I'd hoped.

'You seemed to have managed well,' I said, indicating his trousers.

'Practice.'

'You've been here before then?'

'Yes, quite a few times.'

'Are you here on holiday or for work?'

'Work.'

'It's really a beautiful hotel. Sash booked everything for our trip. She's very good at all that sort of thing.'

'She certainly has good taste.'

'I like to think so, but then I'm probably biased.'

'That's part of the job description for a mother from what I understand with my own.'

'I suppose that's true, yes.'

'You are here celebrating your birthday with your daughter, then? Have you had a good day?'

'Wonderful. Thank you. Sasha's really spoiled me. She bought me this.' I touched the cobalt-blue silk wrap I'd now draped across my chest and shoulders.

'It's very beautiful, and the colour suits you well.'

'Thank you,' I replied, knowing that he was right. Hugh had never had any colour sense and wasn't particularly interested in clothing. Or at least he wasn't until he'd got together with his new girlfriend. It hadn't bothered me particularly but I realised how much I'd missed the appreciation of clothing and style over the years. 'After breakfast, where I had a candle in my fruit salad, which I admit was a first,' I said, laughing, 'we spent several hours in the spa, getting a whole host of treatments. I feel thoroughly pampered.'

'As I'm sure you deserve.'

From some men, this might have sounded cheesy, or trite, or just plain creepy, but not here. And it wasn't just the champagne.

'So, how has your day been? Are you here on business alone?'

'I travelled alone, yes.'

'That's very cryptic,' I replied, smiling. My eyes drifted to his left hand. No wedding ring. But Hugh never wore one either so that didn't necessarily mean anything.

His laugh was easy, warm and rich. 'You're right. It did. In my head, it didn't sound that way. I meant that I travelled to this hotel alone but I've many colleagues here.'

'Oh! Am I stopping you joining them? Please don't—'

Ashok held up his hands. 'No, no. Not at all. This is a most pleasant evening.'

'It is, isn't it?' I agreed, then decided I'd definitely had enough to drink and that it was probably best if I got a glass of water next.

We sat in silence for a moment, looking out over the beautiful landscaping of the hotel gardens, candles flickering in ornate, silver storm lanterns on the tables of the terrace. Classical music played softly in the background and the low hum of conversation, cut through every so often with laughter, made for a peaceful, relaxing ambience. The silence between us wasn't awkward. Usually, I felt the need to fill the gap with words that, once I was home, I'd lie in bed and turn over in my head, regretting what I'd felt was idiotic babble. Something I'd demonstrated perfectly earlier, upon meeting Ashok. But now, sitting on an elegant, but comfortable, cream-coloured sofa in this idyllic place, I didn't feel that way. Clearly, Ashok didn't feel the need to fill the silence either. The last knot unfurled.

Sash strode into view and sat down heavily beside me, crossing her legs.

'Cocktails are on their way.'

Oh, crikey.

'And guess what? I found out something interesting about our new friend here while I was ordering.'

'About me?' Ashok asked, the easy smile in place.

'Oh?'

A small knot began wriggling its way back into place. On the other hand, Sasha was smiling so I grabbed on to the hope that that was a good sign.

'Yes.' She turned to me. 'Did you know that our friend here owns this place?'

I pushed myself up straighter, glancing across at Ashok.

'That's right,' Sash continued. 'This, and several others, apparently.'

'Is that true?' I asked.

'Guilty as charged.'

'Why didn't you say so? We might have said how awful the food was or... I don't know! I mean, it wasn't. Obviously! The food. Or any of it.' The calm silence evaporated as I twittered nervously on. 'But we might have done! How awkward that would have been!'

'Not at all. I'd have been glad to hear it. The only way a business can improve is through honest, considered feedback.'

'That's not really the point.'

A waitress bearing a silver tray with three cocktails and two bowls of nibbles appeared, placed all of them down carefully, checked if we wanted anything else, then retreated. Ashok waited until she had gone to reply.

'No, I suppose not but you were both so kind in inviting me to dinner. It would have entirely spoiled the fact that your generosity was out of pure kindness, not a sense of obligation, but also meant that I got to hear how much you genuinely loved the place. Had you known the position then you may instead have felt compelled to say those things and I wouldn't have known if it was true. But mostly, I think swanning in and saying, "Hi, I own the place," would make me sound, and feel – and excuse me for this, but you can blame English public-school education – a bit of an arsehole.'

I giggled. Which was most unlike me. The current me, anyway. Years ago, I'd giggle at anything. Not in a childish way – or perhaps it was childish? But in that wonderful way that kids do at the slightest thing because they have no inhibitions. No judgements. Somewhere along the way, I'd lost that ability.

Who was I kidding? It wasn't 'somewhere'. It was Paris. That inner child had been left that day years ago at the Gare du Nord in Paris, along with my heart.

A year later, I was pregnant and suddenly, there were lot more important things to do than giggle and laugh at the smallest thing that brought me joy. Sleep being one of them. Not that I saw much of that for a while.

'Mum?' Sasha's expression was half-amusement, half-surprise.

'Sorry. It's just...' I tailed off, suddenly aware that what I'd been about to say was likely going to make me look an idiot. That I could handle but I didn't want to embarrass my daughter.

'What?' she encouraged me on.

'Nothing. It was silly.' I glanced up through my lashes at Ashok, who seemed to be just as intrigued about my answer. 'It's just that you have such a lovely, plummy accent and when you said, "arsehole"...' *Oh, God. Now I'd said it out loud it sounded even worse.* I lowered my gaze, only to raise it again as Ashok laughed, deep and easily.

'My parents sent me to England to study and I came back with this accent. My old friends here still tease me relentlessly about it.'

'I think it's lovely. I didn't mean it as an insult.'

'I didn't think that for a moment. And I'm glad I could provide an opportunity for laughter after what I imagine has been a difficult time.' He took Sasha in his gaze too as he spoke. 'For both of you.'

'Mum's been amazing. I mean, she always is but some couples can get really nasty, can't they?' Sasha took a sip of her cocktail. 'Ooh! This is yum.'

'What did you order?' I asked, glad of the directional change in conversation.

'I asked the barman what he recommended and he said he'd make us something up. No idea what's in it but it tastes amazing! Try it!' She flapped her free hand to both of us. We obeyed. She was right. It was amazing.

'Wow!'

'Very good.'

'I reckon your barman needs a raise.'

'Sash,' I said quietly.

She shrugged and gave Ashok a grin, which he returned.

'You might be right,' he answered.

Sasha turned back to me, playful smugness written all over her features. 'See?'

'Thanks,' I teased our new friend. 'You do realise I'll never hear the end of this now.'

'Sorry,' he replied, not looking remotely like he meant it.

'I'm going to go and ask him what's in it,' Sasha said, pushing herself up again from the sofa.

'Tell him to name it and put it on the cocktail menu.'

She turned back. Are you serious?'

He gave a brief shrug. 'Why not?'

My daughter grinned, turned and hurried off back to the bar.

'She has a joyful soul,' Ashok remarked, looking the way she had gone.

'Yes, she does. She always has done; even as a baby, she was almost always smiling. Almost.' I gave him a meaningful look. 'I've been so lucky.'

'From what I see, she feels the same.'

'Do you have children?'

He shook his head. 'Much to my mother's disgust, I'm afraid. Luckily, I'm still her favourite son.'

'Ah!' I grinned. 'How many brothers do you have?'

'None.' His laugh was warm and infectious. 'But three sisters so I have enough nieces and nephews to make up for it.'

I took another sip from the delicious cocktail and placed it down on a coaster on the glass side table next to me.

'Do you live here? I mean, in the hotel? Or are you just visiting?'

'Visiting. I'm very hands on with my businesses. I find that's important so I like to drop in and meet with the staff, listen to any concerns or ideas they have, etc.'

'How long have you been in the hotel industry?'

'About twenty years now.'

'You obviously enjoy it.'

'I enjoy seeing other people enjoy it. But I also want the

people I employ to be happy. I'm sure that sounds like a cheesy line but I really do believe that if your staff are happy, then most of your problems are already solved.'

'That's very enlightened.'

'It makes sense to me.'

'So what did you do before you built your hotel empire?'

Ashok laughed. 'Hardly an empire.'

'Yet,' I teased.

He paused. 'Yet,' he replied with a broad smile. 'I was a corporate lawyer before this.'

'Ah. Not too much opportunity for dinner with your feet in the water there.'

'Not much opportunity for dinner full stop unless it was billable.' The handsome features momentarily took on a look of strain. 'I hated it but my parents worked hard to pay for me to get a good education; I owed them.'

'But surely if you were unhappy…'

'I didn't tell them. As far as they were concerned, I was living the dream. I graduated in the top 1 per cent of my class at Cambridge, was scooped up by one of the top law firms in the city and then two years later was headhunted by a firm in New York. My apartment had a view of Central Park and I wore four thousand dollar suits every day.'

'Wow. The shiny, polished surface was perfect…'

'Exactly. But beneath all that, I was miserable. I barely slept, my diet was appalling and exercise was almost non-existent.'

It was hard not to notice that something must have changed as the impeccably tailored clothes he wore now only enhanced that Ashok apparently kept himself in pretty good shape.

'So what happened?'

'My parents came to visit. I'd planned a couple of days off but at the last minute, my leave got cancelled. I was so mad.' A shadow dimmed the smile behind his eyes. 'I'd barely seen my family since I'd started work and then that happened. I tried to keep it together, brush it off, but they weren't buying for a moment.'

'It's hard to hide things from people who know you well and care about you.'

'Exactly. They didn't say much but I think the fact that they were finally there after such a long time of not seeing them and me feeling so frustrated that I couldn't spend time with them put it all into perspective. Yes, I was earning a fortune, I had a great apartment and, from the outside, a fabulous lifestyle but I wasn't actually getting to enjoy any of it and certainly not with the people that meant the most to me. There was no balance. It was all work and no life.' He lifted his hands. 'What was the point?'

'So what happened?'

'I handed in my notice, sold my apartment and moved back to India.' He smiled ruefully. 'Some would say that was rather a backward step.'

'Some should mind their own business.'

Ashok laughed. 'That is very true.'

'So how did you go from being a lawyer to being a hotel mogul?'

There it was again, that deep, velvety laugh. I was far from ready for any relationship, especially with a man who lived thousands of miles away, although... I looked around. There were definitely worse places to live, especially when I thought of the cold, grubby slush that was apparently still adorning the pavements of home right now. But something in his easy laugh, the relaxed body language, the simple enjoyment of a meal and easy connection sparked something deep in my soul. Something I'd thought had long since shrivelled and crumbled away into dust. The woman I used to be.

My phone pinged and I checked the message as Ashok called over a waitress and ordered some coffees and then checked his own phone.

> Met some people at the bar and chatting. You OK? Xx

Sasha's text made me smile. How the tables turn as you get older. Now it was the child checking on the parent.

> I'm fine. You carry on xx

She sent me a kissy face and I turned back to Ashok.

'Let's hear it then,' I said, smiling at the waitress as she brought a large cafetière and placed it, along with two fine bone china cups and saucers, on the table in front of us.

'Would you like me to prepare the coffee?' she asked, a little shyly. Clearly, she knew who he was.

'I'll do it, thanks,' he said.

She gave a little nod and hurried off. He leant forward and slowly pressed the plunger down before pouring the coffees and launching into his tale.

5

'I worked in hospitality during school holidays and all through university,' Ashok explained. 'It can be tough. Unsociable hours, poor working conditions, getting the brunt of an unhappy customer's ire because they don't agree with the hotel or restaurant's policy, something that you, of course, had no control over.'

'I can imagine.'

'But I also saw the other side. The joy of people finally getting a longed-for holiday, taking time together. At times, you could practically see the stress evaporating from them. When I came back to India, I spent some much-needed time with my family and travelling, seeing old friends. It was a conversation with one of those, an off-hand comment really, that got me thinking. Someone he knew through business dealings needed to offload some assets, including this hotel.'

'And you decided to buy it?'

'Yep! I just thought, why not?'

'That's as good a reason as any.'

'Exactly!' he said, raising a hand in agreement. 'Obviously, my family thought I was going from the frying pan into the fire but if there was one thing I'd learned from my time as a lawyer, it was about setting boundaries. Both for me and other people.'

'Not as easy as all that, is it?' I replied, thinking of all the times I'd said yes to school functions, PTA duties, school trip accompaniment requests, dinner hosting for my ex's colleagues. I'd smiled and nodded and said yes to everything when all the while, inside I was screaming that I didn't want to. But gradually, the inside voice had got quieter and quieter until eventually, it had faded away. At least I thought it had. But that flicker of life I'd felt, that hint of something earlier... maybe it meant that perhaps the old me, the girl I was, was still in there somewhere.

She'd been a girl who had known what she wanted. She'd set boundaries when they suited her but never said no if she meant yes, or yes if she meant no. For her, life was out there to be explored, to be discovered, to be lived! And she had lived – until she had loved and lost. And that one loss had led to so many others.

From the corner of my eye, I saw Sash sitting at the bar, laughing with the barman and a small group of others her age. I felt the same surge in my heart I always got whenever I saw her happy. Nearly thirty years later and it still hadn't faded. For all the life that I had planned but didn't live, I could never regret it because without that broken heart and those shattered dreams, I wouldn't have Sasha. And she was worth everything.

Sipping my drink, I let my gaze travel, letting it rest momentarily on the woodland of acacias that abounded the outdoor pool and lounge area. From there, my eyes drifted to the palms, their architectural palmate leaves reaching out, dark and glossy. Dotted about, adding height to the design, their trunks wrapped with soft white fairy lights, were tall, thin banana palms. And all around, large bushes, the name of which I had yet to discover, were smothered in tiny, white flowers that almost glowed in the low light. During the day when Sash and I sat by the pool, I'd watch as dragonflies buzzed past, their jewel-bright colours flashing in the Indian sun as huge butterflies flapped from plant to plant, resting and feeding as they made their way around the beautifully landscaped garden.

Ashok had mentioned he had insisted on including lots of pollinator-friendly plants in the redesign of the gardens, not only for colour but with an ecological awareness that, from what he had said, wasn't always shown in his country, but something he hoped would only increase.

My gaze now travelled back to the pool bar, as apparently so had my companion's.

'She has made some friends by the looks of it,' Ashok said, following my eyeline

'She always does,' I said, smiling over at him. 'People gravitate to her. Her father is an academic and very singular and, well, then there's me. So I really don't know where she gets it from.'

'Do you not?'

I understood his meaning. 'You're very kind but it's definitely not from me.'

'I think you do yourself an injustice.'

'I think you're trying to sway me to write an excellent Tripadvisor review,' I said, laughing. 'Don't worry. It was already going to be glowing.'

He did that slight head dip to the side again. 'That is wonderful to hear but not why I said it. It was a true compliment. Even in the short time I've known you, I believe you are far more like your daughter than you think you are.'

I glanced over again just as Sash looked back. Her smile widened and she gave a wave, then held her thumb up as she tilted her head in question. I returned the same gesture.

'Ever get the feeling you're being set up?' I asked, picking up my coffee with a grin.

'I did wonder.'

'Sorry about that. She's impulsive. For all she and I knew, you could be married with five children.'

'While I'm flattered that your daughter thinks I'm worthy of her mother's attention, I get the feeling that the last thing on your mind right now is another relationship.'

I let out a sigh, returning the cup to the table, its marble top cut into the shape of a lotus flower.

'Is that selfish?'

Ashok shook his head. 'Not at all. I was in a long relationship that I once thought would result in marriage. It didn't and it took me a long time after that to realise that jumping straight back into the dating scene wasn't what I needed, despite everyone telling me the opposite. What I actually needed was space and time.'

'That's it exactly. Space and time. You're very wise, you know that?'

Oh, God, that was absolutely my last drink. When was this coffee going to kick in? I used to be able to drink everyone else under the table. What happened?

Several intervening decades and a lack of practice, my brain filled in helpfully.

'Would you like another coffee, perhaps make it Irish this time?' He glanced over to where Sasha had now been absorbed into the group. 'As friends.'

Yes to friends. Absolutely not to more alcohol.

'Both would be lovely, thank you.'

6

Ouch! I squinted as I pulled back the heavy brocade sea-blue blackout curtains in my room. Did someone turn up the sun? Was it having a solar flare? Sliding my feet into the hotel slippers and my arms into the soft robe, I opened the door to my room in the junior suite that Sasha had scored on a last-minute deal.

As a side note, if you're one of those people who goes into posh hotels and can leave the robe hanging with its belt tidily knotted and the slippers untouched and pristine in their paper wrapping, then I don't think we can be friends.

Sasha was sitting on the sofa out on the balcony, legs tucked up underneath her, head in a book.

'Morning.'

She looked up. 'Morning! Did you have a nice evening?'

'Yes, thanks. Although don't think either of us missed your not-so-subtle trick of leaving us together.'

'I don't know what you mean.' Her tone was innocence itself but the grin she sported told the truth. 'Are you seeing him again?'

'Hmm. Not in the way you had planned, no, but as friends, yes. How was your evening?'

'Great, actually.' She shuffled up so I could sit next to her and leant over to kiss me on the cheek. 'It wasn't really a plan to leave you two alone but you did seem to be getting along.'

'He's a nice man but I'm not ready for anything else and, even if he was interested, which I'm not convinced of, he understands that. Did you make some friends?'

'Yes. They were here checking out the place for a wedding venue and we got chatting when I was at the bar. They both come from Goa so wanted to get married here but would you believe they live in London, a couple of streets away from the flat.'

'Really? That's amazing.'

'I know! Small world, eh? Anyway, we're going to meet up when we're all back.'

'Sounds great. And what else?'

Sasha looked up. 'What do you mean?'

'You've got that look on your face. There's obviously something else. You always squidge your nose up and rub it when there's something you want to say but don't want to.'

'Do I?' she asked, sounding genuinely surprised.

'Yep. So spit it out.'

'Apparently, there's a really cool club that's just opened about half an hour away. They asked if I wanted to go tonight.'

'OK.'

She tipped up an eyebrow. 'Now you're the one looking like you want to say something else.'

I took her hand. 'I just want you to be safe, darling. I know you're a grown woman and capable of your own decisions, but you have just met these people. Are you sure?'

Sasha picked up her phone and checked the time. 'I thought

that's what you'd say, so we're meeting them for breakfast in twenty minutes.'

My laughter was a little raspy thanks to a combination of a late night and alcohol, and me having become unfamiliar with more than a glass these days, but it felt good to laugh with my girl. So what if this life wasn't the one that I thought I'd be leading? Sometimes, mistakes can become your greatest blessing.

'And what did they say when you said you had to ask your mum?'

'They're Indian so totally got it!'

I stood up from the sofa, adjusting the robe. 'I'd better have a shower and get a shifty on then. Anything particular you think I should wear?'

Sash frowned. 'No, why?' She stared at me for a moment. 'Oh my God. You do the scrunchy nose thing too!'

'Do I?'

'Yes! How have I not noticed that before? That's so funny.' She stood, placing her book to the side. 'What is it, Mum?'

'I... I don't want to embarrass you.'

'Embarrass me?'

'Yes. I... I know I've got a bit in a rut with clothes and I'm probably not the most stylish fifty-year-old out there. I don't want—'

'Mum. Stop. You have never, and will never, embarrass me. I love you and your dress sense is fine. Don't worry.'

I wrapped my arms around my daughter. 'It used to be so much more than fine.'

'I know,' she said, pulling back a little. 'Until you had me.'

'Oh, my darling!' I took her face in my hands. 'It wasn't you. It was me. I could have still rocked a look if I'd chosen to.' I did a little wiggle but her expression remained serious.

'If you're not happy with your wardrobe, you know you can change it, right?'

'Oh, Sash. I wouldn't know where to start these days, my love.'

'I do. And we will. It'll be fun!'

I had no doubt that it would be. Although whether I had the confidence to change my look after so many years was another thing completely.

'Now,' Sasha continued, 'in the meantime, we've got to be downstairs in twelve minutes so why don't you jump in the shower and I'll pick something out for you.'

'One less decision. That sounds like a very good plan.'

'Excellent.' Sasha hooked her arm through mine and we headed back to my room.

My daughter's new friends were intelligent, fun, and a delight to have breakfast with. Vikram was a consultant neurologist at King's College, London, his fiancée, Mira, was a lecturer at London School of Economics and the third, Alaria, the sister of the bride-to-be, was a high-end events planner. They told me about the new club they wanted to check out as Alaria was considering it as a possibility for future events.

'You should come!' she said suddenly.

I gulped my tea a little more forcefully than planned and my eyes watered as the hot liquid made its way down my throat.

'Are you OK?' Vikram began to rise from his seat.

I waved him back down. 'Perfectly fine, thank you. Although I'm afraid I will have to turn down your offer of the club. My clubbing days are far behind me.'

'Nonsense,' Alaria declared. 'You must come!'

I turned to Sasha, who was nodding enthusiastically. From the corner of my eye, I saw Ashok approaching. He raised a hand in greeting as he did so.

'Good morning, I hope you are all enjoying your breakfasts.'

'It's wonderful, as always,' I replied, the others adding their own agreement and compliments.

'Excellent. I'm glad to hear it.'

'Could I ask if you know anything about Sevens?' Alaria asked, clearly fully informed as to who this man was.

'The new club?'

'Yes. Have you heard any feedback from any of your guests?'

'Not personally, but I can ask my events manager and get her to update you on anything she knows, if that's of use.'

'That would be great, thank you so much.'

'You're very welcome.' He gave a little nod. 'So what are your plans today?'

'We're heading to the beach,' Vikram said. 'Sash, do you want to come?'

'Mum and I are going to have a chill-out day by the pool then head back to the spa today, but I'll see you tonight for the club. Are you going to come, Mum?'

'No, I don't think so. It's very kind of you all to invite me but I fear I would feel very out of place.'

'Not at all.' Alaria waved her hand and the silver bangles on her wrist tinkled together.

I shook my head at Ashok, smiling at their enthusiasm.

He bent down and, behind a hand, stage whispered to me, 'Could I offer you an alternative option of dinner this evening so that you can bow out politely?'

The others exchanged amused glances but I looked at Sash.

'Do you mind?'

'Of course not, Mum. I'd rather you had company if you don't want to come with us.'

'Oh, goodness, that makes me sound terribly sad!'

'Nooo!' She threw her arms around me. 'I don't mean like that. But this is our holiday. Together.'

'And we will be together all day,' I said, reaching for her hand.

'You'll be ready for a break by this evening, you'll be so sick of me.'

'Never,' she said, squeezing my hand.

'Aww, that's so sweet,' Mira said, taking Vikram's hand. 'I hope our kids are that close with us.'

He took her hand and kissed the back of it. 'How could they not be? We're amazing! They'll be lucky to have us.'

'And obviously I will be their favourite auntie.'

'Obviously,' her sister confirmed before Alaria turned back to us. 'So that's settled. Let's meet here for dinner at seven and then we'll get a taxi to the club.' It was easy to see she was a natural at her job.

'I'll arrange a car for you to take there and back.'

All four began to protest but Ashok held up a hand.

'It is not a debate. This way, both Katherine and I know that you are getting there and back safely. During the middle part, you have to take care of each other, OK?'

'OK,' they repeated.

He'd clearly had plenty of adulting practice as an uncle to his many nieces and nephews.

'Meet you at seven in the atrium?' he asked, turning to me.

'Perfect.' I tried not to think of the slight awkwardness of having dinner with Ashok while Sash and her friends were sitting in the same restaurant but at least I wasn't going to feel like a fifth and rather worn-out wheel on their night out.

7

Several hours later, I'd spent one of the laziest days I could remember and then been scrubbed, rubbed and steamed to within an inch of my life.

'When was the last time you did this, Mum?' Sasha asked as we flip-flopped back to our room, wrapped in the fluffy robes, our skin glowing.

'Spent hours doing nothing and then been pampered? I'm not sure I've ever done this. It all still feels a little self-indulgent if I'm honest.'

'And what's wrong with that?' Sasha asked as we stepped inside the lift.

What *was* wrong with that?

'I... I don't know. I suppose I'm just not used to it. It wasn't really a thing that people did as much when I was growing up.' I put a hand to my freshly exfoliated face. 'Oh, God, that makes me sound ancient.'

Sasha slid her arm through mine and pulled me close. 'Not at all. Lots of attitudes have changed in a relatively short time.'

'That's true. I don't know. It just wasn't a thing for everyday women to go and get their nails done every week or two, etc. If people did that, you tended to think of them as being more ladies of luxury.'

'You need to start looking after yourself more now, Mum.'

'Oh, crikey, is it that bad?' I stole a glance in the mirrored interior of the lift as we stepped out into the corridor.

'No! I don't mean it like that. I mean it's your time now. You don't have to worry about Dad or me any more.'

'Darling,' I said as I held the key card against the room door. 'It doesn't matter how old you are, I am always going to worry about you.'

'OK, but the rest of it.'

'Yes, I know.' And she was right. No more keeping the house perfect in case Hugh decided to bring home a colleague for dinner at the last minute to discuss the latest dissertation subjects, most of which went over my head. No more researching recipes for his latest health fad. No more living a life that revolved around others.

'You OK? You look miles away.'

'I'm fine, love, I might just have a lie down if that's all right with you? All this pampering is exhausting!'

'I'm going to do the same.' She leant in and gave me a big squeeze. 'That was so fun. Let's make it a thing. Getting a facial together, or our nails, or whatever. A regular thing, yeah?'

'That sounds lovely, Sash. I'd really like that.'

'Promise?'

'Promise.'

'Love you, Mum.'

'Love you, too.' I kissed her temple as I'd done since she was a baby. 'Have a good nap.'

'And you. See you in a bit.'

I closed the door and hung the robe on the back of the door. It had felt rather licentious heading down to the spa, knowing that I'd only had my pants on beneath. In the lift, I'd voiced the thought to Sash, who'd just laughed and flashed me which had set me giggling too, a distant memory in a dusty corner of my mind lighting up of a girl who, years ago, would have done the same thing. The girl who'd lived in Paris, and being slim and lightly endowed, abandoned wearing a bra as many of the women there did. My initial English hesitance about – oh, the scandal – a hint of nipple very soon dissipated as I fell into the natural way of things in my adopted city, the city I'd fallen in love with. The city where I'd fallen in love.

Poor Hugh. It wasn't his fault. And I had loved him. We'd loved each other. Not in the 'throw all caution to the wind', world-spinning way I'd loved before, but right then, that was all for the better. The other way had split my heart into shards and I never wanted to feel that again. So when I'd run away from Paris, there was Hugh. A friend who, over the course of the following year, gradually and unintentionally became something more. And then, even more unexpectedly, became a father and our lives changed forever.

8

About five to seven, I looked up to see Ashok approaching. I closed my Kindle, and slipped it into my bag as I stood.

'Good book?'

'Yes, thanks. You look very dapper.'

Dapper?

'Well, thank you,' he said, grinning, 'I actually feel quite dapper. Definitely not a word that's used as much as it should be.'

I let out a half-nervous, half-relieved laugh. 'I've no idea where that came from. I'm not sure I've ever called anyone dapper in my life before.'

'Then I'm honoured to be the first.' He did a little bow then offered his arm. 'Ready for dinner?'

'Absolutely.'

I made to step in the direction of the hotel's dining room but Ashok turned the opposite way towards the exit.

'Oh!'

'I thought we'd go somewhere different, if that's all right? I wasn't sure if you might feel a little awkward having dinner with me, even as friends,' his eyes crinkled as he smiled, 'when your daughter and the others were also eating in the same restaurant.'

I glanced up at him. 'That'd be great, thanks, Ashok.'

'Excellent,' he returned and we walked out towards the darkness of the evening.

'I've been thinking today about those fake relationships that you see in books and films...'

'What about them?'

'I'm just wondering whether that might be a route to getting my family off my back about still not having found The One.' His expression was one of amusement and playfulness and I felt once more how glad I was that we were able to be just friends. And, in fact, such good friends already. Connections didn't have to be romantic to fit'. Sometimes, it just worked.

'If such a thing even exists?'

Ashok looked quizzical.

'That might have come out wrong. I just meant, is there such a thing as The One? If you're lucky enough to find The One but then lose them for whatever reason, does that mean you'll never be happy again? That's rather sad, don't you think?'

'True. Who knows? But I do have to say, my mother would love you.'

'I'm going to take that as a compliment.'

'Please do. She's never liked any of my girlfriends!'

'Perhaps your mother just has exceptional taste?'

'Oh, without question. She was absolutely right on all of them. Now, how do you feel about going to the best restaurant in Goa?'

'I feel great about it. Although the food here has been so good, it's going to take some beating.'

'Ah, a compliment and a challenge in the same sentence. I knew I liked you. Challenge accepted. I'll let you into a secret, I'm trying to poach the head chef for a hotel I've just bought in Europe.'

'Oh, really? Does he, or she, know?'

'She does.'

'And?' I asked as we walked out from the cool marble interior of the atrium to the warm, sultry Indian evening, my wrap now over my arm, unrequired away from the hotel's air conditioning. A sleek, midnight-blue Mercedes drew up alongside us. The driver's door opened and a young, uniformed staff member got out, a broad smile on his face, and handed the keys to Ashok. The smile widened as he received a tip which, knowing Ashok and how he felt about his staff, and his naturally munificent nature, would have been generous. Another staff member approached to open the door for me, but Ashok politely signalled he was not needed and opened the door himself before walking back around to the driver's side, sliding in behind the wheel, clicking his seatbelt into place and pulling smoothly away.

The cabin smelled of a mixture of leather, new car and the subtle undertones of Ashok's aftershave. A slight breeze rippled the leaves of the acacia trees lining the road that led from the hotel towards the nearby village as we wound our way along it. I looked out of the window and smiled.

'What are you smiling at?'

'That I'm here. Finally here in India.'

'Hopefully, it will be the first of many visits.'

I turned back. 'You know, I think it might be. So, tell me more about this hotel in Europe and why you want this particular chef to head up the kitchen for it.'

'I want her because I feel she has an ideal mix of innovation, traditional skills and the right personality to lead a creative team. The current one is excellent but I already know he's been poached for a hotel in Malaysia. I want the restaurant to become a destination in itself as well as being in one of the best hotels in France.'

'Ah, France.'

'Yes. Paris.'

'Paris!' It came out on a sigh. 'How wonderful. If she doesn't want it, I'll take it. Aside from the skills, innovation and a fondness for cooking, I'd be perfect!'

'Is that so?' Ashok replied, echoing my laughter. 'Then I'll bear you in mind. It's probably only fair to warn her that she has competition, though.'

'Oh, yes. Definitely.'

He stopped at a turning, checked for traffic and pulled onto another, rather bumpy road.

'So is Paris somewhere that's been on your "to visit" list, like India, or is it a previous love?'

His words were casual but as he glanced over with the question, Ashok's sharp senses picked up something I'd apparently let show in an unguarded, unexpected moment.

'I see,' he said, meeting my eyes as I lifted my gaze. 'Then perhaps we can talk about that over dinner. If you want to.'

And, oddly, I found that I did. Here, in this wonderful, far-flung place with a man I hardly knew but felt more comfortable with than many of the acquaintances I had at home, suddenly I wanted to tell him all. To unpack the whole thing after it had been shut away for so very long in a dark, but never quite forgotten, part of my mind.

'You might regret asking that.'

'No, I don't think I will.'

9

Ashok insisted on driving us to the airport. During the two weeks that we had stayed at his beautiful hotel, he had taken all the time he could to visit and take Sash and me, and whomever of her new friends wanted to come, to see places that the average tourist, including us, would have missed.

It was wonderful to see this incredible country through the eyes of someone who knew, and loved, it so well. Last night, Ashok and I had dined on a rooftop terrace restaurant, surrounded by the heady scent of jasmine and spices, and the evening had already been stored carefully and forever in the compartment of my brain labelled *Treasured Memories*.

'Sounds so romantic!' Sash had grinned when I'd got back and met her down by the poolside bar where she was spending time with her new friends before we left early in the morning.

'It was. But it wasn't,' I'd answered, kissed her good night and hugged the others before heading back to the room, setting two alarms plus a reception phone call before collapsing into the downy softness of possibly the most comfortable bed I had ever slept in. It was one of many reasons I was sorry to be leaving in the morning.

* * *

'Thanks for everything,' Sasha said as she hugged Ashok tight.

'You're most welcome.' He returned the hug and something inside me was sad that he'd never become a father. It was easy to see he'd have been a fantastic one.

'I'll go and see which desk it is, Mum,' she said, grabbing the handle of her case and striding off into the cool air of the airport.

'Tactful.'

'Always,' I replied. 'Actually, no, not always but that's another story.'

'One I hope I get to hear.' He took my hand. 'These last two weeks have been some of my happiest. Spending time with you, and Sasha and the others. It's been fun.' He looked away for a moment. 'Sometimes, as adults, we forget about the simple pleasure of just having fun, don't we?'

'Easily done,' I replied. 'There's always something more important than "fun" on the to-do list, it seems.'

'And yet what could be more important in life than remembering to enjoy it?'

'You're quite the sage when you want to be, aren't you?'

He smiled. 'With that in mind...'

'Uh oh. Am I going to like this?'

'I don't know. But I think you should consider it anyway.'

'OK...'

'I think you should go back to Paris.'

I half-turned away, unintentionally dropping his hand in the process. 'I couldn't. Not now.'

Ashok gently turned me back towards him. 'You could. And

you should. I know you had your heart broken there but you also fell in love.'

'I don't understand.'

'You fell in love with Paris long before you fell in love with anything, or anyone else. And Paris didn't break your heart.'

'It was such a long time ago, Ashok.'

'And yet, when you told me about it that night, it was clear that you still love it, even after all that time.'

'There's a difference between nostalgia and love.'

'There is. Nostalgia doesn't light up a person like love does. Like you lit up when you told me about Paris.'

I dropped my head, studying the vibrant coral varnish on my toenails that the salon had painted the day before.

'Just think about it,' he said, bending his knees to make eye contact with my lowered gaze.

'I'll think about it.'

His smile returned, but there was a tinge of sadness behind it. I knew he doubted that I would follow his advice, and he was probably right.

'Don't take this the wrong way but I'm glad this...' I made a motion with my hand, flapping gently between us.

Without further explanation, he knew. 'I agree. It would be wonderful to meet someone but it's not the right time for you. Not in a romantic sense. But I think it was the perfect time for us both to meet a wonderful friend whom I'm hoping will be lifelong.'

'And now I'm crying,' I said, wrapping my arms around him, and feeling his own tighten around me.

'Happy tears,' he spoke softly. 'That's all I ever wish you to cry.'

I gave him a whack. 'Stop being so bloody nice!'

The rumble of laughter in his chest made me smile. It felt like

I'd smiled and laughed more in the last two weeks than I had in years. Ashok and his friendship had been an unexpected and wonderful part of that.

I pulled back. 'I'll message you when we're home.'

'Please.'

'And let me know next time you're coming to London.'

'Unless you're in Paris.'

Smiling, I shook my head, looking up at him. 'Unless I'm in Paris.'

He leant in, kissed my cheek. 'Now go and find your bloody plane before it takes off without you.'

I gave him another quick squeeze then grabbed the handle of the bright-pink suitcase Sasha had bought me as a present for this trip and headed in the same direction as Sasha had gone, waving one last time before the doors closed.

10

'Paris? Really?' Sasha sat heavily on the sofa in the flat I rented at the end of the Jubilee line when we sold the family home in Surrey. This way, I was within easy reach of Sasha and also of the museums in London.

'It's just a thought at the moment.'

'But obviously one you're taking seriously.'

I gave a sort of shrug and sat down next to her. 'Maybe.'

'Wow. I mean... if that's what you want, then, of course. I just... from what you've said...' She rubbed her temple with her ring finger like she always did when she was figuring something out. 'Whenever I asked about it, you've never said a lot. But you've also never shown any interest in going back to visit. Like ever.'

'I know. And you're right. I didn't think I would.'

'Mum?'

'Yes?'

'You didn't just get homesick, did you? In Paris, I mean.' She straightened and looked at me, my own special mix of blue with hazel reflected back in hers. 'I've never really pushed it because, honestly, it's always felt like you didn't want to talk about it, but from the bits you have said, the photos I've seen, it looked like you were living the dream and absolutely loving it.'

I took her hand. 'I was. And I'm sorry you never felt that you could ask more. I should have told you a long time ago.'

Her hands flew to her mouth, eyes opening wide in a mixture of panic and shock. 'OhmyGod! Is Dad not my dad?'

'Yes!'

Her eyes widened even more.

'I mean, no!'

'What?' she squeaked.

I took a breath. 'Your dad is very much your dad. In every way, including biologically.'

'OK. OK.' Sash moved her hands down to her chest and her breathing began to regulate again. 'Sorry. I mean, I know this is about you but when you said…'

'It's fine. I'm sorry I scared you.'

With the ability of the young, she waved it off, already well on the way to recovery. 'So what is it you need to tell me?'

'I don't *need* to tell you anything. But I'd *like* to tell you about Paris. All of it. If you want.'

'Really?' A tentative but wide smile broke on her face.

'Maybe then you'll understand.'

She frowned briefly but kept the questions to herself for the moment. I knew that my curious, intelligent daughter would have many for me later and where once that would have filled me with dread and stress, I found that now, after pouring everything out to Ashok after so many years of keeping it all buried inside, it no longer did. Another chapter of my life had recently ended and now perhaps it was time to go back and revisit the previous one that had been cut short so long ago.

'Shall we order a takeaway?'

Sash was already picking up her phone. 'What do you fancy?'

'French.'

* * *

'And you never heard from him again?' Sash asked as she poured a glass of the white wine she'd brought with her earlier.

'Nope. Although, of course, back then there wasn't all the different methods of communication like there are now. No social media and mobiles were still ridiculously expensive so we didn't all have one like today. You either had someone's landline and/or their address but that was pretty much it.'

'And did he have either of those?'

I shook my head. 'There hadn't been any need at the time. He knew I lived on the south coast but that was about it, as far as I can remember. We both thought we had plenty of time for all that. He knew my address and phone number in Paris and that was enough.'

'So, what happened exactly? Why did you leave?'

I let out a sigh. 'I met his parents.'

'Oh! So you got to the "meet the parents" stage?'

'No, not really. We hadn't even thought about anything like that. We were just young, enjoying ourselves, thinking we had all the time in the world. But then his parents turned up in Paris unexpectedly. Tomas cancelled the plans we had that day, and to be honest, I didn't think anything of it.'

Sasha took a sip of the wine and tucked her feet up underneath her, watching me.

'The next day, he called and said that his parents wanted to meet me and had booked a table for that evening at what I knew was quite a swanky restaurant. Naively, I thought this was all rather exciting. I was a bit nervous, obviously, but it wasn't until I spoke to Gabby, Tomas's sister, who was a good friend.' I paused for a moment as I thought of her, sadness clouding the memory. 'My best friend, actually. It was talking to her that gave me the inkling that something was up.'

'Oh? What did she say?'

'It was more what she didn't, really. She offered to come round and help me choose what to wear. I was pretty confident in those days but it was still "Meeting the Parents". When Gabs arrived, she was dressed very soberly, which was unusual for her. Did I tell you we were studying fashion together there?'

Sash shook her head.

'Right, sorry. That's how I'd met Tomas. He was a few years older than us but he and Gabby were close so he often came along when we got together. He'd taken a few years off from studying to travel and was now at university too, studying business. Anyway, after flicking through my wardrobe and apparently coming up empty, Gabs pulled out a very conservative, knee-length, black dress from her bag.' I caught a glance at my daughter. 'I know what you're thinking, that sounds exactly like something I'd wear, and you're right. It is now, but back then, I was far more adventurous. In lots of ways.'

'Oh, God, too much info, Mum!' she cried, putting her hands over her ears as she laughed.

'Not like that.' I batted her gently. 'Although...' I placed my finger on my chin in a thoughtful manner.

'Mum!'

I gave her a wink. 'Anyway! I wore what Gabby suggested and we went together to the restaurant to meet Tomas and his parents.'

'He didn't come to pick you up?'

'No, which was also strange. He was always such a gentleman about things like that. I was a bit miffed, to be honest. I asked Gabby about it and she just did one of those Gallic shrugs that sometimes said everything and other times, nothing at all. I think in this case, it was a bit of both.'

'So what happened when you got to the restaurant?'

'Tomas kissed me on the cheek, which was weird for a start. He was so subdued, and dressed in a suit, which I'd never seen him in. His style was far more casual and artistic. Although, I have to say, he looked good!'

'Do you have any photos?'

'No. Not now.' I shook my head, feeling the sadness wash around me. 'I tore up every single one we'd taken together and sent the pieces back to him. Probably a little dramatic but I had been living in Paris for a while by then so...'

'Picked up a little dramatic flair?'

'Apparently. Do you really want to hear all this? It was all such a long time ago.'

'I do, Mum. Really. It was obviously something, and someone, important to you. I want to know it all, especially if you're thinking of going back.'

'I wouldn't be going back for him. That's all past now.'

'Did you keep in touch with his sister?'

'Gabby? No. And that's my biggest regret. We were such good friends, the best, and I know she wanted to. *I* wanted to. But at the time, I just couldn't. When I saw her, spoke to her, all I could think of was Tomas, which probably made me a horrible friend. She said she understood but I know she was terribly hurt.'

'It sounds like it was a difficult situation for both of you and she was stuck in the middle between her brother and you.'

'She really was.'

'So what happened at the restaurant? With his parents, I mean.'

My mind flew back through the decades to that awful evening. Tomas next to me one side, Gabby the other and their parents opposite, scrutinising me.

11

'So, you are studying fashion?' His mother was smiling but it didn't reach her eyes which were cold as she watched me. It felt like all that was needed to complete the scene was a spotlight pointed at me.

'Yes, I mean *oui*.' My reply was stilted and I tripped over my words. The confident young woman I usually was appeared to have scuttled out of the restaurant, replaced with an unsure, insecure version that I didn't like. And yet I could do nothing to switch back.

'We can speak English,' Madame Bertholle said, with a gracious wave of her hand, as though granting a nobleman reprieve from the guillotine.

'Kitty's French is exceptional, Maman.' Gabby's hand squeezed mine under the table.

I didn't return the gesture. My mind was full of confusion. Why was my friend defending me to her parents while my boyfriend, the confident, charming, charismatic man I'd fallen in love with, sat mute the other side of me, his own hands folded neatly on his lap? He'd barely spoken or even looked at me since I arrived.

'I'm sure,' their mother had replied, continuing in English anyway. 'So, fashion? Yes?'

'Yes,' I said again. 'Like Gabby.' This time, I did squeeze her hand, returning the smile she sent me before we both looked back at her mother, who was no longer smiling.

'Yes. Well. We did try to persuade Gabrielle to study something more worthwhile, but...' She made a 'poof' sound. 'She is so stubborn.'

'I'm right here, Maman.' Gabby's cheeks flushed with frustration and embarrassment. Hurt and annoyance for both my friend and myself ignited something within me.

'You don't think fashion is worth studying?' I asked. 'Despite the incredible history it has here in Paris?'

'Fashion is a hobby, not a profession,' Madame Bertholle replied in a manner that suggested that was the end of the discussion. 'Hubert and I have told my daughter this time after time, haven't we, Hubert?' She turned to her husband. He opened his mouth to speak but his wife answered for him. '*Exactement.*'

I looked to Tomas. I didn't need defending, neither did his sister, but it would have been nice if he'd considered it. His eyes were cast down, the hand that ordinarily held mine practically all the time we were together fiddled with the butter knife.

'Tomas. Leave that alone,' his mother snapped.

His hand shot back down and refolded around the other one on his lap. Who was this man? Who were these people? Reducing their children to shadows of their normal selves.

'But, Madame Bertholle, do you not think that Coco Chanel and Christian Dior would have disagreed with your views on their profession?'

'Kitty.' Tomas finally spoke.

I turned and met his eyes, saw the tiny warning shake of his head. He was not only *not* backing me up, but actually telling me to be quiet. I didn't work my arse off to get this placement to have my choice, not to mention my best friend's, dismissed like it was nothing. Of course, I'd hoped that Tomas's parents would like me, but it was obvious that they'd already made up their minds before I'd even walked through the door. This was the reason for their sudden appearance in Paris. Me. Not only didn't I pass, but the man I loved, the man I thought loved me, wasn't prepared to fight for me.

Tears threatened in my eyes but I pushed them back down. I wouldn't let them, or him, see me cry.

'That was a very long time ago, dear.'

I swallowed. 'True. But the brands are still among the most well known in the world, in any field. It's a trillion-dollar industry.'

Madame Bertholle cocked one thin, dark eyebrow, exchanging a look with her husband before fixing her gaze on her son.

'Kitty is accurate. It's an enormous machine of industry,' Hubert spoke and gave me the faintest smile.

Madame Bertholle continued as though he hadn't spoken.

'Tomas, you didn't mention your friend was so...' The pause lengthened... 'Chatty,' she finished eventually.

Still he said nothing. It was like sitting next to a different person. I'd thought we'd known everything about each other. But right now, it felt like it had all been a show. That everything he'd shown me, told me, said to me, was fraudulent. Here, now, was the true Tomas. And I barely recognised him.

'As I'm sure you know, our family owns a large vineyard close to the Champagne region.'

'Yes,' I returned politely.

'As I'm sure you also know – Gabrielle, take your elbow off the table.'

Gabby stiffened and snatched her arm back as though she'd been burned.

'As I said, our family owns a large vineyard. Tomas will be stepping in when he finishes his business degree and will eventually take over the running of it.'

'Is that true?' I turned to Tomas. 'You never mentioned that to me. I thought you wanted to be an artist? That you were doing the business degree so that you knew how to manage the financial side of your own business, not your family's.'

'Oh, for goodness' sake, Tomas.'

'I... I just meant in my spare time,' he said. 'The art stuff.' Finally, he met my eyes. But it wasn't the laughing blue gaze I'd fallen in love with.

'But that's not what you said, Tomas.' I wasn't about to be made a fool of, any more than his mother was already trying to make me.

'You must have misunderstood,' he replied, his eyes locking onto mine, a flash of anger momentarily causing a spark of light to dance in them – the first I'd seen all night.

'You're right, Tomas, perhaps I have, but not about this.' I felt Gabby stiffen beside me as I continued. 'If I remember correctly, you said that you had never been interested in taking over the vineyard and that what you really wanted was to paint.'

From the corner of my eye, I saw his parents exchange looks.

'Then you don't remember correctly,' Tomas replied.

His eyes were shuttered and his mouth a thin line. All the charming, handsome openness his face usually held was gone, replaced with granite-cold looks. Suddenly, he looked much more like his mother.

I dipped my head. I would not cry here. Everything I thought I knew about Tomas had disintegrated in front of my eyes but I was not going to let him or his mother see that pain. I'd thought I'd known him. He'd told me he loved me. I closed my eyes. How stupid of me. I'd fallen for it all, I'd fallen for him but he'd clearly just been saying whatever it was he thought I'd wanted to hear and I'd believed it. But here, now. Here was the man he really was. Under his mother's thumb. God! Gabby had more balls than him! She was the one who'd complimented my French to her mother, defended her friend, while Tomas sat there, silent.

I turned to face her. 'I have to go.'

She nodded almost imperceptibly, tears shining in her eyes. Clearly, her brother had fooled her too about his feelings for me. I knew she wouldn't have let me fall in love with him if she'd doubted his sincerity.

'You're leaving?' Madame Bertholle broke the silence, a hint of surprise in her tone. 'But we've yet to order.'

'Madame Bertholle,' I addressed her in French. 'I may be young, but I'm not stupid. It's clear you invited me here to vet me and decide if I'm good enough for your son. I think it is obvious to everyone that you've already made a decision, therefore I won't waste any more of your and, more importantly, my time.' I stood from the table, forcing a coolness onto my features as I looked at Tomas for the last time. 'And the truth is, today has helped me discover that actually, he's not good enough for me. Enjoy your meal.'

Try not to choke.

I kissed Gabby on the cheeks, picked up my clutch bag and strode confidently out of the restaurant. The summer heat had been building all week. Today, the thick, moisture-laden clouds had blanketed the city all day. As I walked quickly in my sensible shoes back to my tiny rented flat, cool, fat raindrops began to fall, bouncing off the pavements, releasing the scent of petrichor as it fell upon the parched earth and finally, I released the tears and pain, the sky's tears mixing with my own.

12

'When I got back to my room, I tore up all the photos and ephemera we'd collected together, stuffed the pieces in an envelope and posted them back to him.'

'Oh, Mum.' Sash wrapped her arms around me. 'I'm so sorry.'

I held her close. 'It's all right, darling. It was a long time ago now. I was young. As Mr Bennet says in *Pride and Prejudice*, it probably did me good to have my heart broken.'

Her brow rumpled. 'I always thought that was a mean thing to say to his daughter.'

'Yes, well. We both know he had a lot of shortcomings as a father. Unlike your own.' I placed my hand against her cheek. 'It was painful at the time but if I hadn't left after my course finished, then I wouldn't have got together with your dad and had you.'

'But you haven't been happy for a long time, have you?' She took my hand, touching the ruby ring that had been my grandmother's. 'I mean, before you split up. It was more circumstance than real love, wasn't it?'

'Oh, Sash. No. Well, yes. In a way, it was circumstance and

perhaps if things had been different then I wouldn't have gone out with him. He was different. Quiet. But so kind. And I did love him. And him me. And we still care very much about each other even now. We might not have had a particularly eventful marriage but we were happy for a long time.'

'But would you have got married if it hadn't been for me?' She looked up and I saw tears in her eyes. 'I just feel like me coming along made you both settle for something that you wouldn't have chosen for yourselves.'

I took her face between my hands, my throat thick now with emotion. That night in Paris had changed me in a lot of ways. Despite the show I'd put on for the Bertholles, my confidence was shattered. I withdrew into myself, finished my course and returned to England with my heart and dreams in tatters.

'Sasha. You're right. Perhaps life wouldn't have brought us together if I'd stayed longer in Paris. But the reality is it did. And yes, I left that dream, that man, behind. But, oh, my darling, I got a much, much better dream. I got you. Nothing could top that. Ever.'

'But when you had me, you lost yourself.' Sash sat back and wiped her nose on the back of her hand. Automatically, I leant over and offered her a box of tissues. She snuffled her thanks through a tissue and blew her nose.

'What do you mean, love? That I lost myself.'

She took another tissue and wiped her eyes. 'Listening to you talk about your time in Paris, it just shows up all your plans, how...' she waved her hands as she searched for the right word, just as she'd done since a tot. '...alive you were. How vibrant.'

I tried not to be wounded.

'Oh, Mum. Don't look like that.' She wrapped both her arms around one of mine. 'I think you're amazing. You know that.'

I let out a sound that was half-huff, half-laugh. 'It's OK. I think we both know I'm not terribly vibrant these days.'

To be honest, I couldn't remember the last time I'd felt remotely so. Talking about my time in Paris had felt like I was describing a different life. A different girl.

'She's still in there, you know?' Sash nudged me.

'Who?'

'That girl,' she replied, as though reading my mind.

This time, I did laugh. 'Oh, I don't think so.'

Sasha didn't laugh. 'I do. I know she is.' She took a deep breath. 'And I think it's about time you went back to Paris and found her. Look.' Sash grabbed my tablet from the table and switched it on, putting in my passcode.

'I didn't know you knew that.'

She flicked me a glance, rolled her eyes and went back to her task.

'Come on, let's look at some flats in Paris.'

'Flats?'

'Yes. That's what you meant when you said about going back, isn't it? To stay for a while?'

'I...' *Had I?*

She waited.

'I don't know really.' I tried again. 'I'm not sure I'd got that far. I was probably thinking a week or so.'

I got another eye roll. 'Mum. This is your time. Dad's off doing his thing. You've got a good settlement with the divorce and house money and those investments that matured last year. Why not use some of it to go back to Paris and do it properly?'

A thrill chased through my body. And let's face it, it was a long time since that had happened either! However, it was immediately followed by Inner Me, clomping along in terribly sensible shoes, chasing it down and squashing it flat. It was ridiculous to even consider. I was far too old for such silliness!

'Oh, no.'

'What?' I asked. 'I didn't say anything.'

'No. But you've got that look.'

'What look?'

'The one you get when you're about to tell me why what I've suggested or asked to do is a bad idea. Like when I wanted to go to the festival with Carly.'

'You were fifteen.'

'Her dad was going.'

'Her father had even less sense than any of you. And, if I'm not mistaken, Carly ended up in hospital after a reaction to taking drugs some stranger gave her.'

'Not the point,' Sasha mumbled, having clearly forgotten that bit.

'*Exactly* the point. It wasn't a good idea.'

'Fine. Then don't take any pills strangers give you.' She grinned.

'Very funny.'

'Oh, come on, Mum. What is there to lose?'

'What would I do?'

Sash smiled at me. 'Whatever you wanted. Now before you jet off to Paris, I think we ought to go and get our nails done, like we said we would on holiday.'

13

I lay in bed that night with a highlight reel from the evening running on a loop through my mind, preventing me from sleep. Although who am I kidding? Since the menopausal years had hit, sleep and I had had a somewhat turbulent relationship. But Sash's words were still echoing in my brain.

Whatever you wanted.

The next morning, as I checked I had my keys and opened the front door, it was to find Sash standing there, tears streaming down her face.

'Whatever's the matter?' I asked, pulling her close, but she stepped back, a smile breaking on her face along with the still-streaming tears. She reached into her oversized canvas tote and pulled out a metal plaque.

'I got it!' she said, half-laughter, half-choked tears. 'I got my Silver Play Button, my YouTube 100,000-subscribers plaque! It came this morning.'

'Oh! Oh, Sash! That's wonderful!' I pulled her back in for the hug. 'Oh, darling, I'm so proud of you! Congratulations!' My tears joined hers and neither of us cared about the mess our make-up was now in.

Hugh and I had made no secret of the fact that we had both had concerns when our daughter had given up a well-paid job in marketing to focus on her lifestyle YouTube channel, but our first priority was her being happy and it was easy to see the enthusiasm and passion she had for creating content.

To help alleviate our worries, she made a business plan and sat us down to look it over. Unbeknownst to us, she had been squirrelling away a good portion of her day-job salary with a view to being able to fund a career break from the corporate world while she threw all her time and energy into her passion project. Without taking into account the money that she was earning from her channel, funds she only touched to put back into that business, she had enough to live off for six months. She promised that if she didn't hit her financial and business goals by the end of the six months' break she'd budgeted for, then she'd go back to Corporate Land and take another marketing contract. Obviously, she was an adult and could, and possibly would, have done it anyway but knowing she had our support made it an easier, and happier, decision.

And now, with the extra hours Sasha had been able to dedicate to her channel, she'd hit both targets in under half that time and her numbers were only rising.

'Sorry, were you on your way out?' she asked as she peered in my hallway mirror and swiped the smudged mascara away.

'Yes, but that's OK. Are you free?'

'Yep. Why?'

'I'm taking myself out for lunch. Want to come?'

'Yes!'

As we strolled along the pavement on the way to the Tube station, the thin, watery winter sunshine casting half-hearted shadows of skeletal trees lining the avenue, Sash linked her arm through mine.

'You know, I'm liking this new you, Mum. Not that I didn't love the old one too.'

'Less of the old, thank you.'

'You know what I mean.' She squeezed my arm. I returned it and we began chatting about where to go for lunch.

We returned from London several hours later, having taken advantage of the weather to take a walk down the Embankment, gazing over every now and then at the familiar sights of Tower Bridge, its blue-painted iron matching the sky, and then a little further along the looming edifice of the White Tower, more popularly known to the many tourists as the Tower of London.

People bustled along in suits, in jeans, and two Buddhist monks, in their bright-orange robes. London was always interesting. Sasha had filmed much of our day, as usual. I'd always requested that I not be included as much as possible and she had respected those wishes. In a way, I wished I felt more confident in myself to be included on the odd time she asked. But I couldn't. I didn't like having my photo taken these days and in videos, I felt I looked older than I was, and rather frumpy. I didn't know exactly how or when that had happened but I know The Girl From Paris would have been horrified. As would Gabby, if she had known. Assuming she even still remembered me. But then, if Gabby had still been in my life, it wouldn't have happened. I knew that. She wouldn't have let it. On the days that I let myself, I still missed my friend so very much.

That night, Sash and I were sitting on my sofa, feet up on the ottoman, narrowing down choices of Airbnb flats for me to rent in Paris for the six months I'd decided to spend there. We were down to two. One was modern, purpose-built; the other was a conversion of a large period property, now split into six flats.

'Which one are you thinking?' Sash asked.

'The modern one is a useful location, and has all the mod cons.'

She nodded. 'True. But that's not what I asked, Mum.'

I touched the picture of the other one: its shuttered windows, the wrought-iron balconies in front, flower baskets attached to them, red pelargoniums spilling out and contrasting with the black of the iron.

'Obviously, it won't look like this now. That must have been taken in the summer.'

'And yet it's still calling to you, isn't it?'

I shook my head. 'I think I'm too old for things to be "calling to me".'

Sash let out a groan. 'God, Mum!'

'What?'

'You're fifty, not five hundred! That's nothing these days.'

I stayed silent. It certainly felt like something on the days when I looked in the mirror and wondered where the hell the time had gone.

'Book it,' she said.

My finger hovered near the key on the laptop.

'But what if...' I trailed off.

Sasha looked at me, waiting for me to finish but my mind was already tumbling.

What if...

A smile crept on to my face. My hand shook as I pressed the button. Sash let out a squeal of excitement.

What the hell if!

'Oh my God! You're going to live in Paris!' Sasha sounded even more excited than me. 'That is so cool!'

'Come with me!' I said, taking her hands. Immediately, I let go and shook my head. 'Sorry. No, I shouldn't have asked that.'

'Why not?'

'Because it's not fair. You have friends, and a life here. A job.'

'Mum. It's only Paris, not the moon. And, right now, my job is being a YouTuber. I can do that anywhere. I mean, just the thought of the content I could make in Paris... Argh!' She squidged her whole body in excitement.

'Are you sure?'

'Mum. I've been dying to ask you if I could tag along but I didn't want to get in your way. I mean, this is something you need to do for you. Ghosts you need to put to rest and all that. Plus, I wouldn't want to cramp your style.'

'Oh, darling. Why didn't you say something?'

'See above?'

'I'd be so thrilled if you wanted to come. The apartment has two bedrooms anyway and we can each do our own thing so we're not in living in the other's pocket. But only if you're absolutely sure.'

'Mum, I'm sure. I'm literally going to start packing the minute I get back.'

'What about your flat here?'

'Jenny's been dropping hints that her sister is looking for a flat share in London. This way, I get to jump before I'm pushed.'

'You didn't tell me that was going on.'

She shrugged. 'No need. Dealt with now anyway.'

I opened my mouth to speak but Sasha carried on.

'Look, Mum. I know you can do this on your own. You're amazing. I know you don't believe that but I do. I know it. And hopefully, this move, even if it's temporary, will help you see that too.'

'I'm not taking you if you're going to keep making me cry,' I said, pulling Sash in for a hug. 'Thank you,' I whispered.

'Oh my God!' she squealed as we sat back. 'We're going to live in Paris! Are you calling Dad?' she asked as I picked up my phone from the coffee table.

'No.' I pressed the contact name, then speaker. 'Ashok. This is all his fault.'

'Isn't it like three in the morning in India?'

'He's in Spain this week, scoping out that new hotel he's got his eye on.'

'Evening,' the accented voice drifted down the line.

'How's the hotel?'

'Good. They're trying to play hardball, though.'

'Ah. They don't realise they're up against a pro,' I said, laughter in my voice although I knew my statement to be true.

'Exactly,' he replied, amusement lacing his words. 'But on to more interesting topics. How are you?'

'I'm fine, thanks. Sash is here too.'

'Hi, Ashok!' she called.

'Hi, Sash. How's you?'

'Good, thanks.'

'Have you seen the gang lately?' Ashok had taken to calling Vikram, Mira and Alaria 'The Gang' when we were in Goa and were as pleased as we were that they'd all kept in touch. Especially as Vikram and Mira had booked their wedding at his hotel next year.

'Last night, actually. We went to a new bar that had opened but it was a bit naff really. Not much atmosphere and super overpriced. Not sure it'll last long.'

'That's a shame.'

'It was fine.' She shrugged it off. 'We got awesome pizza from a street vendor and went off to a pub that we know really well.'

'Ah. I'm glad to hear it.'

'I'm going to shoot off now, but Mum's got some exciting news for you.'

'Indeed? I'm very intrigued. Lovely to speak to you, Sasha.'

'And you! Bye!'

'Hang on a tic, Ashok,' I said and quickly hugged my daughter goodbye, telling her I'd call her tomorrow about arrangements to tell her dad. 'OK, I'm back.'

'Good! The suspense is killing me. What's this news?'

'I took your advice.'

'Ah. I'm glad someone listens to me. Which bit exactly?'

'I'm going back to Paris.'

14

'Paris?' Hugh repeated, looking between us across the restaurant table. 'Both of you?'

'Yes, Dad.'

'Why?'

'Because "Paris is always a good idea"?' Sash returned, throwing me a smile as she quoted the line from *Sabrina*. Her natural and very welcome joie de vivre had been a godsend these past few weeks whenever I felt the beginning of a wobble beginning to surface about my decision. I watched her latest YouTube video announcing to her followers that she was moving to Paris for six months, excitement radiating through the screen. As she had told them, we didn't have definite plans yet, but if they had any ideas of places they wanted her to go, eat at and see, then to put them in the comments below the video. I scrolled through after I'd watched it, reading the suggestions as well as the good wishes and her followers' own excitement at this new chapter.

'I thought you were all done with that,' Hugh said, turning to me.

'With what?'

'All that Paris nonsense.'

'Dad!'

'It's fine, Sash.' Hugh and I had managed to keep the divorce pretty amicable but there were moments my ex did raise my hackles. Like now. I turned back to face him. 'It's not nonsense, Hugh. It wasn't nonsense then either. Let's remember that I haven't judged you on your choices.' I let that sit a moment. The fact that his girlfriend was twenty years his junior had surprised me a little but other than that, if she made him happy then that was all that mattered. Sasha, on the other hand was, understandably, still having trouble getting her head around the fact her dad was dating someone only a few years older than her.

But if he was going to be snarky about my decision, there was ammunition there enough to launch at least a warning shot across the bows. Such as the fact that they went to Glastonbury last year, for example. And that he'd paid for it all, according to Sash. This was a man who felt six people at dinner was a crowd. But that had been his choice and Paris was mine.

'No. No, of course not. Obviously, I didn't mean it like that.'

Can anyone say backpedal?

'No, I didn't think you did.' I tried not to smile.

'So? When are you leaving?'

'Saturday.'

'Oh. So soon?'

'We arranged it all several weeks ago but you were travelling in the Andes and out of contact.'

'Oh. Yes. Yes, I see. Of course.'

Hugh and the girlfriend had recently trekked to Machu Pichu as part of an overland hike, with 'wild camping', whatever that meant. I'd once suggested a glamping weekend at a luxurious-looking place in the Cotswolds. Hugh's reaction had been more akin to suggesting he parade through Bourton-on-the-Water in his underpants and mortar board. But then I wasn't thirty-one with perky boobs and a backside you could bounce coins off, so there was that.

'Did you enjoy the trip?' I asked. Hugh had always had a slim frame but he looked thinner than I'd ever seen him and although his comment had irked me, I'd spent a long time married to him, and had loved him. It was hard to turn concern for someone off like a light switch when you closed the door on a marriage. At least it was for me.

'Marvellous. Yes. Absolutely. Incredible sights.' The words rushed out.

'You always were shit at lying, Hugh.'

Sasha's head snapped towards me.

My ex held my gaze for a moment, his body tense before he went soft and dropped his head momentarily. When he looked up again, a hint of smile played around his lips.

'Oh, God, Katherine. It was bloody awful!'

'Camping not really your thing?'

'No. As I'm sure you already knew.'

'As did you.'

He gave a small nod. 'The views and monuments were spectacular. I can't deny that.'

'I'm sure you enjoyed the opportunity to learn more about the region and its history.'

'Absolutely fascinating!' he said, his face coming alive as it always did when he gained new knowledge. Hugh had an insatiable thirst for learning. It didn't matter what it was about. When I'd discovered I was pregnant with Sasha, he'd thoroughly researched how it was possible, bearing in mind I'd been on the pill at the time. I'd advised him that that particular aspect was moot now and he'd moved on to more useful fact harvesting.

By the time Sash was born, there wasn't a book on babies that

Hugh hadn't read and made copious notes on, including the intricacies of the birth, which he was looking forward to finding out more about during my delivery. That particular part had, however, remained mere theory as he'd passed out within seconds of the first sign of blood. But as young parents, his thirst for knowledge had, when tempered, been inordinately helpful in us navigating our way.

'I've never felt so bloody ill in my life. Honestly, I thought I'd contracted bloody dysentery!'

'Dad!' Sash's face flushed as the couple on the next table looked over, horrified.

Hugh and I burst out laughing. Ageing could be a bitch but the one thing it did have going for it was that you cared a lot less about what others thought.

'I thought you looked thinner.'

'I lost nearly two stone through my arse!'

My snorts of laughter did nothing to lessen my daughter's embarrassment but on the plus side, the tension of earlier was now well and truly broken.

'I'm on probiotics, fermented food and all the rest of it, trying to get my stomach to talk to me again.'

'I'm sorry you didn't have the best time.'

'Are you?' he asked with a smile.

'Yes. I am,' I replied, honestly. 'I'm not surprised, if that's what you're getting at, but I am sorry.'

'I should have listened to you when you reminded me about the glamping thing.'

'People change.'

'I don't.'

I raised my eyebrows a little. He'd always been a bit snooty about men who went off with younger women to 'pander to their ego'.

'OK. Point taken. But not about bloody camping. I've told Tania that's it now. If she wants to do anything else in that line, she'll have to go on her own or with a friend. I'm afraid I value my creature comforts far too much.'

'How did that go down?'

'Better than expected. To be honest, she was pretty embarrassed about me having to stop every five minutes and find a convenient rock to disappear behind so...' He shrugged.

'I'm not surprised,' Sash spoke.

'It could have happened to anyone, Sash,' I said, defending her dad.

'I know.' She shrugged. 'Just...' She gave a shiver. 'I'd have been mortified if it was my boyfriend. Ugh. It sounds so weird describing you as someone's boyfriend, Dad.'

'To be honest, it feels weird being described as such.'

'If you care about someone and they're in distress or ill, you don't, and shouldn't, give a damn about what other people might be thinking, Sash.'

As I'd never been able to get Hugh to agree to my much longed-for trip to India in all the time we'd been married, due to his 'dodgy tum', I'd been pretty miffed when Hugh had told me of his plan to conquer the Andes with his nubile girlfriend. However, events appeared to have shown that he'd been right to be concerned. Although I would have been sensible enough to stick to the hotel food, as we had in Goa, despite how appealing some of the street food had been. But eating street food in South America apparently did more for Tania's TikTok likes.

'You looked like you were having a great time,' Sash said.

'Shows you shouldn't always believe everything you see on social media,' her dad replied with a wry grin. Hugh had always shown a distaste for social media and, wisely enough, worried about the implications of it when everyone else was lauding it as the new messiah. Although, of course, he made an exception for Sash's YouTube and accompanying Instagram, he was still constantly reminding her to be cautious and keep herself safe. Seeing him grinning out of a social media post that wasn't his daughter's had been very odd when Sash forwarded me a picture her friend had sent on to her. Having been married to him for nearly three decades, I, however, had immediately seen the tension in his eyes, the way his jaw was rigid. To the world viewing the picture, he was living the dream with his young girlfriend, striking out on new adventures in exotic places. But to the person that knew him best, it was clear he was miserable.

Sasha was about to reply when her phone rang. She glanced at it, ready to ignore as she generally did when she was with us, but her finger hovered over the button.

'It's a brand I really want to work with. Do you mind if I take it?'

'Not at all.' I nodded at the phone. 'Good luck.'

She blew me a kiss and answered as she pushed her chair away from the table and walked towards the door. Hugh watched her go.

'Our daughter, the entrepreneur.' Pride shone in his eyes as he turned back to face me. 'We did good, Katherine.'

'We did.' I took a sip of my wine. 'Are you sure you're OK now? Healthwise, I mean.'

Hugh nodded. 'Yeah. On the road to recovery.' He shook his head. 'Stupid bloody idea, really. I don't know what I was thinking.'

'I do,' I replied as I replaced my glass on the table, laughter in my words.

He looked at me for a moment before his own laughter bubbled out. 'Fair point. But oh, God, Katherine. It was amazing to see the places but what I wouldn't have given for a comfy armchair in my study with a fire in the grate, a whiskey in one hand and a book in the other.'

'That does sound more like you. But, as I said, people can change.'

'I don't want to change, though. That's the thing. I'm quite happy with all that. I've just described my perfect evening.'

I screwed my nose up. 'What are you going to do?'

'I don't know. She's a great girl and we do have fun together. I think it's something we'll have to have a discussion about sooner rather than later.'

'I hope it works out for you.'

'Thanks. From anyone else I'd have thought was sarcasm but not you.'

'We're too old to play silly games like that, Hugh, don't you think?'

'I don't know about being too old. Fifty is the new thirty and all that. But I do agree about the games. You never were one to play games. It was one of the many things I loved about you. People know where they stand with you. Although I do think sometimes those same people walked over you.' He dipped his head. 'And when I look back, I'm ashamed to say that I likely did the same at times. I took you for granted far too often and I'm sorry for that.'

'Water under the bridge. It was up to me to stand up for myself a bit more.'

'You were a little firecracker when I first met you at school.'

'Yes, I suppose I was. I was going to conquer the world!' I said, laughter in my voice, but even I could hear the note of sadness in it.

'You could have done too.'

'Maybe.'

'No maybe about it. You were fierce!' He pulled a face. 'Is that the right word? It changes so often, I can't keep up!'

'I literally have no idea but I like the sound of it so let's go with that.'

He clinked his sparkling water against my wine and we drank to my past self.

'I hated that Tomas bloke for taking that from you.'

I looked up at my ex. 'What?'

'You went away one person, full of determination and dreams, and came back another. A shadow of the one that went. It's like he switched the lights off.'

'May I remind you that you married that dull person?'

He shook his head and reached for my hand. 'I never said you were dull. Not at all! I thought you were hot at school and I still thought you were hot when you came back from France. But you were different. More reserved. Less sure of yourself. He did that and I've never forgiven him.'

'You never said anything.'

There was a sigh. 'Never seemed the right moment before.' Hugh glanced over to the window where we could see Sash still talking animatedly on the phone, her hands flapping around as she spoke. 'Looks like it's going well.'

'Yes. Good.'

'Do you know who it is, this brand?'

'No idea. I'm sure she'll tell us when she gets back.'

'I'll miss her.'

'She's already said she's going to come back as often as you're available to see you.'

His brow wrinkled, the sprinkles of silver through his blond hair hadn't touched his eyebrows and they drew together.

'When I'm available? I'm always available for Sash.'

I held up a hand. 'Don't get defensive with me. I'm telling you what she told me.'

'Have I appeared uninterested in her? Has she said something to you?'

'No, Hugh. You haven't. Obviously, the Andes thing made communication a little patchy but she knows you're allowed to have a holiday just as we all are.'

'But she couldn't tell me about Paris because I was away.' He scratched his chin.

'She's fine. You are, and always have been, the best dad. We might have grown apart but you and her are two peas in a pod and always will be. Whatever, and whoever, comes along, she will forever be your little girl. And she loves that. She loves you.'

He glanced back at the window. Sash caught his eye, waved and did an excited thumbs up. The concern that had clouded his features moments ago dissipated like magic. The magic of a father's love.

'She'll always be my little girl,' he echoed.

'I know. They're grown-ups but they're still our babies.'

'She doesn't like that I'm seeing Tania, does she?'

'It's not that she doesn't like it. It was a bit of a shock, I think, and her being so close in age... she'll come around.'

He blew out a long puff of air. 'Between you and me, she might not need to.'

'Don't make any hasty decisions. Talk it over with Tania and see where you are.'

'Hmm. Yes, you're right.' He looked up from where he was making chess moves with the condiments. 'Never thought I'd be getting dating advice from my wife.'

'Ex-wife.'

'Yes. Of course. You know what I mean.' He made another

move. From what I could see, the mustard had just taken the salt. Hugh had always done this. It was one of his little quirks. At times, it had irritated me but eventually, I'd realised that he only did it when he was turning something over in his head. God knew we were both negotiating uncharted waters right now. All we could do was take it one day at a time. At least that's what I'd decided after my panic last night when I'd nearly backed out of the whole thing.

'What is it, Hugh?'

'What?' He looked up.

'You're playing Condiment Chess which means there's something on your mind.'

'Oh. Oh, yes. Sorry.'

'It's fine.'

'Drives Tania mad.'

'She'll get used to it. I did.'

He gave me a look that suggested he wasn't so sure.

'So what is it? Spit it out.'

'This Paris thing.'

'Yes?'

'Is it... are you going back to him?'

'Who?'

'Tom.'

My newly shaped and tinted eyebrows raised. Sash had, as tactfully as possible, advised that I couldn't launch a new life in Paris with unruly brows. They weren't actually that bad, I thought, but apparently bad enough and the next day, I'd been booked in for the full works and consequently both my brows and lashes were now dyed, shaped, waxed, and therefore perfect for emphasising the surprised expression Hugh's question elicited.

'You mean Tomas?'

'I suppose so.' He gave a wiggle of his head, and a slight roll of his eyes. 'If you want to be fancy.'

I couldn't help but laugh. My usually eminently sensible ex had momentarily turned back into the twenty-something I'd got together with all those years ago.

'What?'

'You. Calling him Tom and acting all sullen.'

'I'm not.'

Just the one brow this time.

'OK. Fair enough. He was never good enough for you.'

'You never even met him.'

'I didn't need to.'

We sat in silence for a moment, both likely remembering how different the girl who'd come back from France was from the one who'd left Heathrow three years earlier.

'I'm not going back for Tomas. I'm going back for me. I don't even know where he is now, and I'm not interested. If his mother had anything to do with it, I suspect he's married to an heiress of another lucrative vineyard. In fact, any heiress would probably have satisfied her.'

'She sounded a treat.'

'Oh, she was. Luckily, I ended up with far nicer in-laws.'

'They're devastated we've divorced.'

'I know.'

'They keep asking if we might get back together.'

'Do they know about Tania?'

'Oh, yes. They've met her.'

'And?'

'Don't ask.' He put a hand to his head momentarily. 'Just... don't ask.'

'OK, I won't. Although obviously I'm dying to know.'

'I'll tell you when I've recovered from the mortification a little more.'

'Ooh! Sounds like a goody.'

'I'm sure at some point, I will look back and laugh.' He cleared his throat. 'Maybe. In the meantime, no Tomas then.'

'No Tomas. Just Paris.'

'What brought all this on? Was it something you've been thinking about and you just never told me?'

'No. Not at all. I was talking to a friend on holiday and he—'

'He?'

'Yes. He. He made me see that it wasn't just Tomas I'd fallen in love with back then. It was Paris too. Paris hadn't broken my heart but I'd put it in the same box as those difficult memories and pushed it away.'

'But?'

'But, talking about it to Ashok—'

'The friend?'

'The friend,' I continued, ignoring the hints to elaborate. 'Talking about it with him made me realise that I'm desperate to see it again. And that I'll get to share it with Sash is the absolute icing on the cake.'

'I'll miss her.'

'I know. She knows that too.'

'OK. So, this friend on holiday...'

'Just friends.'

'Was that the bloke in the pictures Sash posted?'

'I don't know.'

'Middle-aged, ridiculously handsome, wealth and style oozing from every pore.'

'Sounds like him.'

'Hmm.'

Our eyes met and we giggled like we had when we'd first got

together. Hugh was a good man and he was a wonderful father. We just didn't fit any more.

He looked over my shoulder. 'She's coming back. Looks happy!' He gave me a tiny double thumbs up and I felt a wash of love flow through me. Not romantic love, not now, but familial and I knew that still having that made me one of the lucky ones.

'Go OK?' Hugh asked, doing his best to sound interested but casual.

'Oh my God! They really want to work with me. I can't believe it!'

'They'd be idiots not to.' Hugh caught the eye of a waiter. 'Let's order and you can tell us all about it.'

The waiter approached. 'Good evening. What can I get for you tonight?' He pulled out a pad and pencil. I loved that this restaurant, one of our favourites, stayed old school and hadn't switched to tapping out things on a tablet or, even worse, ordering by QR code.

'Could we have a bottle of Nyetimber to start with?' Hugh grinned at Sash. 'We're celebrating!'

15

There's something romantic and magical about a train ride. Hang on, let me quantify that. I'm not talking about commuter trains running consistently late with too few carriages and too many people. But as we sped through the French countryside on a beautifully blue-skied but freezing-cold morning, I felt a sense of fairy-tale wonder.

I'm actually doing this!

I sipped on the strong black coffee I'd bought on board the Eurostar and watched as the view outside the windows changed from urban to countryside and eventually became more urbanised once again as we began approaching the outskirts of Paris. Across from me, Sash was resting her head on a makeshift pillow created from a bundled-up scarf, eyes closed. It had been an early start to catch the train at St Pancras and she'd been shooting footage to document it all, her excitement palpable. Hugh had come to see us off and there were tears between the two – more so from Hugh – but Sash had reassured him she'd be back often and that it wasn't forever. I'd given them space, taking in the beautiful architecture of the building. The Victorians, in my opinion, still couldn't be beaten when it came to knowing how to design and build for both function and beauty.

Sash's eyes fluttered. She sat up with a start. 'Did I fall asleep? Where are we? Why didn't you wake me?'

'You were tired and needed the sleep.'

'Mum!' she replied, exasperation in her tone as she grabbed her vlogging camera. 'I need to document all this!' Immediately, she began shooting out of the window, steadying the shot by resting her elbows on the table.

After a few minutes, she put it down. 'Sorry. I just don't want to miss anything.'

'I know.' Inside, I worried as to whether Sash was missing out, forever looking at life only through a lens, but I'd been a mum long enough to know not to say this. Especially when an offspring had just woken up.

'Are we nearly there?' she asked, scribbling something in her notebook.

'Not far,' I said, checking my watch against the stated arrival time. And yes, I'd returned to wearing a watch. That was something else I'd decided on. This way, I didn't have to look at my phone to check the time and then get pulled into a black hole of deleting spam emails and glancing at offers from companies I'd bought something from once, six years ago. None of us had had mobiles when I'd been here last and we'd experienced everything with our whole selves. The memories were imprinted on my mind so indelibly that I could remember it like it was yesterday. I'd waited so long to come back that I wanted to make sure I experienced it fully again.

'*Mesdames et messieurs...*' The tannoy announcement told us, first in French and then in English, that we would soon be arriving at the Gare du Nord, Paris.

Sash looked across the table at me and grinned, her momentary grumpiness gone. The one thing I'd kept with me from those days was the language. Mostly. It was certainly a little rusty but I'd done my best to keep it up, reading books in French, and occasionally watching the odd French film. Those weren't my favourite, though. I liked a nice tidy ending and some joy. French cinema was rarely either of those things and they were proud of it. I'd wanted to teach Sash but she hadn't been interested at the time. Of course, now she was wishing she'd taken me up on the offer and was currently learning via an app on her phone.

We followed the instructions I'd written down as a back up, catching the Metro to the nearest stop to our apartment in the 15th arrondissement. Disembarking from the train, we stepped out onto the streets of Paris, pulling the cases we had brought with us. Some further luggage was on its way via a shipper. Sash dropped her sunglasses down from the top of her head and looked around, already looking effortlessly chic in her Breton top, cashmere cardigan, jeans and boots, a midi-length trench completing the ensemble. I, on the other hand, felt suddenly even more drab than usual. I'd dressed for warmth rather than style. I'd always been aware that the long puffer coat I wore now was far more caterpillar than couture but here it seemed amplified.

'You OK, Mum?'

'Huh?' I looked over. 'Oh, yes. Fine, fine.' I pulled my phone from my eminently sensible handbag and pressed the Maps icon. I'd put the apartment in as a favourite earlier to save hassle and now pressed start to lead us the correct way.

The wheels of our suitcases rumbled over pavements. Above us, a bright-blue sky hosted a low-hanging winter sun. Stylish locals swished by as I took in the city that I'd once known like the back of my hand.

'Is it far now?' Sash asked.

I shook my head without checking the map. Last night, when I couldn't sleep, I'd gone over the route several times on Google Maps and the buildings around us now were familiar to me.

'Just on the right down here,' I said, steering us both down a narrow side street. 'It should be just...' I checked the numbers. 'Here.'

We both looked up at the apartment building. Cream with black shutters and wrought-iron balconies, finished off with an elegant set of oak double doors. I punched in the code I'd been sent into the keypad of the small wall safe and the door pinged open. I retrieved our keys and placed one in the lock. With a turn and a heft of the door, we were in.

'Wow!' Sash trailed her case to the bottom of the stairwell and looked up. A wrought-iron staircase spiralled majestically up the centre of the building accompanying the polished stone steps, all of which dipped slightly in the middle from centuries of use.

'Do you like it?' I asked as I headed over to the row of post boxes and, with the second key from the safe, opened the one belonging to our apartment. Inside lay one more key. The key to the apartment itself. I took it out, locked up the box and joined Sasha at the bottom of the stairs.

'Ready?'

'Do you want to take the lift?'

'There is no lift.'

Her perfectly laminated brows rose. 'Really?'

'Really.'

'Oh.' She looked at our cases. 'OK.' And we began the climb to the fourth floor.

'You OK, Mum?' Sash said as we finally reached the door to the apartment, her slightly ahead of me.

I held up a finger as I took a few moments to find some breath to shove into my lungs so I didn't actually die before completing one day of my second Paris adventure. In the end, I put a thumb up. Far less effort than finding extra air, or energy, to speak. I was also in a little bit of shock-slash-denial as I remembered how I'd lived in a similar, although far less elegant, version of this building all those years ago and would jog up and down the stairs every day like it was nothing. Oh, God. I was so unfit.

I handed the key to Sash but she pushed it back towards me.

'No, Mum. You should do it.'

'I don't think it matters, darling,' I said, my breathing finally getting back to normal.

'It does, Mum. This is your adventure. A new chapter in your life. And this is where it's all going to start.'

I pushed the key into the lock, opened the door and walked in, wheeling my suitcase beside me. Behind me, I heard Sash wheel hers in too and close the door.

From somewhere deep within me, laughter bubbled up and burst out along with a wash of unexpected tears. I put my hand to my face.

'Mum?' Sash asked. As I turned, I saw her perfectly made-up face – how she always looked like this even at the ungodly hour we'd got up this morning is beyond me. Even in my youth, I didn't have the energy for that.

'What am I doing, Sash?'

'Come on. Let's make a cup of tea and sit down. You're just over-tired.' She took my hands. 'Mum. This is going to be great! Loads of people have said how cool it is that you're doing this and how they'd love to do something similar but don't feel brave enough, or wish they had done when they had the opportunity. I have the coolest mum!' She shrugged a slim shoulder. 'I mean, I already knew that but still.' Her smile was wide but I knew my daughter and could also see the hesitation behind it. The last thing I wanted to do was freak my daughter out within an hour of arriving in Paris.

'You're right. I'm just tired.'

'It's OK. It's a lot. I'm kind of "argggghhhh" about it too if I'm honest.' She put her hands to her face to accompany the sound. 'But it's also amazing. It's going to *be* amazing. I just know it.'

I mentally hoiked up my big-girl pants – the hold-it-all-in kind, obviously – I was in Paris, after all.

'You're right. It *is* going to be amazing!' And right then, right there, I was damned if it wasn't going to be. I knew I was privileged to be able to come back to a place I had once loved to make new memories, memories with the daughter I might never have had if things had been different all those years ago. It was a case of sliding doors, but the door I thought I'd go through had slammed shut in my face. At the time, I'd thought it was the worst thing that could ever have happened. But I'd made a life. Admittedly, it hadn't been a terribly exciting life but it was a comfortable one and there was something to be said for that. And the best thing about it was here with me now. It was time, as she had said, to start a new chapter.

'Let's put the kettle on and explore.'

I'd had some email correspondence with the owner of the property who it turned out was married to a Brit. Clearly knowing our need for a cuppa, she had kindly offered to make sure there was a small amount of fresh milk in the fridge for our arrival. I took off my coat, laid it over the chair and walked to the kitchen part of the open-plan living area. Filling the kettle, I switched it on and after a bit of rummaging found two china mugs and set them next to the kettle.

'Here you go.' Sash appeared next to me with our emergency stash of teabags we'd packed in a small tin. There was a large box in my suitcase. Obviously.

'Thanks. Let's go and have a nose around.'

The main living area looked exactly like the pictures we'd seen online, thankfully, and the high-ceilinged room was painted a soft shade of off-white. Luxuriously thick, pale-blue curtains hung at the full-length windows and complemented the cornflower-blue, squashy sofa that faced them. Two other cream-coloured armchairs provided more seating and a dark wood coffee table sat on a large, pastel, floral rug in the centre of these.

'Isn't it lovely that the seating is centred around the coffee table and not the television?' I commented as I tried the sofa. 'Ooh, this is lovely.'

'I don't think there is a telly,' Sash said, looking around.

'Good.'

She looked unsure.

'Obviously, you can still access things on your devices, but, personally, I'm looking forward to reading more.'

'Oh. Yeah. Of course.'

I walked to the window opposite the sofa and pulled back the sheer curtains that lay behind the others.

'Oh!'

'What's the matter?' Sash caught up with me. 'Oh!' she echoed.

I twisted the key, unlocked the doors and stepped out onto the tiny balcony.

Paris! I missed you.

Below sat a small, cobbled courtyard. A few benches were scattered about, a couple placed under the currently bare branches of some trees. On one sat an older man wrapped up, stylishly of course, against the chill of the weather, reading a hardback book that, at a glance, looked older than my daughter. Here and there was the odd evergreen shrub adding some colour to the scene. Various large planters were dotted about which, although currently empty, I could picture spilling over with spring and summer blooms.

'Is that ours?' Sash asked.

'It's shared between these three buildings.' I replied, my hand moving to encompass the three similar houses that surrounded it, as well as this one.

'Are they all apartments?'

'I don't know. Possibly. I suppose some of them could still be houses.'

'They'd be massive!'

'They would. And pricey.' Even back in the day, it had cost a fortune to rent my one-room *pension*. I knew I was lucky to have secured such a great apartment this time around. Just as well as I was long past staying in ratty places like I'd been willing to back then. These days, creature comforts were high on the must-have list.

'I think I'd feel a bit weird sitting down there when other people I didn't know could be there too.' Sash pulled a face.

'That's how you meet people. But, even if you saw someone, it doesn't mean they'll want a conversation anyway. That gentleman looks engrossed in his book, for example.'

'Yeah. I suppose.'

We'd been lucky enough to have a large and fairly secluded back garden in our family home in Surrey. It wasn't surprising that to have to share outside space now might come as a bit of a shock to my daughter.

'At least there's somewhere to go if you want to and it'll be lovely as the weather warms up.'

She looked again. 'True. I'm sure it will just take a bit of getting used to.'

'Exactly.'

'It's gorgeous though, isn't it?'

'It is,' I agreed. 'It really is.'

Sash insisted on taking the smaller bedroom, although I'd told her I was happy to have it. Both had been tastefully furnished and were scrupulously clean. Mine also had an en suite which left the main bathroom for Sash to use as her own.

'I can't believe you have a bath in your bedroom!' Sash said as we finished exploring. 'That's so extra!'

'I know! I've always loved the look of it. We stayed in a hotel room one time many years ago that had one in it. I thought it was fabulous. Your dad wasn't quite so keen.'

'Why not?' Sash asked as she took the tea I'd made and headed over to the sofa.

'I suppose it's just a bit different from what we're used to. He didn't fancy the thought of standing up in the bath and baring all and sundry to anyone who happened to be in the vicinity.'

'Ew, Mum. Too much info.'

'Sorry,' I said, laughing as I took a seat next to her. The panic of earlier was wearing off a little now as we relaxed in the beautiful apartment with our soothing cups of tea.

'Do you mind if I film a tour?'

'No, not at all. Best to do it while it's still tidy,' I teased. 'I think I'm going to pop out and get a few groceries anyway so I'll be out of your way.'

'Are you sure? I mean, I can do this later if you want me to come with you?'

'No, you go ahead. I won't be long. It'll do me good to stretch my legs anyway.'

'OK, if you're sure,' she said, pulling her camera out of her bag.

'Perfectly.' I stood and took the cups to the kitchen, popping them in the top tray of the slimline dishwasher before picking up my coat and slipping it back on. 'I'll be fine.'

'OK. Have you got your phone?'

I held it up to show her before dropping it back in my bag, smiling at the reversal of roles. How many times had I asked her the very same question over the years? Although, like most people these days, that was the one thing she was unlikely to forget. I picked up the spare set of keys Olivia, the owner, had left on the side and headed out.

From the research I'd done, together with helpful information Olivia had sent over, the nearby market would be open tomorrow so I only planned on getting a few bits in for now. One of the many things I'd loved about Paris, and France in general, was the easy availability of high-quality fresh food and I was looking forward to getting up early tomorrow and heading across to the market. I suspected it would make great content for Sash too – although what did I know? I'd suggest it to her anyway. In the meantime, there should be a little supermarket down this road somewhere around... aha! Here.

I got a few basics, pausing to nose at things I'd whizz past at home. Supermarkets were always far more interesting abroad.

'*Bonjour!*' I greeted the checkout girl with my best accent.

'*Bonjour,*' she replied in a tone that suggested it was not a particularly '*bon' jour* as far as she was concerned and would rather be anywhere else but there. Oh well. I tapped my card to pay, gathered my goods in a canvas bag I'd brought with me and tried again.

'*Au revoir.*'

Silence.

Worth a try.

Next stop, the boulangerie.

Oh, God. Bread! And pastries! I double-checked to make sure I wasn't physically drooling as I entered the shop. The smell alone had probably just added five pounds to my hips but I didn't care. I was in heaven and calories didn't count up here.

'*Bonjour, madame!*' A cheery greeting knocked me back to earth.

'*Bonjour!*' I replied.

'What can I get you?' she asked in rapid French.

I chose a baguette (I know. So sue me), and two strawberry tarts that were so beautiful, it would be a crime to eat them. But eat them I definitely would! Well, one of them, assuming Sash was quick enough to grab the other.

I paid, cheered by the fact that I'd managed a conversation, albeit short, with my rusty French. I'd even braved asking the lady where the nearest fromagerie was. If there was one thing that this bread was crying out for, it was a rich and creamy brie. The other thing I knew for sure was that I was going to have to up my exercise now I was back in Paris. Thirty years ago, I could eat all the wonderful offerings and never gain a pound. That speedy metabolism was sadly a distant memory now but that was a problem for a different day. Today, I had decided, after my initial wobble, that I was going to enjoy the day, eat the food and just 'be' in Paris.

Stepping back out onto the pavement, I looked up the street to where I'd been directed, and began walking. But the further I went, the less confident my steps became. The feeling I'd had as we'd stepped out from the station reared up again. As I noticed the people who strode past me, I felt smaller and smaller – and dowdier and dowdier. How different from the girl I'd been the first time when I'd felt – and been – so confident and relaxed in my style. I knew who I was and what I wanted. Now... who was I? I was 'Professor Collins's wife', or 'Sasha's mum'. But who was I really? I was no longer the first and although I would always be the second, and loved it, surely there was, or at least should be, more to me than being someone's mother alone. Who was *I*?

There was no doubt what I wasn't, though. And that was stylish. I tipped my head down, lowered my eyes and hurried along to the shop. Had I been here alone, I knew that I would have hurried back to the apartment. But I couldn't. She might be a grown-up but Sash was here and we needed lunch.

Ten minutes later, I had some ridiculously creamy brie which the chap behind the counter had insisted I try before I bought. That had brought my smile back, even if only temporarily. I'd forgotten what an experience food shopping was here. I couldn't wait for the market tomorrow now. As I walked back in the watery sunshine, I glanced down at my cosy, but, let's face it, very ugly coat. It hadn't seemed out of place at home but now? I pushed the thought out of my mind and, head down, hurried back to the flat.

Sash waved as I entered.

'And here's Mum, back from getting us some lunch for our first day in Paris.'

I frowned and shook my head. Sash paused and lowered the camera she'd been talking to.

'What is it?'

'I don't want to be in it, Sash.' The thought of my daughter's one hundred thousand-plus subscribers seeing her dowdy old mother made me cringe.

'Why not?'

'Because I don't love.' I placed my purchases on the island and shrugged off the coat like a caterpillar's chrysalis. Except I didn't feel like a butterfly either. Maybe I was more of a moth. A dull, greige moth.

'But you've been in other ones.'

'Very briefly! And that was only on special occasions.' *When I was scrubbed up, made up and dressed up.*

'What's the difference?'

'Quite a lot,' I said. 'Do you want tea or coffee with your bread and cheese? The chap at the fromagerie got me to try some of this before I bought it so I know it's good.'

'I'll have a coffee.' She put the camera down on a side table. 'I'll make it.' From our emergency stash, she pulled out a sachet of ground coffee and the filters that Olivia had told us would fit the machine here.

I set about cutting the bread and setting out the cheese as she busied herself with the drinks.

'Is there something wrong, Mum?'

'No, love. Not at all. Where shall we eat this?'

16

'So how is your first day in Paris?' Ashok asked on the video call.

'Wonderful. And strange. And a few other emotions I've yet to quite work out.'

'From what you told me in India, I'm not surprised. But you *will* work them out. It'll just take time.'

'Oh, stop being so bloody wise,' I said, laughing.

His warm smile across the miles made me momentarily forget my insecurities.

'So what's on the cards for tonight?'

'We're going to dinner at a nearby café that looks nice and has good reviews. Apparently.'

'Sasha has been busy?'

'Incredibly! There's a list of places as long as my arm to try, visit and see.'

'That's good. That's what she's there for.'

'True.'

'But don't forget what you're there for too.'

I swallowed. 'Sometimes, I regret opening up about all this to you.'

'No, you don't.'

I rolled my eyes. 'No. You're right. I don't. But I should.'

'Nah.' He laughed this time. 'Plans for tomorrow?'

'Food shopping in the morning at the local market.'

'Your eyes lit up when you said that.'

'I'm excited! Then I'm thinking back here to cook something fresh and amazing for lunch. Well, fresh at least.'

Ashok wagged his finger. 'Ah ah! Sasha told me what a great cook you are, so no false modesty there. And then what?'

'I don't know, to be honest. I'm sure Sash has a whole itinerary but I'm a little less organised.'

'That's OK. Are you free in the evening?'

'Tomorrow? I expect so. I've not quite got around to making our apartment the "salon" to come to just yet.'

'Would you be available to meet me for dinner, with Sasha, of course?'

'Dinner? Tomorrow?'

'Yes.'

'Where?'

'Hotel Vert? Do you know it?'

'No, but we can find it.'

'I will send a car.'

'Ashok, you don't need to do that.' I could see him about to object and I knew from previous occasions that I would not win this battle. Ashok was like a stick of rock with the word *chivalrous* stamped through the middle. But I had a more important question. 'Are you in Paris?'

'Not yet. But,' he glanced at his watch, 'if my flight is on time, I will be in about eleven hours.'

'How come?'

'Is it not enough to say I wanted to see you?'

I pulled a face. 'Smooth but untrue.'

'Fine,' he grinned. 'I want to do some surreptitious snooping of the hotel in Paris I just bought and I'm in talks for another. I have a meeting the day after tomorrow with the current owners and many, *many* lawyers.'

'That sounds fun.'

'Indeed.'

'So you want to eat there tomorrow to check it out before they know who you are?'

'*Exactement!*' he replied with a chuckle.

'And let me guess. You're staying there too to see how things are being done?'

'Correct again.'

'Won't they recognise your name when you check in?'

'Somehow I doubt the staff have any idea who I am so I'm not concerned.'

'You're sneaky.'

'I prefer to think of it as being thorough in my business.'

'But surely you'll be changing things anyway?'

'Only if they don't work. If there's something I particularly like about the style or way of doing things, I'll be careful to maintain that. But it gives me an insight into what may need to be changed and what won't. All of which is to say that I'd very much love to have your company there tomorrow.'

'That would be lovely.'

* * *

'Oh, Mum, I can't! Sorry,' Sash replied when I told her about Ashok's call. After I'd hung up, I'd got undressed, slipped on my robe and begun running a bath before going back into the living area to get a glass of pre-dinner wine to have in the bath.

'Oh. OK.'

'You can still go, though. I mean, you have to!'

'He'll be sorry not to see you.'

'I know and I'd have loved to have seen him too but I'm meeting a couple of other YouTubers who are based in Paris for drinks and dinner tomorrow. Sorry, I was going to tell you but I could hear you were on the phone.'

'Not to worry. That's lovely, though. Do you know them at all already?'

'We all follow each other but I've never met them in person, no, but I love what they do and we're even thinking of doing a couple of collab vids. I'm so excited!'

'That's great, darling. I'm so glad you're making friends already.'

'Are you going to be OK, though? I mean, I assume he's sending a car or something because, well, it's Ashok.'

'Bingo. And yes, it's absolutely fine. We always said we would each make our own plans here. The last thing we want to do is get on each other's nerves.'

Sash had been sitting on the floor but at this, she stood up with the grace of a young antelope. Once upon a time, I'd had a similar grace but these days, it felt like I had at some point unknowingly traded it in for something more bovine in nature.

'Mum, that's not going to happen.' She wrapped her arms around me and hugged me tight before pulling back. 'I can postpone this if you want me to come. I don't mind.'

'No, no, no!' I pushed back the tears that were threatening for reasons I was still unsure of. I was sure I'd be back on a more even keel once I'd got a good night's sleep. 'It's lovely that you're making friends already. I was worried you might get a bit lonely stuck here with me.'

'Mum...'

'I shall pass your regrets on to Ashok. The sale of this hotel is pretty much a done deal, from what he said, and if he's looking at another here too, maybe we'll see more of him anyway.'

'Are you running a bath?' She craned her head around to look behind me.

'Oh, God!' I ran back to the bedroom and launched myself at the taps that were just disappearing under bath foam that had now scented the entire room with French lavender. I'd also bunged in some bath oil I'd been given one Christmas and had forgotten about, only discovering it when we'd begun packing the house up for the sale.

'All right?' Sash stuck her head around the door.

'Yes. Thank goodness. That would be a good start, wouldn't it? Flooding the place on the first day. Right, I'm going to have a soak and then get ready for dinner.'

After a long, luxurious soak with a new book, I stood up to step out of the bath. From there, everything went rather downhill at quite some speed. My arms windmilled uselessly as my feet did a comedy run on the spot before I plummeted face first towards the water, landing with a large splash back in the tub.

'Mum!' Sash came barrelling in just as I finished wrapping a large bath sheet around me with one hand. I was bent over, with the other hand gripping tightly to the side of the bath.

'I'm fine.' In truth, my face hurt so much that an entire paragraph of 'Fuuuuuuuuuuuuuuuuuuuuuuuuucks' wouldn't make a dent but as far as my daughter needed to know, I was fine.

'Mum!' She marched over, unpeeled my hand from the bath and stood there until I acquiesced in allowing her to assist me out of the bath.

'I've no idea where you get your stubborn side from.'

'Obviously it's you, Mum,' she replied and handed me my robe to swap for the towel. 'What happened?' she asked while she grabbed a flannel and ran it under the sink tap then handed it to me.

'What's that for?'

Sash moved me in front of the mirror. There was a small gash on my head and my nose was bleeding. Excellent. *Bienvenue à Paris!* I chose to deal with my nose first as that was gushing the most.

'What happened?' Sash repeated her question. 'Did you get dizzy?'

'No.' I went to shake my head and thought better of it. 'I just forgot how sodding slippery bath oils are. My foot slipped as I was getting out and I hit my face on the side of the bath.'

Sash scrunched up her face in sympathy. Something I was currently unable to do.

'Ouch.'

'Something like that.'

'Shall I get you some ice? I put some in earlier when you went out.'

'Thanks. That'd be great.'

'Let's get some food delivered tonight,' she suggested on her way out.

I followed her, now holding a new flannel to my nose which, thankfully, seemed to have slowed its flow.

'No, I don't want to mess up our plans.'

'Honestly, Mum. I'd rather. It was a really early start and the thought of getting out of my joggers now is less than appealing. I'd happily just sit on the sofa with you and watch something on the tablet and just veg.'

My whole face throbbed and a headache was now knocking at the door to join the pain party but I didn't want to spoil things.

'I mean it, Mum. I didn't want to say anything earlier because I know you were looking forward to going out.'

'Are you sure?'

'Very.'

'OK. Do you want to choose something?'

'Done. Go and get your jamas on and I'll get a plaster for your head and some ice for your face. Hopefully, it won't swell up too much if we do that.'

* * *

That hope was sadly misplaced. The following morning, after a sleep that was helped by the codeine painkillers I'd had to take for my face, I padded to the loo and caught a glimpse in the mirror of my face.

'Oh. Bugger.' I blew out a sigh and then padded into the living room.

'Morning. Oh, wow!'

'I don't do things by halves, do I?' Ironically, I was closer to that particular truth than I'd meant as I had not only one, but two, black eyes. The cut on my head was healing nicely. I'd refused the plaster last night, hoping that leaving the air to get to it would heal it faster. In one way it had. But beneath the now nicely healing thin line was a purple, bumpy bruise.

'What are you going to do about dinner tonight?'

'Urgghhhhhh.' I tipped my head back momentarily before discovering that made it hurt more. 'I'd forgotten about that with all the excitement.'

'I can try and put some make-up on over it for you, if you like?'

'Can you try that now? I'm desperate to go to market but I'd rather not look like I've gone three rounds with Frank Bruno before stepping out the door.'

My daughter wrinkled her forehead. 'Who's Frank Bruno?'

Sasha did her best but the truth was, nothing less than professional stage make-up was going to hide the blooming disaster of matching black eyes I was now sporting.

'Can you ask Ashok to postpone it?'

'This isn't going to go overnight and I can't imagine he's here for long.' I twiddled my neat bob that was someway between chin and shoulder – a sensible style, like everything else about me these days – and longed for the thick mane I'd had the last time I was here, not least to help cover some of my face in a chic, Veronica Lake look.

'True. What are you going to do?'

I shrugged. 'I either cancel and not see Ashok, which would be a shame, or brazen it out.'

We exchanged a look.

'I know,' I said, reading the expression she was trying her hardest to hide. 'Brazening anything out is not exactly my style.'

'I didn't say anything.'

'You didn't have to,' I replied with a wry smile. 'I've spent a lifetime reading your face.'

'It's not that I don't think you can do it. I just know you'd rather not,' Sash said.

'Very true. But here we are.'

Sash covered what she could with a thick layer of foundation and concealer and we headed over to the market. The clear skies of yesterday had been swapped out for overcast ones but Sash insisted that wearing the sunglasses she handed me was a good idea.

'You'll just look chic and mysterious.'

Chic was pushing it in my caterpillar coat but I liked the sound of mysterious. It made me feel more interesting than I had in decades.

As it was, once we got to the market, I forgot about everything but the fabulous array of foodstuffs laid out on stall after stall under the cover of the bridge of the Metro that rumbled above. Sash was in heaven, filming it all, and, although she didn't think I noticed, I knew she'd snuck a couple of shots of me asking about some fish and buying some vegetables for a ratatouille I planned on making for dinner tomorrow night. Caught up in the excitement of it all, I let it slide. The glasses she'd lent me were oversized and I'd draped a pale-pink scarf around my neck, covering a little of the bland polyester. Admittedly, it would take a lot more than a pretty scarf to salvage this outfit but it was a start.

* * *

'Hi, it's Ashok.' His voice came through the intercom for the apartment and a warm feeling of familiarity rushed through me on hearing it.

'Hi! I didn't realise you were coming in person. Come up!' I buzzed him in and went to the door to greet him. 'Ashok's here.' I turned to Sash, who was just grabbing her bag to go out.

'Oh, great! I thought I was going to miss him.'

I opened the door ajar and moments later, our friend's handsome face peeked around it. '*Bonsoir!*' His eyes met mine. 'Holy shit!' He pulled me into a hug. 'Are you OK? What happened?'

'I slipped in the bath. Oh, it's so good to see you! I can't believe you're here.'

'I know. I was so hoping you'd be free. It feels like so long since Goa but what is it, two months? Is that right?'

'About that. And now I'm here in Paris and it's all your fault!' I laughed then hugged him again. 'Come and sit down while I finish getting ready.'

Sash rushed into the room and a hug. 'Ashok! I didn't think I was going to get to see you!'

'A fleeting visit but so long as I get a hug, I'll call it a win. Katherine said you were meeting some fellow YouTubers?'

'Yes. I'm a bit nervous, to be honest.'

'Are you?' I asked. She hadn't mentioned that to me but then, as I'd discovered on our holiday, Ashok had a way of drawing out people's secrets.

'Yeah, a little.' She scrunched up her face. 'What if they don't like me? Or don't think I'm as... I don't know, sophisticated as they are. I don't want to look like an idiot.'

I pulled her into a hug then stood her back, my hands holding hers. 'I highly doubt any of that. If they do think that, then they aren't worth knowing in the first place. You are brilliant, beautiful and strong. That's all you need to know.'

Sash's eyes flicked to Ashok.

'What she said,' he agreed, tilting his head my way.

Her smile returned. 'Thanks, Mum. I love you.'

'I love you, too. Have a great night and keep in touch, OK? No walking home on your own.'

'Mum, I'll be fine. Stop worrying.'

'Yeah, that's never going to happen,' Ashok put in. 'Also, can we talk about this?' He made a circular motion around his face.

'I'll leave you to it.' Sash grabbed another hug from Ashok, told him to come back soon before kissing me on the cheek and heading out, closing the door behind her.

'She'll be fine.' Ashok touched my hand and I realised my gaze had lingered on the door.

'Yes, I'm sure.'

'So?' he asked, pointedly. 'You said you slipped?'

I rolled my eyes and quickly stopped as apparently, that's ridiculously painful when you've got two black ones.

'Yep. And headbutted the bath on my way down.'

'One night in Paris and the bathtub has managed to offend you?'

'No. Actually, it was all perfect! And then I ruined it by forgetting how slippery bath oil can make surfaces.'

'Ah. Are you sure you want to go out?'

'No, but neither do I want to miss the opportunity to spend time with you.'

'We could eat in.'

'But you wanted to check out the hotel.'

'Ideally, yes, but not if you're sore or it will make you uncomfortable.'

'It's not ideal, I agree. Sash lent me some sunglasses to go out to the market. That felt a bit odd to start but I forgot about them after a while. However, wearing sunglasses inside, at night, would seem a little bit too "extra", as my daughter would say. I'll whack a bit more make-up over the worst bits in a minute.' I paused. 'Does it make you uncomfortable?'

'Me? No.'

'People might... you know... look at us a bit funny.'

'Let them.'

I'd learned in India that Ashok had a very healthy attitude to people whose opinions didn't matter. His philosophy was 'let them'. As in, let them think what they want. It doesn't actually matter. Which was both true and sensible and something I was very much still struggling with. Twenty-year-old me would have, and did, agree with this wholeheartedly, only faltering when it had come to my friends' mother that fateful day. But the self-belief I'd had then, like many other things, was much changed over the years.

'Take a pew and give me a few minutes,' I said to Ashok before disappearing back into the bedroom. Foundation in hand, I dabbed on another couple of layers. The bruising was softened but there was no denying its presence.

I stared at my reflection in the dressing-table mirror, took a breath, grabbed hold of those big-girl pants once more, yanked them until they were pretty much under my chin and walked back out to where Ashok was taking in the evening view from the window.

'Let's go.'

17

The hotel lobby purred rather than screamed chic with marble flooring, comfortable, pale sofas and chairs, low dark wood coffee tables and the whole lit with two huge, glittering chandeliers. I watched Ashok from the corner of my eye subtly taking mental notes as we entered.

'*Bonsoir*. Can I help you?' The man at the desk smiled. Kind of.

'*Bonsoir*. I have a table reserved in the name of Shukla?' Ashok's French was fluent and smooth with a perfect accent. Of course it was.

The receptionist nodded and directed us to the restaurant, the other side of the lobby.

'I didn't know you spoke French,' I whispered.

'I took some intense lessons when I began considering a purchase here,' he spoke quietly back. 'I wanted to make sure I understood any potential side conversations that might happen during the negotiations.'

'Good to be prepared. Although learning a whole new language is quite the preparation.'

'True. But you've met me, right?'

'Quite.'

'*Bonsoir, madame et monsieur.*'

'*Bonsoir,*' I replied, as did Ashok. Like the receptionist, the greeter here was doing a great job of pretending I didn't have two swollen eyes that were turning a different shade with every hour that passed.

We were shown to our table and seated, and Ashok ordered one bottle of still water and one of their most expensive champagne. The waiter nodded once and left.

'Is that another test?'

He shook his head. 'No, I'm just celebrating dinner with a friend.'

'Then the second most expensive probably would have sufficed.'

Ashok laughed and then asked how it felt to be back in Paris.

'Honestly?'

'Of course.'

'I'm wondering if I made a mistake.'

'Why? It's not as you remember?'

'It's not that. I mean, of course things have changed but Paris is still as beautiful as it ever was. But I've changed.'

'I don't think any of us are the same people we were thirty years ago. It'd probably be a bit weird if we were,' Ashok offered.

I made to reply as the waiter appeared with the champagne, an ice bucket in a stand, and two stunning cut-crystal glasses that made the reflected light from another large chandelier above dance. He showed Ashok the bottle, and he nodded before picking up his phone and tapping away briefly as the waiter made an understated display of opening it. He then poured a small amount into the glass before Ashok and stood back, awaiting Ashok's decision. My friend tasted the champagne, gave the waiter a nod and we paused our conversation until we had each been poured half a glass and the bottle been placed it in the ice bucket. Once this was done, the waiter then gave a tiny bow and moved away.

'So what weren't you happy about? Or is it that you're particularly impressed by something?' I tilted my head towards his phone.

'Oh. Was it that obvious?' Ashok looked momentarily unsure, an expression that looked unusual on his features.

'Not to anyone else,' I reassured him. 'But I know you barely look at your phone when you're in company. And,' I leant closer to him, 'I also know this is an undercover operation.'

'Busted!'

His laugh was warm and I felt the stress of earlier melting away, even, for a moment, forgetting about the state of my face. How wonderful it was to have friends who you could absolutely be yourself with, without judgement. And if you could make them laugh, and they you, it really didn't get much better than that.

'As for my secret scribblings, I noted that he didn't show you the wine, just me. You should have been included as neither of us had known what he would bring.'

Ashok picked up his glass and I did the same, waiting for the toast.

'To Paris.'

'To Paris.' I echoed and touched my glass carefully against his, the soft ring of the glass perfectly clear.

The bubbles tickled my nose as I tipped the golden liquid up and took a sip. It was light and smooth with a hint of spring.

'You like it?' Ashok asked.

'Yes, I do.' I leant over and turned the label towards me as I hadn't been able to see it when the waiter had shown Ashok. 'Shit!' I whispered the expletive. 'Ashok!'

Quickly, he put his glass down on the crisp, white, linen tablecloth.

'What is it?'

'Cristal? You didn't need to order that! It's ridiculously pricey!'

He shrugged, picking his glass up by the stem once more. 'It's a business expense.' A smile slid on to his face, hooking itself higher the longer he looked at me.

'What?' I asked.

'Katherine, just drink the damn wine and tell me why you think you made a mistake.'

I paused, let out a sigh and took a big slug of the champagne. Classy, I know. With mortification hovering over me like a cloud, I proceeded to tell him just how dowdy and plain I felt amongst all the beautiful people of Paris.

'Bollocks.'

'*Pardon?*'

'Bollocks. You have your own style. You don't need to follow and copy anyone else.'

'It's not that. My style is... I don't even know! It's... mumsy!'

Ashok looked at me. 'I don't really know what that means.'

'Old-fashioned. Dull.' I thought again. 'Boring.'

A waiter, noticing our glasses were getting low, began to move towards us but Ashok subtly waved him off, then topped up my glass while I pondered, our conversation unhindered by interruption. 'I was always so interested in fashion and style. I never followed it slavishly but I enjoyed it, if that makes sense.'

He nodded agreement as he concentrated on pouring his own glass. The bottle made a satisfying crunch as it settled back into the crushed ice of the bucket.

I continued on. 'What we were saying earlier about having changed in the last few decades, of course that's happened but aren't you supposed to get to know yourself better as you age? If

I'm honest, I feel like the older I've got, the less I know who I am. When I was here before, I felt, I don't know, stronger, I guess. I knew what I wanted, what I was going to do with my life.'

'I think that changes for many of us. I was convinced I was going to be a train driver on the Toy Train, hauling carriages up the Himalayas.'

'Really?'

'Oh, yeah. Absolute dream job.'

'I don't think you'd be sipping Cristal on those wages.'

'That is also true. Compensation for sitting in an office instead of behind an engine. So you don't feel you know who you are now?'

I looked past his shoulder. It felt stupid to say it out loud now, even to someone who was as close a friend as he was.

'The truth is, I feel like a nobody. Like I'm invisible.'

'You're not invisible, Katherine. It's rather more that others don't see, and that's their fault.'

'Hmm.' I took another sip. 'When I came back into the apartment yesterday, Sash was filming. She turned the camera on me. I got a bit grumpy and asked her not to film me. I told her I didn't want to be in any of her vlogs.' I sipped my drink as I got the words right in my head. 'She, quite rightly, pointed out that I'd appeared in some before, which I have. Hugh and I both. But those were special occasions and I'd done my hair and make-up and so on. It was the best version of me and to be honest, that's not even that special.'

'Don't.' Ashok's voice was sharp and I snapped my attention back from where it had been wandering, surfing the décor behind him.

'What?'

'Don't say things like that. Don't put yourself down like that.'

'I'm not. Not really.'

He sat back and folded his arms, an expression of 'don't bullshit me' arranging itself on his features. I'd seen it once before when we were on holiday. Sash and her friends had returned early from a night out, fed up that they hadn't been able to get into a swanky bar that they'd all been looking forward to trying. They'd been told by the bouncer it was full even though they'd gone early. Ashok had packed them and us into a town car and driven them back to the club. He and I had walked up to the entrance and magically, the rope had been set aside at his natural air of success and wealth. As he stepped past the rope, he turned to the bouncer and with the look he'd just given me, advised him that 'as they apparently weren't full after all', he had a few friends joining him. At his sign, the other four strode in, heads high. He'd made a point of telling them to look confident, that they belonged there and not that they were being granted some magical access that they should grovel and be thankful for. They'd done exactly that, the girls swishing in with swaying hips and all of them with confidence to spare, whether real or imagined. The bouncer had shifted his weight, opened his mouth to say something then taken one look at Ashok's face and wisely changed his mind.

Once inside, the kids had all chattered over each other with laughter and excitement. I'd loved Ashok even more for that act. The fact he wasn't about to let people he cared about be arbitrarily judged 'not good enough' by a bouncer and then showed them they were entitled to be there just as much as anyone else and have the confidence of knowing it was so kind and so Ashok.

'Look around you, Ashok! Everyone is stylish and chic. You, for a start. And then there's me in a dress I've had twenty years, the one I always pull out for "nice dinners" because it's plain and sensible and familiar.'

'Chanel always said you couldn't go wrong with a little black dress.'

'Oh my God, Chanel would cut me dead! I dread to think what she'd say about my style, or lack thereof.'

'True. But she judged everyone harshly. OK. Bad example but the sentiment remains.'

'I know, but... I used to know what made me feel good. What I looked good in and now I don't feel like I know myself at all. I've been someone's wife, someone's mother for so long – not that I haven't enjoyed those roles – but somewhere along the line, *I* disappeared.'

'Then perhaps this isn't a mistake after all, returning to Paris, I mean. You say when you were here before, you felt you knew who you were. So take the time to explore not only the city, but yourself. I'm pretty sure you're going to find yourself in Paris once more.' He paused and pulled a face. 'Out loud that sounds a bit wanky but you get the gist.'

I burst out laughing, the tension I'd been holding onto evaporating as I did so.

'Such poetry!'

He was laughing too now. 'I know. I'm a businessman with the heart of a poet.'

'Clearly.'

The worries of earlier dissipated in the company of such a good, uplifting friend. Perhaps he was right. Perhaps this was the balm I needed to salve my practically non-existent ego and begin, slowly, to rebuild the confidence I'd once had. One step at a time. I'd put all this pressure on myself but the truth was, I didn't need to.

'You should explain to Sasha how you feel.'

I shook my head. 'I can't. She'll just tell me I look great and I'm fine.'

'I know. But what does she think at the moment?'

'I don't know,' I replied with a shrug. 'That I want my privacy, maybe.'

'Despite having not objected before?'

I turned that over for a moment then sighed. 'Fine! I'll tell her. Now can you stop being all Wise Guru Man and get us some food? I'm starving.'

18

Having placed our orders, I sat back and took in the luxe surroundings.

'What do you think?' he asked.

'About the hotel?'

'Yes. I'm interested in a second opinion.'

'OK.' I rested my chin on my hand. 'Well, it's obviously popular, the restaurant at least. That's a good sign. The décor is rich without being too intimidating.' I cast my eyes over it again. 'Actually, that's a lie. It's incredibly intimidating but to be honest, everything feels a bit intimidating to me at the moment but it didn't feel that way when I walked in with you. You're a human intimidation shield.'

He laughed. 'Go on.'

'It's probably just preference but the welcome at reception was a bit aloof for me. I mean, I'm sure that is "cool".' I made bunny ears with my fingers. 'But the slightly snooty air didn't really hit the spot for me.'

'I agree. Anything else?'

'The wine thing? You were right about that. I mean, I don't

know my Chardonnay from my elbow but still. Actually, the most I know about Chardonnay is that the woman two doors down from the house we just sold named her baby that and the woman next door was livid and thought it was bringing down the tone of the neighbourhood.'

'Really?' Ashok leant forward, his eyes glittering with mirth at the gossip. 'And what did you think?'

'I thought it was hilarious that next door had got so worked up over a baby name and took the new mum some barely worn baby clothes I'd found in the loft when I was sorting out for the move.' I took a sip of the crisp wine, letting the bubbles play on my tongue and tickle my throat as I swallowed. 'Poor girl. She looked shattered. I remember those days.'

'I expect it feels like yesterday?' His voice was soft, sensing that memories of times long gone were drifting in my mind.

'Sometimes. Sometimes, all of it feels like yesterday and then some days, it feels like everything was so, so long ago and I'm not exactly sure what I've done with all the time.'

'Raised a child?'

'Yes.' I took another sip. 'Anyway, what else?' I steered the conversation back on course, afraid of the memories more reminiscing might drag to the surface. There was a lot of my time in Paris I wanted to remember and fall in love with once more. But there were also parts of that time I wanted to stay buried. No good would come of that particular exhumation.

Together, we discussed things we liked and loathed about hotels in general and very occasionally, Ashok made a note until the starters arrived.

I looked over with suspicion at Ashok's snails. Despite being adventurous in my taste as a young woman, I'd still not conquered the snails. They were, and always would be, garden creatures. *Slimy* garden creatures.

I took a small forkful of my steak tartare and nearly cried as the flavours exploded in my mouth – the sharpness of the capers and cornichons, the richness of the steak and egg, cut through with the zinging warmth of French mustard. It was like heaven in a mouthful.

'Good?' Ashok asked.

'So good,' I said, closing my eyes.

The main course of sole fillets in a rich, buttery, lemon sauce with dauphinoise potatoes and charred *carotte de garde* was just as delicious.

'And for pudding?'

'I'm full!'

'No! You can't be.' he replied, laughing. 'You're my accomplice in undercover dining. You have to choose something.'

I didn't take too much persuading and before long, a syllabub, lighter than air and flecked with vanilla, arrived and was finished far too soon, while opposite me, the glossy dark-chocolate bombe that Ashok had ordered was now nothing but a few scrapings of decorative drizzled chocolate and raspberry coulis.

'I think we can put the food in the "Excellent" column.'

'Definitely.'

'What time is your meeting tomorrow?' I asked.

'Ten a.m. Thank God it's France. I'd probably be looking at six thirty if it was the States.'

'Whoever invented breakfast meetings needs a stern talking to. At least.'

'Definitely. I refuse them if it's at all possible.'

'Don't blame you. Are you going straight home after that?'

The smile faded. 'Sadly, yes. The hotel you stayed at is hosting a wedding for a top Bollywood actress at the end of the week and although I know my team are more than capable, the bride-to-be has requested my presence for the entire week of celebrations.'

'Tricky to wriggle out of.'

'Impossible.'

'Shame.'

'Very much so. But with taking over this hotel and, if things go well tomorrow in talks for the next one here, I'll likely be back and forth for a while. All of which gives me a legitimate excuse to come back to Paris as often as possible.'

'I'll be keeping my fingers crossed.' I did the action for added emphasis and Ashok echoed it with both hands.

'Would you like coffee?'

'Could I be terribly uncouth and ask for tea?'

He gave a chuckle. 'I'm Indian so can't be convinced there is anything uncouth about tea.'

'I'm just going to nip to the loo.'

Ashok nodded and signalled for the waiter as I headed off towards the ladies'. A few minutes later, ablutions done, I checked my appearance in the ornately framed mirror above the sink, took a thick towel from the pile and dried my hands before reapplying my lipstick. Despite Sash's best efforts, there was no disguising that I had two excellent shiners. The bright-red lipstick I'd applied was striking but there was no detracting from the eye make-up nature had given me following my argument with the side of the bath.

I took one more look, sighed, gave my hair a fluff and walked back out into the restaurant.

'Kitty?' The nickname pulled me thirty years into the past. I stopped momentarily before continuing. Of course it wasn't me being called. There were very few people who had ever used that name and they'd been gone from my life for a very long time.

'Kitty?' This time, I turned towards the woman's voice. 'It is you!'

There, in front of me, was the friend I hadn't seen in three decades, still looking as glamorous as she had done all those years ago, if not more so.

'Gabby?'

'Oh, *mon dieu!*' And suddenly, I was wrapped in the biggest hug, and enveloped in a cloud of perfume with a heady, but not heavy, scent. As it had always been with Gabby, enough but not too much. She pulled back, her hands moving to my forearms, not letting go. 'You haven't changed a bit!'

'Hi,' I said, immediately feeling pathetic that was the most I could come up with.

My old friend didn't seem to mind. 'Hi!' she replied. 'Oh my God,' she said, laughing. 'Thirty years and all we can say is "hi".'

'I know. Sorry.'

'*Non, non, non.*' She waved an elegant hand topped with a perfect manicure. 'But what is this?' She touched my face gently. 'Are you in trouble? Can I do anything?'

With an overwhelming feeling of mortification, I felt the tears begin, powerless to prevent them. Gabby immediately led me back into the ladies'.

'Now. Tell me everything.'

19

When we returned to the restaurant twenty minutes later, my make-up was repaired, care of my old friend, and a small piece of my heart that had been missing for thirty years finally replaced neatly in the gap that had remained there ever since it was lost. As Gabby had patched up my make-up, we'd each given the other a brief, potted history of our lives from the end of term until now. The one subject we'd both avoided was her brother.

'Ashok will think I've climbed out the bathroom window and abandoned him.'

'Is that him?' Gabby slowed our pace as we walked arm in arm back to my table.

'Yes.'

'Wow. If you do decide to climb out of the bathroom window, let me be the first to know, won't you?'

'It's not like that. We're just good friends.'

'But why not?' she asked. 'I think perhaps it should be. You've seen him, right?'

'Yes, and I know. There just wasn't that spark. But he's now one of my best friends and somehow, I think that's even better.'

Gabby made a 'poof' sound and shook her head.

'Then we must agree to disagree because I would definitely not be putting him in the Friend Zone.'

'It was Ashok who suggested I come back to Paris.'

'Then I like him already. *Vite!* Come, introduce me!' She grinned at me and we giggled as though we were still the twenty-year-olds we had been. For a moment, all those intervening years melted away and it was just us and a handsome man catching our eye.

Ashok stood as we approached the table, his gaze flicking momentarily to Gabby before focusing intently back on me.

'Is everything all right? I sent out a discreet search party and was assured you were in good hands but still...'

'Yes. I'm so sorry for leaving you for so long! It was just...' I looked at Gabby and began to laugh again, unable to think of any words to finish the sentence. I wasn't sure what it was at the moment apart from... wondrous!

He waved away the apology. 'So long as everything is OK.'

'Perfectly. Ashok, I'd like you to meet Gabby.'

His eyes flicked to me, recognition of the name flashing in them. I knew he would remember her from the stories I had regaled him with on our evenings out in Goa when he had asked me about Paris.

'Yes. That Gabby,' I beamed and answered the unasked question.

'*Ooh la la!* It sounds like I have a reputation already. I only hope I can live up to it.' She shook Ashok's hand.

'Somehow, I don't doubt that for a second. *Enchanté.*'

My gaze flicked from one to the other. There had been no romantic spark between me and Ashok but right now, I could practically see a bonfire evening's worth leaping between the two of them.

'We were about to have some tea when I so rudely abandoned Ashok. Would you be able to join us? Sorry, in all the excitement and blubbing, I completely forgot to ask if you were here with someone!'

'And I completely forgot I was!' She laughed as she spoke, her eyes drifting back to Ashok.

'It would be lovely if you could join us,' he enthused. 'I've heard a lot about you.'

'Then I really should and put the record straight,' she replied, her smile still wide.

'Believe me. It's all been good things.'

She stuck out a hip. 'I should think so.' Her smiled faded a little. 'As much as I would love to, I'm not sure it will be possible this evening.'

'But Ashok's leaving tomorrow,' I told her. From the corner of my eye, I saw him cast a glance at me.

'Oh.' Her face fell. Gabby had never done the aloof Parisian thing naturally. Certainly, she could turn it on when she felt like it but her natural personality was open and warm. The disappointment showing on her features was no act.

'If you have company, they are, of course, welcome also,' Ashok added, clearly keen to find a way to continue their acquaintance.

Gabby suddenly looked uncharacteristically tense, her eyes darting to me. And I knew.

'Gabby?' The voice was deep, smooth and ridiculously sexy. Despite not having heard it for nearly three decades, I'd have known it anywhere. Tomas.

20

And of course, *of course*, in all the time I could have run into him, it had to be tonight.

Gabby and I both turned. I saw shock register in Tomas's eyes before they flicked to Ashok and darkened with anger.

'Kitty?' There was so much more contained in that one word than I could even begin to put into words but somehow, I understood all of it immediately.

'Kitty, you remember my brother, Tomas?'

I shifted my bruised eyes to her, not knowing whether to laugh or cry. Gabby, in turn, had an uncertain expression on her face. After all, how did you introduce the once love of someone's life to them after a gap of thirty years, especially when it had all ended so badly?

'I do, yes,' I replied, almost automatically, my mind still running round in circles, trying to decide which emotion to pick. 'Hello, Tomas.'

'Hello, Kitty.' God, I'd always loved the way he'd said my name and it turned out, from the suddenly squishy feeling in my stomach, that, at least, hadn't changed. The sensible part of my brain strutted over and gave me a kick and I gave an almost physical start.

'Kitty and I ran into each other by the bathroom! Isn't that incredible? They've asked us to join them for coffee. We do have *so* much to catch up on. This is Kitty's friend, Ashok. Ashok, this my brother, Tomas.'

Ashok, only a fraction shorter than Tomas, held out a hand in greeting.

Tomas had never been good at hiding his emotions back then and apparently, little had changed in that respect. It was also evident that he didn't think them joining us this was the fabulous idea the rest of us did. But he took Ashok's hand and shook it.

'*Bonsoir.*'

'*Bonsoir.*'

'Wouldn't that be wonderful, Tomas?' Gabby gave him a verbal prod, accompanied by a look that few would argue with. Tomas, unless he'd very much changed, was one of those few.

His gaze shifted back to his sister. 'I thought you wanted to get back early this evening?'

So, no, apparently he hadn't changed, at least not in that aspect.

'No, not particularly,' she replied lightly.

Ashok, who'd barely been able to take his eyes off my old friend since we'd approached the table, signalled a waiter and requested in perfect French for two more chairs to be brought. I didn't miss the glance of appreciation from Gabby as he did so, nor the suspicious one from Tomas. Chairs were found and Tomas was overruled. Fresh coffee and teas were ordered – the one Ashok had ordered for me earlier having long gone cold as Gabby and I caught up in the ladies'.

'I can't believe you're here!' Gabby started, her hand taking mine as I rested it on the white linen of the tablecloth. 'I've hoped for years that I might run into you one day.' Her eyes filled with tears and I felt like a shit for not keeping in touch with my friend. It wasn't her fault that her brother hadn't stood up for the woman he professed to love.

'This is actually my first time back in Paris since... back then.'

I felt Tomas's eyes on me but refused to meet them.

'No!' Gabby put her other hand to her chest. '*C'est vrai?*'

'Very *vrai*, I'm afraid. You know... life and all that.'

'Oh,' she replied as we waited for the waiters to place the white bone china cups and saucers down on the table, so fine they were semi-translucent, along with a large cafetière, glass teapot and all the necessary accoutrements and condiments. The waiter asked if we required anything else, was advised by Ashok with a smile and thanks that we didn't and moved away.

Gabby turned to me, her hand still holding mine. 'Well, you are here now so. *Alors!* Tell me everything about your life now.'

We'd given each other some brief details in the loos but now I gave a potted version of the last three decades, purposely avoiding looking Tomas's way when I recounted my wedding, the birth of my daughter and more recently, my divorce.

'Do you have a photo of your daughter?' Gabby asked.

'Thousands!' I said, laughing, pulling my phone from the chic clutch bag Sash had lent me for the evening. Quickly, I opened the gallery app and scrolled through a few. Gabby took the phone and continued. 'Oh, she is so beautiful.' She glanced at me. 'She takes after her *maman.*'

'I'm not sure about that,' I replied, the automatic self-deprecation kicking in as usual.

Tomas leant towards his sister so that he could see the screen. 'Gabby is right. She does.'

It was the first time he'd spoken since his attempt to avoiding joining us. His gaze flicked up from the phone and met mine.

'Thank you,' I said, for lack of anything else to say while my brain momentarily set itself to pause without my permission.

'Perhaps you have already explained to my sister, but why are you bruised?' he asked, looking for a moment at Ashok before turning back to me.

'Oh!' My hand went automatically to my temple. Caught up in our memories, I'd temporarily forgotten about the state of my face. 'I slipped in the bath last night.'

It was obvious he didn't believe me. This was what I'd worried about on Ashok's behalf. A more kind and gentle man I'd never met and I hated that anyone might think he was in any way responsible for my injuries. His earlier dismissal of my worry had settled my concerns somewhat but the fact that Tomas doubted my explanation bothered me more than it should have. Strangers thinking something was easier to ignore but then again, what was Tomas to me now but yet another stranger? I felt my hackles rise. What right did he have to judge me or my friend? He'd given up that right the moment he'd let his mother treat me like I was well below par as a potential partner for their son. 'My daughter was there if you feel you need confirmation, Tomas. If not, then I'd appreciate it if you'd stop giving Ashok dirty looks.'

Wow! Where the hell had that come from?

For years, I'd been the peacemaker. The smoother of ruffled feathers amongst our acquaintances and family, but Tomas had pushed a button.

'It's fine, Katherine.' Ashok shrugged the suspicion off. *Let them*, he had said. But for some reason, I wasn't able to 'let' Tomas.

'No, Ashok, it's not fine.'

For a few long moments, silence settled over the table. Tomas and I locked eyes and despite the boundless love I'd once felt for him, all that burned in me now was anger and hurt and I wasn't sure if that was because he'd refused to accept my word, thereby insulting both me and my friend, or for reasons that went far further back. He swallowed then broke the gaze, turning to Ashok.

'My apologies.' He held out his hand to Ashok. Ashok hesitated for a fraction of a moment before taking it.

'Accepted. Thank you. Shall we begin again? It's a pleasure to meet you, Tomas. I'm Ashok, a friend of Katherine's.'

'Tomas Bertholle. I used to be a friend of Kitty's.' As their hands separated, Tomas's eyes once again met mine and for a moment, there was a flicker of a smile. 'I was young and stupid enough to mess that up – something I've regretted ever since.'

I felt frozen in place. Part of me wanted to go to him, to have him hold me as he'd done so many times. The other half wanted to scream at him that he had no right to say those words. He'd had his chance and I'd moved on. Made a life. Without him.

'Well said!' Gabby said, placing her coffee cup back on the saucer. 'Glad to see the old Kitty is still in there somewhere, putting my brother back in his place.' She turned to Ashok. 'Kitty was one of the few who always stood up to him.'

'This is true,' Tomas agreed. 'If I hadn't met Kitty all those years ago, I dread to think what kind of person I'd have become. Unbearable, I suspect.'

Gabby wiggled her head to and fro. 'There are still plenty of times you are unbearable.'

Her brother grinned and my stomach flipped before my brain sent down a very sternly worded message telling it to behave.

'Probably also true.'

'So what are you doing in Paris?' Gabby asked Ashok. 'Apart from visiting your friend.' She darted a look at her brother and I smiled inwardly. The days of attempting to make him jealous on my behalf were long gone, whatever platitudes he spouted.

'A business trip,' Ashok replied. 'Sadly not a long one.'

'But perhaps you might be back again soon?'

'I very much hope so,' he replied as they exchanged a flirtatious smile.

'And what business is it that you are in?' Tomas asked.

'Hospitality. Specifically hotels.'

'I first met Ashok when I stayed at one of his beautiful hotels in Goa last year with my daughter.'

'You got to India then?' Tomas replied, his eyes softening as the faintest of smiles tipped his lips. 'I'm glad. I remember you had always wanted to go there.'

My heart swelled with a mixture of emotions that were hard to separate or even name. When I looked up, I saw some of those same emotions reflected in Tomas's eyes. Travelling India together was another one of the many plans we'd made that had never become reality.

'Did you ever go?' I asked, making sure to keep the question light and conversational despite my insides churning like a washing machine on super spin mode.

He shook his head.

'You really should. It's an incredible country.'

A smile that got lost long before reaching the deep blue eyes touched his lips. Just as quickly, it was gone.

'So what are you doing here? I thought you had planned to move to Provence?' I focused on Gabby, pulling myself away from the look on Tomas's face.

I wasn't going back there. I couldn't. I'd put those memories, the many plans we'd had away in a corner of my mind and gradually, other memories had piled up in front of them but they were never quite hidden. As much as I tried, a glimmer always remained.

'Oh, I did. But I've been back in Paris for about ten years now, since my divorce. Tomas has an exhibition at a local gallery not far from here. For my sins, I am his agent.'

'An exhibition?' Ashok asked as he signalled the waiter for more tea and coffee.

'My brother is an artist.' Gabby's eyes flicked towards me. 'A painter.'

The decades crumbled away and suddenly, I was back in that restaurant with Tomas, Gabby and their parents, attempting to make sense of the surprise and shock that Tomas was apparently due to be crowned heir of the family winery. All the talks of his wish to paint, the endless discussions we'd had about his longed-for career as an artist as he painted and I watched, dismissed not only by his mother, but also by him. The end of the dreams he'd confessed to me – and the end of us.

'But... I thought... the winery?'

The still dark brows raised momentarily. 'Ah, yes!'

His hair was short but still thick, silver touching his temples which only added to the air of distinction he'd always had about him.

'I took up my place as my parents wished me too. Not for a couple of years after...' He cleared his throat. 'After I finished my degree, but yes, eventually, I did go back to be crowned "King of the Vineyard".' His words suggested amusement but the tone of them spoke otherwise.

'So you paint in your spare time?'

'No.'

It was like getting blood out of a six-foot three-inch rock.

'*Mon dieu!*' Gabby threw up her hands. 'We will be here all night at this rate. Not that I mind.' She squeezed my hand but I didn't miss the fleeting look thrown Ashok's way too. 'It is a good job you paint and not write, Tomas. The books would be thousands of pages long!'

Tomas gave his sister a look only a sibling could which she shrugged off, raising her right shoulder for emphasis, just as she always had. Some things never changed.

'Basically, Tomas was shit at running the family business.'

I had always been jealous of how, whichever language my friend swore in, she still sounded chic and elegant! Yet another thing about her that I'd loved and was glad to see hadn't changed.

'Which, in my defence, I had always told my parents I would be,' Tomas said, before taking another sip of coffee.

'That is also true. Unfortunately, they refused to listen until it was too late.'

'Too late?' I asked.

Tomas drained the strong black coffee he'd poured and replaced the cup onto its saucer, the china looking even more delicate in his large hands.

'Nearly bankrupted us.' He spoke the words with the shadow of a smile playing on his generous mouth, before turning to Ashok. 'Not all of us have your obvious talent for business.' There was no meanness in the words. It was merely a statement of fact. Tomas had been romantic in many ways, but entirely pragmatic in others. Whether the romantic side still lived on was unknown, and also none of my business. But clearly the pragmatism still survived.

'On the other hand, drawing a stick man is stretching my artistic talent. There's a reason we all have different strengths.'

Gabby turned to me but pointed at Ashok. 'Why aren't you married to this man? Or at the very least engaged? Something?'

'Too perfect.' I shrugged.

She looked back at my friend, resting her chin on steepled fingers, pretending to study him for a moment before returning her attention to me. 'I can see that.'

'Oh, I definitely have faults.' Ashok leant into the conversation. 'Which I'm more than happy to go into at length over lunch tomorrow?'

'I thought you were leaving tomorrow?' I said.

His handsome features took on an impish grin. 'It might have to be an early lunch.'

Tomas glanced towards me. 'I have a feeling you and I aren't invited.'

Ashok blushed and I laughed before turning to Tomas. 'Luckily, I have plans tomorrow, otherwise I might have been offended.'

His gaze hooked mine. 'That's a shame. I was hoping you might be free for dinner. That way, we could both be snubbed together.'

I wanted to look away but I couldn't. Thankfully, my friend's perfect manners came to the rescue.

'I apologise.' Ashok's hand was on his chest. 'I never meant to imply that you, either of you, weren't—'

'Ignore them,' Gabby instructed him, laying her hand on his forearm. 'My brother thinks he is soooo funny. All these years and still he believes it, despite me reminding him on a regular basis it really isn't so. I would love to have lunch with you. At any time.' Ashok's discomfort disintegrated and Gabby turned her chair ever so slightly towards him.

'I guess that told me,' Tomas said, a faint smile on his face as I looked away from the other two, back towards him. 'The gallery hosting the exhibition is just around the corner. I...' He hesitated, appearing to momentarily second-guess himself.

'I'd love to,' I replied. The words fell out of my mouth without consulting my brain, likely knowing that the answer would have been a categorical 'Absolutely not'.

And then there was that smile. It was Tomas's smile that I'd fallen in love with first. It was warm, a little lopsided and when he really smiled, like he did now, his almost navy eyes always seemed to hold a promise of mischief. Back in the day, that was often followed up on. But that had been long ago. Mischief had disappeared from my life around the same time as Tomas and Gabby had.

'I'm going to show Kitty the exhibition.' Tomas tapped Gabby's shoulder, leaning behind me to do so, the bulk of his body close to mine, brushing my bare arm briefly. A spark crackled through me at his touch. For a moment, I let it fizz and pop and burn within me but then I remembered that I wasn't twenty years old any more and I certainly wasn't about to let Tomas Bertholle get to me like he had all those years ago. Even if, like his family's wine, he had only improved with age – in looks at least. Something at the time I hadn't thought would even be possible. But he'd proved me wrong. Of course.

It was hard to believe that tonight was the first time in decades we had all seen each other – the familiarity, the comfort between us had slid straight back into place. But Ashok was a new addition and it was obvious he was more unsure – both from an etiquette side but also because he knew the whole sorry story of me and Tomas. He looked across at me, a question in the kind, brown eyes. I gave him a nod. *I'm OK*, it said. Understanding immediately, he returned it.

'Meet you in the bar in an hour?' Tomas suggested.

'*Parfait*,' Gabby responded before catching my eye. 'I hope you enjoy the exhibition. Tomas is an amazing painter. Personally, I think this collection is his best.' There was something about the way she said it that made me pause. Our eyes connected for a second before she turned back to Ashok.

Tomas held my coat as I slipped my arms in and belted it closed. I watched from the corner of my eye as he then shrugged into his own pure cashmere overcoat. It fit the still broad shoulders perfectly, as though made to measure. I kicked myself. It probably was made to measure! Gabby and Tomas came from a wealthy family and, apparently despite Tomas's best attempts at bankruptcy, it appeared that wealth still existed. I shoved my hands into the pockets of the Marks and Spencer mixed-fibre coat I'd bought in the sale around five years ago and reminded myself the money hadn't mattered to me back then and it didn't matter to me now.

The first bit was right but the second was an outright lie. Back then, I'd had confidence in spades. Somewhere along the line, that had seeped away and now I felt acutely aware of my lower-priced, slightly worn wardrobe.

'Ready?' he asked.

I nodded and followed him to the door. He opened it, waiting until I was through before following.

21

Outside the clouds of earlier had ganged up and were now producing an insistent drizzle.

'Wait here,' Tomas said, ducking back through the hotel door. I stood under the canopy, gazing out onto the rainy Paris street. Unlike at home where I'd have rolled my eyes at another damp day, here I stood and watched and saw nothing but beauty. I knew from experience that that wouldn't last. The weather in Paris wasn't all that much different from home and once the initial shine wore off, it could be just as annoying if you had plans. Or the hairdressers. But now, in this moment, it was beautiful. The pavements, glossy with rain creating an Impressionistic version of the view above, the colours melting and indistinct.

'Here we are.' Tomas appeared beside me and I jumped. '*Pardon*.' His hand rested on my arm for a moment. 'You were miles away?'

'No. Right here, actually. I'd forgotten how beautiful it could be.'

He opened the large umbrella, offered me his arm, ensuring I was sheltered, and we stepped out into the rain.

'It's hard to believe you haven't been back in all this time.'

I gave a small, thoughtful sigh. 'At first I didn't want to…'

He nodded but remained silent.

'And then, well… I didn't think there was anything to be gained by coming here.'

'And yet here you are.'

'Ashok suggested it might be a good idea.'

'You are close.' It was a statement, not a question. 'And yet you've not known him long.'

'Is it a requisite of friendship to have known someone for a certain length of time?'

'Of course not. That's not what I meant.'

'If you're concerned about Gabby, don't be. I'd trust him with my life.'

'That's a strong statement.'

'We have a strong friendship.'

'So I see. And no, I'm not worried about Gabby.' He paused. 'Frankly, I'm more inclined to be worried about Ashok. He might not know what's hit him.'

Tomas had a point but it made me smile. 'I'm pretty sure he can look after himself.'

We walked on a little further in silence that was, if not quite companionable, less awkward than I'd expected.

'Clearly he knows the history you have with Paris.'

'He does.'

'I'm a little surprised he spoke to me at all then.'

'Don't worry. We'll bitch about you later.'

His laugh was as warm as I'd remembered, wrapping around me as we huddled close under the umbrella.

'It was all a long time ago, Tomas. We've all grown and had lives since then.' It was easier to say the words walking along, not looking at him. It made it easier to avoid thinking what might have been. 'Now I'm here, though, I realise I should have come back to Paris a long time ago but at least now I get to share it with my daughter.'

'Then I hope she loves it as much as her mother.'

'Me too.'

'The gallery is just here.' He pointed to the next window front along, slowing as we approached. I stepped away and looked at the single large painting displayed in the window. Tomas followed, keeping the umbrella above me.

I'd have known that scene anywhere. The sparkling blue of the lake, the deep, rolling green of the trees behind and to the right, rows and rows of deep purple lavender that when you got close would be alive and humming with the sound and movement of thousands of bees.

'It's beautiful.' I turned to look at him. 'Sorry. That's probably a very banal description of your art.'

'I prefer that you use the words that first come to mind when you think of it.' He paused, both of us looking at the painting. 'You remember?'

'Yes, Tomas,' I replied, my eyes remaining on the image in front of me. 'I remember.' I could hear the tension in my tone. Looking at the painting, I could feel the breeze on my skin, smell the heady scent of lavender in the air and remember the mixture of nerves and thrill that had raced through my body on that day. The fact that Tomas thought I'd ever forget the place I'd lost my virginity to him sparked a flash of anger in me. I squashed it back down and gave myself a mental kick. What did any of it matter now?

'I apologise.'

'Don't be silly. I shouldn't have snapped,' I replied, pasting on a smile. 'I'd blame it on jet lag but I don't think a few hours on the Eurostar qualifies.'

Tomas flicked his own brief smile back. 'Shall we go in?'

The gallery was sparse-looking. Plain, white walls that wouldn't compete with the art, a couple of uncomfortable-looking but likely extremely expensive chairs were placed opposite a marble-topped desk with gold hairpin legs. Lights were artfully installed in order to highlight the pieces to their best advantage.

'It doesn't open until next week. There's still a little tweaking to do with the set-up.'

I looked around, my mind tumbling back to halcyon days when we'd jump on a train to somewhere and spend the day together in quiet company, Tomas transferring the scene in front of us to a canvas balanced on a homemade easel he'd knocked up from some bits of wood he'd found in a skip we'd passed on the way back from a bar one night. I'd sit or lie beside him, reading, doing coursework or just dozing in the warmth of the sun. How simple those days had been. No Internet to drag me down rabbit holes, no social media to doom scroll as I sat beside him. Just us and nature and paint.

'Do you want to just look around? I can wait over here.' He pointed towards one of the uncomfortable-looking chairs.

'Would you show me?'

His shoulders relaxed a little and his face creased into that beautiful smile once more.

'I'd love to.'

We moved to the first painting. The warm cream walls of the Palais du Luxembourg resting stately in the background, its neutral walls acting as the perfect foil for its gardens where fiery accents of brilliant oranges and warm, rusty reds contrasted with swathes of cornflower blue, the colour of summer. I could practically feel the sun as it warmed the stone of the building and the bare shoulders of the woman in the white sundress, bending to smell those same flowers.

Next was a riot of colour in the Parc Floral de Paris. We had loved spending days there, the colours changing with the seasons.

'I can smell the flowers.' I turned to him and found his eyes on me. 'You always loved painting there.'

He nodded in agreement. 'Like many gardens, there is always something new to see, to paint. I love their everchanging nature.'

'Sasha told me they host jazz festivals there now.'

'That's right. Do you like jazz? I didn't think you did but... it's been a long time.'

'It has. And no,' I screwed up my nose, 'not really. I mean some is OK but the freeform, to me at least, still sounds like a lot of notes just thrown in and left to get on with it.'

His laugh echoed around us. 'I completely agree.'

I moved away from him, towards the next painting.

'You've captured her so well.'

'Thank you.'

In front of us was a large canvas of Gabby, champagne coupe in hand, bubbles clinging to the glass on the inside as condensation coated the outer. Her head was thrown back in laugher, and her neck, long and slim, held the gold cross necklace that she had worn ever since I had known them first. It had been a christening present, ostensibly from her older brother – according to family legend, he had chosen it, declaring that only this one would do.

'Does she like it?'

'Yes. Thank God!' he replied, arranging his features into an expression of overstated mock-relief.

'I'm glad. It shows the inner joy she has.'

'It was that I wanted to capture most. It's easy to paint a picture of a beautiful woman, but, for me at least, there has to be more to it than that. Just as there is so much more to a beautiful woman than her looks.'

'So enlightened.' I threw the tease to him.

'You know my sister well. Do you think I would ever have any choice but to be?' He was smiling but it faded as quickly as it had arrived. 'I'm so sorry that what happened between us caused your friendship to fail too.'

I shook my head. 'It didn't fail, Tomas. It was just too painful at the time.' I didn't want to talk about that now. Think about that now. 'What's next?'

We wandered together through the rest of the exhibition. An atmospheric scene of Passage l'Homme caught my eye, the vivid greens of the early summer trees contrasting with the cobbles of the street and the antique cream stone buildings with their faded, shuttered windows. Tomas's paintings took me on a tour from steep steps leading to the Sacré-Cœur as it gazed from its position over the city, before plunging us deep underneath the streets of Paris to the catacombs housing the bones of around six million Parisians, before we were back above ground and into the lavender-scented air of Provence.

As we approached the very last painting, I stopped. The last thirty years fell away and there, in front of me, was the girl that had come to Paris all those years ago, full of hopes and dreams and confidence. The girl who had made wonderful, meaningful friendships and had loved her studies that had never felt like schoolwork, who merely studied for interest and joy. The girl who had fallen in love with both Paris and Tomas Bertholle with her whole heart and in that moment, that exact moment captured on the canvas before me, was happy and relaxed, a gentle bronze to her unlined skin, and all of those dreams still vivid and intact.

'I can see Sasha in her.'

'Yes.'

The silence settled once more. I had so many thoughts, so many questions but none of them would become cohesive and stick long enough for me to utter.

'Are these all for sale?'

'Yes.' Tomas repeated his one-word answer and I turned to him.

'Aren't you supposed to have a model release or something for this?' That hadn't been one of the questions zooming around my brain but it had apparently shoved its way to the front and made itself known.

'I didn't know how to find you. You didn't leave me an address.'

'So… what?' I asked, my hands going to my hips. 'What I don't know won't hurt me?'

'No, that's not what I meant.'

'What did you mean then? I was good enough to paint and sleep with but not good enough for you to defend to your parents?' *Oh, shit. Where the hell had that come from?*

Bloody Tomas and his paintings, drawing me back into the past! *That's* where it had come from! The box where I'd stuffed all those memories had been dragged out into the open and the lid so unexpectedly lifted. I dragged in a breath and let it out again slowly.

'I'm sorry, I shouldn't—'

'No. You should.' His hands wrapped gently around my upper arms and I could feel the gentle strength in them. 'You have every right to be angry at me.'

'No, Tomas. It's all long in the past and we've both moved on.'

'I haven't.'

I tilted my head up to meet his eyes. 'What?'

'I never moved on from you. Anyone I ever met was always a poor imitation of you so it never worked out.'

I took a step back. 'Don't you dare blame me for your failed relationships!'

He shook his head. '*Merde!* No, I didn't... I am not explaining this well.' He checked his watch. 'We have to be back at the bar shortly.'

'I think that's probably for the best.' I pulled my coat around me and belted it tightly as I walked towards the door. Behind me, the gallery once more fell back into the low light it had been bathed in, except for the artfully lit window display.

We stepped back onto the pavement, still shiny with the earlier rain. Thankfully, it had now stopped and there was no need to cram together under the umbrella as we began the short walk back to the hotel.

Eventually, Tomas spoke. 'I'm sorry you didn't like it.'

'It's not that. The paintings are incredible. You always were so talented. But it's...' I turned and stopped. 'It's so many things, Tomas! The last person I expected to run into tonight, or ever, was you! I'd packed away all those memories and then at the gallery, they all came tumbling out again.'

'They aren't good memories?'

'Of course they're good memories, you idiot! That's why it's so hard!' I punctuated the word 'idiot' with a punch to the biceps, causing Tomas to wince, which had been oddly satisfying. For some reason, Tomas was bringing out the worst in me.

'I'd forgotten what a good left hook you have.'

'And I'd forgotten what a pain in the arse you are!'

We stood there staring at each other for a moment, my breathing short and shallow with annoyance and a whole host of other emotions I'd shut the door on and wasn't ready to open back up yet – if ever. And then, out of nowhere, laughter bubbled up inside of me and burst out. Tomas looked as surprised as I felt.

A hesitant smile, shot through with a clear streak of confusion, crept onto his lips.

'Is... everything OK?' He reached out and laid the briefest touch on my cheek with the back of his hand, light as a butterfly, before withdrawing. 'Perhaps we should get you to a hospital. You obviously took quite a fall.' His eyes scanned my face, lingering on the worst area of bruising. 'Head injuries can be more serious than at first thought.'

'Oh, Tomas! I'm not deranged.'

'No, of course I didn't mean...' He stopped under the scrutiny of my focus then tipped his head back to the light-polluted sky and let out a sigh. 'I have replayed this scenario in my head so many, many times over the years and not once has it been even half as disastrous as tonight has been.'

'You have?'

He pulled his eyes from the cloud-obscured heavens. The pain in his eyes told me more than words ever could.

'Tomas, I—'

A rumble of thunder jolted us back to the present, away from the thoughts of times past and what might have been. Tomas opened the umbrella once more as the clouds unleashed another downpour. Without thinking, I hooked my arm around his and he wrapped his other arm around my shoulders, pulling me closer under the brolly, and to him, as we hurried back towards the hotel. The ornate glass doors to the foyer were opened in anticipation as we dashed through and Tomas handed back the borrowed umbrella with thanks.

'You're OK?' he asked. I caught sight of my reflection in a nearby gilt-edged mirror and winced, the pain of which made me wince again.

'I'll have to do.' I heard the forced buoyancy of my tone as I took in the reflection before me. My hair, tonged into loose curls earlier in a vain attempt to distract people from the bruising, now hung straight and limp. My make-up, remastered by Gabby earlier, hadn't fared too badly but seeing the painting earlier when I'd looked so vibrant and happy, it was hard to dredge up anything other than disappointment at the rest.

'Whatever it is that you are thinking, it's not true.' Tomas's voice was deep and mellow beside me.

He always had been able to read me like a book. It was only when I'd left Paris that I'd been determined to close that book for good. To let people think what I wanted them to think, not the real feelings hidden below.

'The painting of Gabby, that was recent?'

'Last summer.'

'And she looks so alive, so vibrant still. And she is! It's obvious immediately to anyone who meets her.'

'And that's not how you feel?'

I shook my head. 'Not even close.'

'Why?'

I turned to face him instead of our reflections. 'So many reasons, Tomas.'

'Was I one of them?' He held up a hand. 'I'm sorry. I shouldn't have asked that. It's none of my business, not to mention it sounded far more arrogant out loud than it did in my head.'

'I don't know the answer to that, or any of it, if I'm honest. Just one day, I looked up and there was no sign of that girl any more. Absolutely no trace.'

Tomas echoed the wiggle of the head Gabby had done earlier. 'I'm not so sure. So far tonight, you have put me back in my place a few times, quite rightly, I might add. Not to mention proving you can still pack a punch when required. I don't think you're as far removed from her as you think you are.'

'Well, you bring out the worst in me.'

'And you bring out the best in me. You always did.'

'Tomas...'

'I'm sorry. I know...' He made a zippy motion across his mouth. 'As I said earlier, I've, how did you used to say? Buggered this up from the start.'

It was impossible not to laugh. The deep timbre of his voice, the undoubtedly sexy accent and the blunt English phrase made unlikely companions.

'Let's go and find my sister and Ashok.' He held out his arm, almost hesitantly, but I wasn't pedantic enough to reject it. It was likely just as much a shock for him to see me this evening as it had been for me to see him and I had to allow some grace for that. I very much hoped that Gabby and I could rekindle and retain our friendship but Tomas was another matter. But for his sister's sake, we needed to put the past behind us and move forward.

'That sounds like a very good idea. I hope there's wine.'

'I hope there's champagne!'

Tomas got his wish and somehow the three of us – Ashok had wisely declined more after a couple of glasses, citing his important meeting in the morning – got through three bottles before the night was over.

'I'm going to regret this in the morning,' I told Gabby as she tipped the last dribbles from the last bottle into my glass.

'Nonsense,' she replied, waving a hand of dismissal at my words, catching Ashok with a slap across the forehead as she did so. 'Oh, *merde!*' Her hands went to his face. '*Je suis très, très désolée!*'

'It's fine,' Ashok replied, laughter in his voice and admiration in his eyes as Gabby laid her hand against one cheek and placed a kiss on the other.

I shot a look under my lashes at Tomas. He'd always been

protective of his younger sister, just as she was of him. He turned his glance towards me at the same time, our eyes meeting as we shared a private smile.

'You're not about to challenge my friend to a duel, are you?' I leant over a little too much as, beside me, Ashok and Gabby fell deep into flirtatious conversation. 'Oops!'

My elbow slid off the table. Tomas caught my arm and gently tipped me back up. 'No. I've matured a little since those days, although I don't believe I ever went quite so far as a duel? However, hopeless romantic that I was, I wouldn't have put it past me.'

'He's a good man.'

'I can see that. Also the fact that he's clearly a confidant of yours is more than enough recommendation for me. You always were a good judge of character.'

'Oh, I don't know,' I batted back. 'I chose to go out with you.'

He gave a nonchalant, very French, shrug. 'Everyone has off days.'

I nodded in agreement, intending for the gesture to be a wise, knowing acceptance, but I was on the verge of one too many now and dangerously close to tipping into nodding dog territory. I rested my chin on my hand purposefully in order to cease the movement.

'So do you not consider yourself a hopeless romantic any more?'

'*Quoi?*'

Ha! Not quite as sober as he was trying to make out. Both he and Gabby had always reverted to their native tongue if we'd been speaking English when they were either angry, frustrated or drunk. I was pretty sure I could rule out the first two and the fact I wasn't the only one swimming in a pleasant fug of pre-hangover made me oddly happy. I'd always been pretty good at holding my own when it came to alcohol back in the day – practice made perfect – but it had been a long time since I'd practised this well. Not to mention, Tomas had size on his side. He was tall and broad and had been drinking wine from a young age as per the French custom, especially if your family owned a vineyard. I'd done a good job of making up for my slow start during my teenage years and honing the talent when I'd lived out here but there was no denying Tomas's six foot three frame that held nothing but muscle gave him a distinct advantage.

'A minute ago, you said that you were a hopeless romantic. Past tense.' I pointed backwards for emphasis. 'Does that mean you're not one these days?'

He mirrored my position and rested his own chin on his hand and looked at me, eyes soft. Although that might have been the wine. At some point between the second and third bottles of champagne, someone had nipped in and fitted a soft-focus filter on the whole world. It was really rather pleasant.

'No, I would say definitely not.' He thought for a moment. 'As I'm sure most of the women I've dated would testify to.'

'Ohhhh! But you used to be so romantic!' I touched his hand. The sensible part of my brain which had been taking a nap suddenly woke at the contact and gave me a sharp prod. I snatched my hand back. Sensible Me stomped back to the corner. 'You know... back then.'

'French men are supposed to be romantic, aren't they, and I was trying to woo you so... I had a reputation to uphold.'

'Woo me?' I sputtered out a laugh.

'Yes. Is that funny?' Laughter lines around his eyes that hadn't been there when I knew him before crinkled as the smile spread.

'It is.'

'Why?'

'I don't know. Probably because it feels like I've drunk my body weight in champagne and also because it makes me feel like a fourteenth-century maiden. Although,' I tapped my fingers against my cheek, casting my mind back over the fashion history degree I'd studied for, 'they did have some fabulous clothing.'

'I could see you in one of those pointy princess hats with the veil thing.' He made the shapes with his hands as he spoke.

'Yeah, I reckon I could have rocked that look.'

'You rocked any and every look.' Our eyes met and... did he lean towards me or I towards him?

'Oh, no.' I wagged my finger as I pulled back. 'No, no, no. Nopedy nope.'

'Nopedy nope?' The laughter lines deepened.

'I'm not falling for you a second time.'

His smile now was sad. 'I wouldn't expect you to. I know I had my chance and messed that up.'

'So why did you lean in like that, just then?'

'I didn't. I already got punched once this evening. I'm not drunk enough to ask for another! Your chair was tipping. I leant forward to steady it but you righted yourself before further emergency measures were required.'

'Oh. Oh, right. Good.' I cleared my throat. 'Good to be clear on these things.'

'Absolutely,' he replied, smile still firmly in place. 'Although – and I apologise if this is inappropriate or out of place – it's not always easy to keep up these days.'

'Agreed. I gave a nod of agreement, just to be absolutely clear.

'I had forgotten how cute you are when you get drunk.'

'I was cute when I wasn't drunk.'

'You were. You are. Incredibly.'

'Also, I am not drunk,' I stated. Drunkenly.

'No. Of course not. My apologies.' He did a fake bow from his sitting position before hooking my gaze with those mesmerising navy-blue eyes.

Bugger.

22

'Oh, wow.' Sasha's cup of coffee was frozen halfway to her lips as I emerged from the bedroom like a bear emerging from the depths of hibernation, all squinty-eyed and matted hair. Was the world always this bright? Was there a dial somewhere I could use to turn it down just a teeny bit?

'Hi.' My voice sounded like I'd gargled with rocks.

Sash was still staring at me. 'Someone had a good night! I'll have to have words with Ashok next time I see him, leading you astray like this.' There was laughter in her voice. 'Would you like a coffee?'

I put up a thumb in grateful acceptance and skated over the comment about Ashok leading me astray. Right now, I didn't have the energy or brain power to explain that I'd run into my old friend, Gabby, not to mention the man I'd once been certain I'd marry and found him, much to my chagrin, just as interesting and complex as before. Also, he'd aged really, *really* well. Git.

'How was your evening?' I croaked out.

'Oh my God! It was soooo good. Sorry I didn't message you. It just flew by so quickly!'

'That's OK. I took it as no news is good news.'

She threw a smile as she placed a large mug of the freshly brewed coffee down in front of me, excitement at her evening making her words tumble out quickly.

'Thanks, love,' I squeezed in as she did so.

'They were both super nice and we talked over some great ideas for content. We're going to do a chatty vlog with all of us too, to try and get some cross-over of followers. They've told me about some really cool places off the tourist trail to go to. I thought we might do some together, if you're free?'

'That sounds great, love. And, of course, I'd love to.'

'I mean, I know you don't want to be filmed or anything now, but I can shoot around that. It'd still be nice to go together and also to the places you'd told me about too.'

'Of course.' Her comment about not wanting to be filmed sent a spike of guilt through me – but I couldn't do it. Not at the moment. Maybe not ever. Judgement for anyone on social media was harsh – I'd comforted Sasha plenty of times when some troll with more time than brain cells had posted something nasty on one of her videos. I was glad that she had now employed a friend from her marketing days to take over the moderation of her channel. It was one less worry for her – and us as her parents. 'Absolutely, Sash. That sounds great.'

There was so much to say. To think about. To tell her. But not right now. Staying upright and focused on not spilling a scalding-hot coffee was the most I could concentrate on right now. Also, I needed to get some things straight in my own head first before speaking to my daughter. Like why could I not stop thinking about Tomas Bertholle as though I was still some lovesick teenager? Champagne had a lot to answer for. I was sure, once the fog cleared and the percussion section of the Paris Philharmonic stopped warming up inside my skull, things would be a lot clearer.

'How was the hotel? Do you think Ashok is still happy with the investment?'

'Yes, I'd say so. He made some observations about things he did and didn't like while we were there but nothing major.'

'So how come you got plastered?' Sash was grinning at me.

'I did not get plastered, thank you very much.' The cacophony in my head would suggest otherwise but it was the principle of the matter. I was supposed to be the responsible adult here. Although from the look on my daughter's face, I was fighting a losing battle.

'If you say so.'

'Actually we, or rather I, ran into some old friends at the hotel.'

'Oh, wow, really? Like from back in the day?'

'Yes, from back in the Dark Ages!' I gave her a wink, which felt a little easier today. Hopefully, that meant the bruising was healing. I'd yet to get up the gumption to actually look in a mirror.

She rolled her eyes. 'So, who was it? Someone you studied with?'

'Yes. Gabrielle. Gabby, that I told you about.'

'Oh, wow! Amazing! And you just ran into her?'

'Literally. Coming out of the loos of all places.'

'Did she recognise you?'

'Yes. Much to my astonishment! Apparently, I haven't changed a bit.' I pulled a face.

'Why do you say it like that?'

'Well, we haven't all aged as well as Gabby. She still looks fabulous.'

'So do you!' Sash replied loyally.

I pulled her towards me and kissed her. 'Thank you, darling. That's very kind.'

'It's not kind. It's true.'

'OK, then let's say Gabby still looks unbelievably stylish.'

'She's French,' Sash said with a shrug as if that said it all. Which it kind of did. 'And you have your own style.'

I smiled, and decided not to take that particular train of thought past its current station.

'Wait,' Sash continued. 'Isn't she the sister of that arsehole that dumped you?'

'There wasn't really any dumping as such. We just... broke up.'

'But that's her, though?'

'Yes. She is Tomas's sister.'

'Well, at least he wasn't there,' she said with a snort. 'God, can you imagine?'

I drank the last remaining dregs of my coffee and remained silent.

'OhmyGod!' She sat bolt upright. 'He was there!'

I looked over the rim of the mug and met my daughter's wide-eyed expression.

'Yes. He was.'

'Well, I hope he's fat and bald and you wondered what you'd ever seen in him!'

'Unfortunately not.'

Sash gasped.

'I mean to the first bit. He's actually aged very well.'

'Is he married?'

'No.'

'Ah. Divorced. See?' She threw up her hands. 'He'd have been unreliable anyway.'

'Sash. I'm divorced.'

She paused as the penny dropped. 'That's different.'

The logic of that particular comment escaped me but I didn't have either the brain capacity or energy this morning to dispute it.

'As far as I know, he's never been married.'

His words of last night floated back to me. *Everyone I met was a poor impression of you.*

'Lothario.'

'I don't know. We didn't discuss his love life.'

Sash pulled a face. 'Thank God for that. Do they both still live in Paris then? I thought you said Gabby had plans to move to Provence.'

'She did for a while but she's back here now. Actually, it was really rather lovely. Ashok and her really hit it off. I think he's smitten already and Gabby barely took her eyes off him all night.' Just thinking about it made me smile. My daughter, though, looked less thrilled.

'What?'

She shrugged. 'I always kind of hoped you and him would get together. He'd be soooo good for you, Mum.'

She plopped down beside me on the sofa.

'And he is good for me, Sash. As a friend. A very good friend. Don't forget that I'd never have even considered returning to Paris if it hadn't been for him.'

'And so far, that seems to be working out more to his advantage than yours.'

'That's not true. I was heartbroken that my friendship with Gabrielle became a casualty of my relationship with Tomas failing. Meeting her again last night was incredible and I'm very grateful that I was in the right place at the right time to start rekindling that.'

'Anything else you might be rekindling?'

I got up and walked to the cupboard, reached up for a glass and filled it with water and popped out two paracetamol from a packet on the top, gulping them down with the water. When I turned back to face the living area, Sasha was watching me, apparently still waiting on an answer.

'I thought I was supposed to be the mother in this relationship.'

'You are but that doesn't mean I don't worry about you.'

'Sash. I'm a big girl. You don't need to worry about me. I'm more than capable of looking after myself. So if you're alluding to me rekindling anything with Tomas, then no. I have no plans in that direction.'

'I know you're capable, Mum. But you can be a bit naïve sometimes.'

My brows raised and Sash held up her hands.

'And I don't mean that in a bad way.'

'Is there a good way?'

'It's just that you and Dad kind of kept to yourselves or stayed within the realms of Dad's academic circle. I'm not saying you don't know what's going on in the world or anything.'

'Well, thank you,' I interjected with a shovelful of sarcasm.

'Don't be offended.'

'I'm doing my very best not to be.'

She shifted in her seat. 'People can take advantage of others who might not be as street smart as them,' my daughter continued in a knowing way.

'Sash, I know you mean well. And you're right, me and your dad did keep a fairly small life, compared to yours, but that doesn't mean we're unaware of things. Believe it or not, we were once your age and despite not having smart phones, rolling news and being connected twenty-four hours a day, seven days a week, somehow we managed to survive this far. People using others for whatever purpose is as old as time itself. I might not know the latest Taylor Swift song or how to do what you do on YouTube but I'm not entirely hopeless.'

Sasha was quiet for a moment, flicking her thumb. This usually meant she was thinking something over, a tic she'd developed as a small child. As I had said, I might not know facts about the latest fad but I knew my daughter and right now, I knew she was pondering over whether to continue this debate or withdraw. Thankfully, and wisely, she chose the latter. With a raging hangover, I wasn't in the mood to continue it either.

'I'm just trying to look out for you, Mum. He obviously really hurt you before and I don't want that happening again.'

I held out my arms and Sash came over and allowed herself to be wrapped in a hug.

'I know. And he won't.'

She pulled back suddenly. 'So you are seeing him again?'

'No. Not like that.'

She frowned.

'I mean, possibly not at all. He has an exhibition at a local gallery. That's why they're here. I mean, Gabby does live in Paris again now, but now I think about it, I never asked Tomas where he was living now. It never occurred to me, if I'm honest.'

'Well,' Sasha said, straightening, 'that's a good sign. It shows you're not interested.'

I wasn't entirely sure it showed anything of the sort other than the fact we'd had thirty years to catch up on in the space of a few hours and certain things naturally got left out or forgotten.

'Why don't you go back to bed for a bit?' my daughter suggested.

'No, no.' I waved my hand. 'I'm fine. I want to hear all about your evening.'

'Mum. Don't take this wrong, but you look like shit and I'm not sure you'd be absorbing much of what I tell you anyway.'

'Thanks.'

'I mean it in the nicest possible way.'

'Of course.'

'How's your face?'

'A little sore, but better than yesterday.' Without the dulling aid of alcohol, my face was in a battle of wills with my head as to which hurt the most. Right now, my head was definitely winning.

'At least it doesn't look any worse.'

'That's something then.' I finished the glass of water and pushed myself up from the sofa. 'You know what, I think I will go back to bed and see if I can get a bit more sleep then perhaps we can go and have some lunch together if you're free and you can tell me all about last night and what you're working on next.'

'That sounds great, Mum.' The tetchiness between us had evaporated and I was glad of it.

'Do you want to choose a café in the meantime? Maybe one on your list you want to try or near somewhere you want to film?'

'Any preferences?'

'Nope. Wherever you like.'

'OK. I've got a few ideas. I'll do a bit more research while you're getting some rest.'

'Perfect. I'll see you in a bit.' I headed back into the bedroom, pulled the heavy curtains across and climbed into bed, sinking into the soft mattress. I closed my eyes and Tomas's handsome face drifted into view, the smile that had won me so many years ago still the same. Still as handsome. But I was different person now, I told myself. Romantic relationships with Tomas were a thing of the past. Hopefully, we could be friends now, for Gabby's sake at least. So why had my stomach done that long-forgotten flutter every time he'd looked at me?

My head thumped and I shuffled over onto my side and snuggled down into the duvet. Within a few minutes, I was asleep.

23

Sasha had put a poll on her channels, asking her followers if there was anywhere they wanted her to visit on their behalf and had been flooded with suggestions, many of them linked to the Netflix series *Emily in Paris*. So, after I'd had a nap, a shower and brushed my hair, I was feeling a little more on the human side. Pulling one of my comfy secret pyjama dresses from the wardrobe, I slipped it on, did my best with some concealer and foundation to hide the worst of the bruising and went back out into the living room.

Sash looked up from her laptop. 'You look better. How do you feel?'

'More like a resident of this planet, which is something.'

'Good start.'

'Did you find somewhere you wanted to go?'

'Yes. It's one of the places from *Emily in Paris* that got a lot of votes. Is that OK with you?'

'Absolutely. So long as it has strong coffee and good food, I'll be happy.'

'I'm pretty sure that's a given here.'

I scrunched my nose. 'There's definitely a few places aimed specifically at tourists which don't always have the best cuisine but I reckon we can avoid them.'

'I'd love to go to some of the places you used to go to.'

'As would I. And now I'm back in touch with Gabby, she'll probably remember some that I don't, as well as being able to tell us whether they're still there or not.'

'That's true.' There was hesitancy in her voice.

'I can't wait for you to meet her,' I added. 'Obviously, she already loves you from how I was gushing about you last night and I'm sure you'll love her too. Most people do!'

'Including Ashok by the sounds.'

'That's probably a bit strong but he did seem keen. As did she.'

Sash sighed. 'Well, if it can't be you, I hope it's someone that deserves him.'

'And she would, if it goes that far. Don't forget he lives in India and she lives in Paris. Not the easiest commute. We'll see.'

'I wonder how his meeting is going?'

'I'm sure he'll update us later.' I tied the laces on my platform Converse trainers and grabbed a coat. Sash had bought the shoes for me for Christmas, insisting they were the comfiest shoes I'd ever wear and I'd certainly need them with all the miles we'd be doing exploring Paris. I'd been a little unsure as to whether they were a bit 'trendy' for me but Sash had told me not to be so daft and insisted I'd try them on. She hadn't been wrong about the comfort.

We took the train to Montmartre and followed Google Maps on Sash's phone, wandering among the Bohemian history of the quarter until we arrived at a pink-fronted restaurant with Kelly-green shutters. Groups of tourists were standing and taking photos and, of course, selfies in front of it. We shuffled around them to the door and made our way in. Le Maison Rose was brimming even in the off season but we managed to snag a table and settled ourselves in. Many of the others there were clearly also tourists – the show had done wonders for their business by the looks – so at least I didn't feel too out of place in my caterpillar coat which, despite looking uglier each time I put it on, had at least kept me warm as we'd walked from the Metro station.

Sash peeped over the top of her menu. 'Do you think the chef is as gorgeous as Gabriel? I mean, I know this one isn't "his" restaurant but still?'

'Gabriel?' I repeated vaguely as I perused the menu and concentrated on not drooling. It was a short menu which I always took as a good sign and although Sash and her followers were more interested in its TV connection, it was its history and its farm-to-table ethos that appealed to me.

'Mum!'

'Hmm?' My head snapped up.

'Did you hear me?'

'Yes. Gabriel.' *There. Covered that well.*

'And who is Gabriel?' she asked.

'I didn't realise there would be a test,' I shot back teasingly.

Her shoulders sagged. 'Mum, I thought you were going to watch the series before we came.'

'The series? Oh! Yes. Well. I was but I will.'

'It's a bit late now we're here, isn't it?' She looked down at her own menu.

'Not at all. This way, I get to recognise it when I do see it on the telly.'

She flicked at her thumb. 'I suppose.'

'So who is Gabriel?'

'He's the chef at her local restaurant. And he's gorgeous.'

'Does she end up with him?'

'I'm not telling you that! You have to watch it.'

'Fair enough. And I will do, Sash. I promise.' I made a mental note to start tonight. 'Do you know what you're having yet?'

For once, due to the restaurant's no-filming policy, she'd been able to take in the place and the menu far sooner than was usual.

'The fresh vegetable tart, I think,' she replied.

The same puff pastry tart had caught my eye too.

'Tarts for two then!' I chuckled.

'Mum,' she whispered, but I saw the amusement in her eyes. 'Will you order?' Sash asked.

'Why don't you do it, love? I know you've been practising.'

She scrunched her nose. 'I've sort of fallen behind a bit with it.'

'OK.' I didn't mind. I'd been hoping that Sash would learn the language but she was an adult and I was way beyond telling her what to do. From experience, I found that it was only when you wanted to learn that you actually did.

The tarts were a good choice. Eminently Instagrammable, which Sash obviously took advantage of, and as delicious to eat as they were to look at. When asked if we'd like to order anything to go with our après lunch coffees, Sash chose a cheesecake which, when I tried a piece, literally melted in the mouth. I'd plumped for a slice of carrot cake which hit just the right balance of fruit, spices and icing, not to mention being perfectly moist.

'This used to be a painter's studio, apparently,' I said as I sipped a rich, dark cup of Illy coffee.

'Did it?'

'Yep. Pals with Picasso amongst others.'

'Wow. Cool.' Her enthusiasm was less than mine had been when we'd sat over coffees thirty years ago, having deep discussions about fashion and art and everything else that came to mind.

To Sasha and many others, it having featured in one of the biggest series on television was a far bigger draw, which was good too. Either way, it was great to get back to exploring and I'd loved getting out into the city this afternoon. Plenty of water, strong coffee and good, healthy food had chased away the last remnants of the hangover and I leant back in my chair, soaking it all in, my mind drifting back into the past.

Tomas and I had passed many an hour wandering this artistic quarter and more than once, sitting on the steps of the nearby Sacré-Cœur, had watched the sun rise over Paris. I thought back to his declaration about no longer being a romantic and wondered if it was true.

'You're miles away, Mum.'

'Oh, sorry. Just enjoying the atmosphere.' *Mostly*. 'So where did you want to go next?'

'Do you know this area?'

'I used to.'

'Will you show me?'

Happiness flooded through my veins. 'I'd love to.'

* * *

We'd just stepped off the Metro close to home when my phone rang. I grabbed it out of my bag, not checking the screen.

'*Allo?*' I answered, pressing my phone against my ear as a three-wheeler delivery van rattled past.

'Kitty?' Gabby's voice floated through the ether. 'Ooh, you sound so French! I love it!' Her laughter made me smile as it always had.

'I'm trying to get back in the habit.'

'*Bon*. Now, you're coming to the opening night next week, aren't you?'

'Am I?'

'But of course! Tomas invited you?'

'Then Tomas forgot to tell me.'

'Ugh! My brother is such an imbecile at times.' Somehow, her warmth softened the insult. It was clear from the previous evening, not to mention the fact that she was managing his business, that the two were still close. I was glad of it. I hated to think that relationship might too have been fractured in the fallout of ours. 'Of course you are invited. And darling Sasha, *bien sur*! I cannot wait to meet her!'

I glanced over at Sash, a wide smile on my face. She gave a questioning frown in response.

'Hang on.' I held the phone to the side so that Gabby could still hear. 'Gabby would like to know if we'd like to attend Tomas's opening night at the gallery.'

'Tell her she can have all the exclusive content she wants!' my friend practically bellowed into the phone and we both laughed at the enthusiasm bursting through the airwaves.

'Seriously?' Sash asked quietly.

I gave a shrug. 'Want to come?'

'Definitely!'

'That's a yes, then!' I put the phone back against my ear. 'Thank you.'

It was strange. After thirty years apart, and one evening together, talking to Gabby now felt like none of that had happened and we were picking up exactly where we'd left off. And it was wonderful.

'*Fantastique*! Unfortunately, Ashok can't come. He's had to go home.'

'How did it go?' I asked as I handed the keys to Sash to unlock the main door so that I could gossip with full concentration.

'Ah, *mon dieu*. Kitty. He is perfect! We had lunch together after his meeting and I came home to a delivery of twenty-four yellow roses. You remember they are my favourite? I don't even remember telling him, but perhaps I did.'

'Actually, he asked me.'

'He did? He is so sweet. Which is terrible!'

'It is?'

'But of course! He is too good to be true, which means there has to be something wrong with him!' She laughed but I caught the catch in her voice. After all this time, I could still remember her tells.

'Nothing drastic that I know of but there are obviously some. We'll winkle them out.'

Gabby gave a snort of laughter at my phrasing and I got a burst of warmth. Childish humour for the win! Hugh wasn't always a fan of it, especially when he was surrounded by his academic pals.

'Oh, I know one! He's always, *always*, early.' For many, that could be seen as a good thing but, with this disclosure, I was about to see how much my old friend had changed.

'Ah! See! I knew it! I knew there would be something!' Gabby laughed. 'Although you will be pleased to hear my timekeeping has improved... a little.'

Gabby's tardiness had often driven her brother up the wall but to be the successful businesswoman she clearly now was, I guess that it had improved more than the little she was teasing about.

'OK. I have a few meetings this week but shall I come around a couple of hours earlier before the exhibition and we can gossip some more?'

'That sounds perfect!'

24

Within minutes of us entering the gallery for Tomas's opening night, Gabby was summoned by a very glamorous elderly lady dressed from head to toe in Dior. I'd never used my degree in anger but I could still spot Dior at a hundred paces. The clever lighting not only highlighted the artwork on the walls, but also the diamonds that glittered on her hands, ears, wrist as well as the enormous pendant at her throat.

'Sorry, I have to...' Gabby gave us an apologetic look.

'Go, go!' I whispered. 'Good luck!'

Gabby gave me a private fingers-crossed sign and then strode away confidently as if she already knew the deal was done. Dior lady put her hand on Gabby's arm and they moved to a quieter part of the gallery where an extra couple of small sofas had now been installed, I assumed for instances such as this. Silently, I wished Gabby, and Tomas by default, luck and turned back to Sasha.

'There is a *lot* of money in here,' she spoke out of the corner of her mouth.

'Yep. I've never felt so out of place.' Well, apart from that one time long ago… But according to Gabby there was no chance of that happening tonight at least. Their father had passed some time ago but their mother was still around, although now living a much quieter life in the countryside. It had occurred to me that she might have been attending her son's exhibition but Gabby had mentioned, even without me asking, that her mother no longer came up to the city. The fact I'd even had a moment's thought about coming face to face with the woman again irked me at the time but Gabby had made me laugh, as usual, and knowing that she would not be here tonight allowed me to relax. Sort of.

'Why?' I turned to find Sash staring at me, her brow creased in apparently genuine surprise.

'Because,' I said, almost laughing at her reaction, 'this is very much not my world.'

'Just because you don't normally come to things like this, or might have less money—'

'There's no might about it. I'm practically blind from the sparkle of that lady's diamonds.'

'Yeah, they were amazing,' she agreed with just a hint of longing. I felt the same way. 'But just because someone has less money doesn't mean they're any less entitled to be here and enjoy the art.'

'No. I know. It's just—'

Sash put her hand up. 'There's no "just", Mum. That's it. That's the whole statement. You and Dad always taught me not to look down on people, and not to let people look down on me. That it is people's actions that determine their merit, not their bank balance or how many houses – or diamonds – they own.'

I swallowed hard. My daughter was right. We had done our best to instil those values in her and it seemed to have worked. But all the time I'd been making sure my daughter was never made to feel as inferior as I had been made to all those years ago, I'd forgotten to take that lesson on board myself.

'Besides, *you* were invited by the artist himself.' She pulled a face that didn't entirely mask her disapproval but tucked my arm through hers anyway. 'Come on. Let's go and look at the paintings. I can't believe Gabby has let me film in here and get an exclusive!'

'Yes, that was very kind of her.' I knew that Tomas must have agreed too. They were his paintings, after all, but as Sash's reaction to the mention of him the other night hadn't exactly been warm and fuzzy, and she was so excited about it right now, I decided to omit mentioning him any further for the moment. Likely she would meet him later anyway.

'Where do you want to start?'

'Let's go this way,' she said, pointing in the opposite direction to where Gabby had gone. I stayed silent as Sash filmed, the press lanyard Gabby had prepared for her stopping anyone questioning her. When she lowered the camera, we exchanged comments on the paintings in front of us, all of them positive and not just because we 'knew' the artist. The scenes were just as intoxicating as they had been the night Tomas had given me a private viewing. The rain gleaming on wet Paris streets, so real I could practically feel it, reminding me of the many times the three of us had run through the rain, squealing and laughing as we got soaked to the bone before warming up back at either my tiny studio flat or the larger one that Tomas and Gabby shared, huge bowls of hot chocolate cupped in our hands as we thawed.

The cool rain was contrasted in the next painting where heat shimmered above endless rows of lavender in a hot, dry summer. A mass of purple marching away from the viewer until they halted, stopped by the foot of mountains.

'You can practically smell the lavender,' Sash sighed and snapped me back to the present.

'Yes. Yes, you can.' My reply was soft as my mind travelled back to those fields.

'I might not like him but he's certainly talented.'

A couple next to us pretended not to hear but I noticed the shared private exchange of minutely raised eyebrows.

'Shh,' I whispered. 'You can't say that in here. Besides, you don't know him.'

'Why not?' she asked in the way that many of her generation did. 'I'm allowed an opinion, aren't I?'

'Of course,' I said, keeping my voice low as I steered her away from flapping ears. 'It's just not polite to say so in the middle of the man's exhibition.'

She shrugged. 'OK. I was complimenting his art, though. It's not like I said that was shit.'

'No, I realise that, but let's just keep our thoughts about other things for later, shall we?'

'Fine. I still don't like him, though. Not after what he did to you.'

'It was all a long time ago, Sash. And anyway, he didn't do anything, not really.'

'That's rather my point,' she fired back, one laminated brow arched. 'He just let you sit there and get talked down to by his mother and made no effort to stand up for you. Unlike his sister. Perhaps you should have dated her.' She gave me a half-smile, signalling that she was done arguing.

'Maybe I should,' I replied, returning her smile.

'Gabrielle would certainly have had your back every time,' a deep voice behind us agreed.

We both spun round to find Tomas standing there looking unbearably handsome in a suit the colour of midnight and a crisp, white shirt, the collar unbuttoned. Both Armani, if I wasn't mistaken.

'Tomas!' I wondered exactly how much of the conversation he had heard. As our eyes met, I knew. Every single word.

'Kitty.' He hesitated for a moment until receiving the almost imperceptible nod I gave him then bent, kissing me on both cheeks. 'Thank you for coming.'

'Thanks for inviting us.'

He nodded along with the game. Gabby was the one that had invited us, telling me that although Tomas had wanted to, he felt that it might be better coming from her. And, from Sasha's point of view, he'd probably been right.

'Tomas, this is Sasha, my daughter.'

'Hello,' she said, her face not quite a smile but doing its best as she studied him and stuck out her hand. Tomas didn't miss a beat.

'Hello,' he replied, shaking it. 'I'm so glad you could come. I've heard a lot about you.'

'Oh?' Sash flicked me a look.

'Yes. Your mother is extremely proud of you. You are a social media influencer, I understand?'

'That's right.' She gave a glance around. 'Thank you for letting me film here this evening. My viewers are excited for the video. Mum didn't tell me you were quite so well known.'

That's because Mum hadn't had the first clue!

'You're very welcome. I'm glad that it is of interest to you, and your YouTube audience.'

'Perhaps you could do an interview with Tomas to go with it?'

Both of them turned to me with polite but utterly horrified expressions.

'Just an idea,' I said, less enthusiasm behind my words this time. I'd thought it was a great idea. Apparently, I wasn't destined to be a YouTuber.

An awkward silence descended.

'It looks busy. That's a good sign.' With a now ex-husband who never felt the need to fill any silences at the few social gatherings we had gone to, I'd become accustomed to doing so, even though it was usually with some inane comment as I'd expertly just demonstrated.

Tomas, however, didn't appear to notice anything amiss and merely picked up the thread of conversation. 'Gabby is always excellent at getting the right, and the right amount, of people to attend the opening night.'

'Who are the "right" people?' Sasha asked, her chin tipped a little in challenge.

'Those who have shown an interest in previous works of mine, and have the money to invest.'

'Isn't that rather an elitist view?'

Oh, crikey.

'Sash.'

'What?' She turned to me, her face a picture of innocence. I'd thought that sharing my past with her would bring us closer, and it had. But what I hadn't bargained on was the defensiveness she now felt on my behalf against the man who she now knew had broken my twenty-year-old heart. 'I'm interested.'

Tomas held up a hand. 'No, it's a valid question. And yes, I can see how it would seem elitist. But the truth is, as much as I would love to paint for free, and sometimes do, I also need to earn a living. Creative pursuits, as in your own case, often start out as hobbies. If we are lucky, they eventually are able to support us.'

The awkward silence returned but this time I bit my tongue, almost literally, to stop myself from filling it. This was for Sasha and Tomas to sort out.

Sash cracked first. 'I suppose that's true. Although I'm pretty sure my income and yours are in very different areas of the spectrum.'

'Perhaps.'

I gave Tomas an 'oh, come on' look. The briefest phantom of a smile touched the corner of his mouth.

'Your mother still has the ability to call me out, it would seem.'

'Good job someone does.' The comment was under her breath but there was no doubting Tomas, as well as I, heard it.

'Sasha,' I said, more cross this time.

She swallowed and glanced away for a moment.

'What I intended to say was that, yes, I have been lucky that my work has been noticed now. But it took a long time. You are just starting out.'

'I've actually had my channel for eleven years.'

'That shows you have commitment. But, from what I understand from my godson about things, it is a very competitive field, and some, as with me in my field, are lucky to have been standing in the right place when the limelight swept past and can make an exceptionally good living from their channel and associated sponsorship and connections. This is right, yes?'

'True. Your godson sounds well informed.'

A waiter with a tray of champagne flutes balanced on one hand drifted past. Tomas stopped him and took two, handing one each to Sasha and me before lifting one for himself.

'Would you let me show you around the exhibition?' His question was directed at Sasha. 'You're clearly a woman unafraid to give an honest opinion and I appreciate that. Perhaps it is an inherited trait.' He gave me a side-eyed glance.

Sash still hadn't relinquished her rein on defensiveness. 'I do. I don't believe in pretence.'

'Neither do I. As such, I would be very interested to hear those opinions, if your mother can spare you?'

'I'd be more than happy to keep the lady company until you come back.' A mid-Atlantic twang curled itself around the words as we all turned towards the person who'd spoken them. A similar build to Tomas, he was perhaps ten years younger, with a wide, orthodontically perfect smile and pale-blue eyes. 'Hi. Frank Delaney.' He held out a hand and I shook it.

'Katherine Collins. Pleased to meet you.'

'If I was being corny, I'd say that I'd guess this was your sister, but that's not my style.'

Tomas gave a grunt at this before the new arrival continued.

'But I'm assuming she's your daughter.'

'I am.' Sash held out her hand, this time with far less confrontational energy behind it. 'But Mum did have me very young.'

'That I can see.' He flashed us the smile again. 'Nice to see you again, Tomas.' He pronounced it in a standard English – or American – way and I saw a tiny muscle begin to pulse in Tomas's jaw. It was something you'd only notice it if you knew him well, knew what to look for.

'Francis,' Tomas parried back.

Oh, for goodness' sake.

'I'm fine here, darling, if you want to go with Tomas for a tour.' I made a point of saying it correctly and felt it was probably an ideal opportunity to separate these two boys before they started putting itching powder down each other's pants.

'OK. Have fun!' She winked at me, making sure Tomas saw.

The flicker increased and I shooed them away.

25

'So! It seems like you two are the best of friends,' Frank said, briefly watching Tomas's retreating back before swinging his full focus back on to me.

'We used to be.' I took a sip of my champagne and idly wondered if it was actual 'Champagne' or from their family's vineyard. I guessed the latter and took another sip. It really was truly excellent.

'That sounds like a story.'

'As does the fact you two were acting like ten-year-olds.' I kept my eyes on him as I took another sip.

'Touché.' Throwing a glance over his shoulder, he looked back to me. 'She's a little younger than Tomas's usual dates.'

'That's because my daughter is certainly not his date. Right now, she's not exactly a fan.'

'Aha, there are two of us then.'

'She has her reasons and she's here because I wanted to come and because she's working.'

'I saw the press badge. Interesting.' He took another sip, his eyes never leaving mine. 'Gabrielle and Tomas are usually super cagey about the media.'

'Gabby and I are old friends.'

'Gabby and I used to be friends.'

The penny dropped. 'Ah.'

'Yep. I was stupid and Tomas never forgave me.'

'I take it Gabby has, bearing in mind you're here.' I drained my glass then pointed it at him. Normally, I wouldn't have been this intrigued. Or flirtatious. Was I even *being* flirtatious? It felt like it. But then again it had been literally decades since I'd attempted anything remotely in that arena – I actually had no idea! 'Am I being too nosy?'

Frank laughed, easily and openly. From the corner of my eye, I saw Tomas and Sasha look round. Sash grinned. Tomas scowled.

'Not at all. It's refreshing for someone to actually say what they mean rather than talking in riddles. Between you and me,' he leant in conspiratorially, 'these kind of things are usually pretty stuffy.'

'That's because,' I said, gesturing with my glass again, 'I'm not usually at them.' Oh God, I *was* flirting. Note to self, do not drink on an empty stomach. Or, actually, maybe do!

'You know, ma'am. I think you might just be right. Can I get you another drink?'

Inner Sensible Me was frowning. *No. I definitely need to find food before any more bubbles.*

'That would be lovely.' *Oops!* Inner Me gave a disapproving huff and stomped off.

'Be right back.'

'Great.'

Frank moved confidently through the crowd to the small bar that had been set up in the corner and I turned away so as not to make it obvious I had been watching him go. Nice bum. Good shoulders...

'Kitty?' Gabby returned to my side, her eyes shining with mischief as she followed my line of sight. 'I see you've met Frank.'

'I have. Or is it Francis?'

She rolled her eyes. '*Ooh la la*. I didn't realise he'd already spoken to *Tomas*.' She pronounced her brother's name in the same way Frank had.

'Oh, yes. That was fun. I sent him off with Sash to give her a tour before they started giving each other wedgies.'

'Good plan.'

'So, he says you were friends.'

She did the head-tilt thing. 'Somewhat more than that. But he fucked it up so now we are not so friendly.'

'Yes. He said something about being stupid.'

'Ha! Yes, perhaps he has learned his lesson. Men, as we know, can be highly intelligent yet incredibly stupid at the same time.'

I gave a small huff of agreement. 'So what's the discord between them then?'

'They never hit it off from the start. Tomas didn't think Frank was right for me. Said he didn't trust him.' She shrugged. 'Most of the time, it didn't matter as they didn't see each other much, although I'd have liked them to be friends, of course. But then, on one of those occasions, a friend of Frank's took a shine to my brother and they started dating. I think he actually really liked her, although trying to get him to admit it, as always, was like getting blood out of a stone. You probably already noticed that change, eh?'

I nodded.

'He always used to be so open until... well.' She waved her hand. We both knew. 'Tomas and I had a meeting with a gallery in New York. Rich people don't always seem to have much of a schedule so they both came with us. Actually, we flew over in Frank's private jet.' She widened her eyes in amusement.

'Ooh, fancy!'

'I know,' she said, laughing. 'Tomas was dying to protest and fly commercial but I told him I'd never speak to him again if he did.'

'Wow. You really liked this chap then?'

'It was more that I'd never been on a private jet and I was desperate to!' She giggled. 'Anyway, we got there, and the next day, Tomas and I went off to the meeting. It didn't really go well. The commission they wanted was absolutely extortionate and not what we'd initially discussed so it all felt like a huge waste of time.'

'Except for the private jet.'

'Except for the private jet,' Gabby repeated with a grin. 'So we headed back to the hotel early. Tomas's room was a few doors up from mine so he heard the screams and came running back.'

'Screams?' I touched her arm, all levity gone.

'Oh, no, it wasn't me. It was Tomas's girlfriend screaming. First at the sight of me walking in on her in bed with my boyfriend. And then as she was trying to avoid the many, many things I was throwing their way.'

'Wow. So your boyfriend slept with your brother's girlfriend?'

'*Oui*. So terribly French, eh? Except they are both American.'

'*Ooh la la.*'

'Quite!'

'Now I get why Tomas gave him such a cold look. I'm surprised he's here though, bearing in mind he cheated on you?'

'I was angry at the time but I wasn't in love with him. I was more upset for Tomas. She was never going to be the love of his life and I think she knew that.' At this, she threw me a glance. I looked away. 'He's never hidden that from the women he's met.

That he's not looking for The One. But he did like her. However, his fury was purely directed at Frank and the fact he'd cheated on me. In the end, I had to practically lock him in his room to avoid having to pay for removal of blood from the hotel carpet.'

'And I guess you already had to pay for all the things you threw.'

'Ah, *non*. The room was booked in Frank's name so...' She shrugged one elegant shoulder and winked.

'Karma.'

'*Exactement*,' she agreed.

'But I'm still not entirely clear as to why Frank is here tonight.' I caught sight of him returning. 'Oh, Lord, he's coming back.'

'Much to his and Tomas's chagrin, Frank collects French artists as investments and also loves Tomas's style. Art is about the only thing they ever agreed on. Also,' she whispered as he approached, 'he is very, very rich!'

'Gabrielle.' He handed me my drink as Gabby offered the two-kiss greeting. 'How lovely to see you.'

'And you, Frank. We were just talking about you, actually.'

Frank looked from her to me then back again. 'Yeah, I bet you were.'

The rift between Gabby and Frank seemed, as she had said, to be healed. Unlike that between the two men. As the three of us continued chatting, Tomas and Sasha, having finished the private tour, now approached. Frank still being here was clearly not what Tomas had hoped for. His dark brows drew together, forehead creasing as the blue gaze flicked between Frank and Gabrielle.

'Ah! Sasha.' Gabby turned, her arm naturally sliding around Sash's waist. 'And what did you think?' She threw a look at her brother. 'And be honest. You know these artists and their egos. It doesn't do them good for everyone to pander to them.'

'Actually, I thought they were all... incredible.' The body

language between them wasn't quite as rigid as it had been earlier but I knew my daughter too well to imagine that a few beautiful paintings would be enough to sway her that quickly. Gabby, on the other hand, she had connected with from their first moment of meeting, just as I had hoped she would. 'The final one was especially interesting, I thought,' Sash spoke again, sending a penetrating look my way.

'Oh?' Frank asked. 'Which one is that?'

'The pretty young woman in the yellow sundress,' Sasha told him.

Frank was scanning the sleek brochure. 'Is that what it's called?'

'Have you even seen it?' Tomas asked, his clean-shaven jaw radiating with tension.

'Not yet. I got caught up chatting to two beautiful women. As much as I love your work, *Tomas*, much to both our disdain, I'm afraid it can't beat good conversation with interesting people.'

Tomas picked a glass from a timely passing server, rolling his eyes as he did so. 'Anyone else? Sasha?'

'That would be lovely, thank you.'

Tomas handed her the glass, nodding politely in acknowledgement.

'Oh, is this it?' Frank looked up from the brochure. '*Summer's Bliss.*'

'That's it,' Sasha replied when it was clear Tomas wasn't going to and Gabby was doing a good job of avoiding the question entirely.

'You recommend that one then?' he asked, looking at Sasha.

'For what?'

'My collection. An investment.'

'Oh... I've... erm... no idea how much it is.' Her voice was low in reply. This wasn't a place where – *quelle horreur* – prices were discussed, or even mentioned.

'Doesn't matter.' He flashed her a grin and my mum spidey sense prickled. As too, it appeared, did Gabby's very recently acquired auntie spidey sense. Her narrowed eyes locked onto Frank's face. Tomas got there before both of us, standing just that little bit taller next to my daughter.

'Don't even think about it, Francis.'

Frank held out his hands. 'What?'

'Why don't I take you round and you can make your own decision?' Gabby said, linking her arm through his, steel wrapped in silk. Frank was going, whether he wanted to or not.

'*Summer's Bliss* isn't for sale,' Tomas stated as Gabby made to steer Frank away. By the brief look that passed between the siblings, this was new information to her.

'It's a special piece,' his sister seamlessly picked up the thread. 'It was sold prior to the exhibition.'

'So how come it's still on display?' Frank might act the playboy but there was clearly an astute mind behind the façade and he'd picked up that something was going on.

'Oh, darling,' Gabby said, looking up at him under her lashes. 'You of all people know how this works. Sometimes, one receives an offer they just can't turn down.' She offered an innocent look, all raised brows and big eyes, which was anything but. And Frank knew it.

'Nicely played, Gabs. OK, so show me the ones I am allowed to buy.'

'*Bien sur!* With pleasure. Shall we get another drink on the way?'

Sash was watching, adoration clear on her face.

'She's amazing!' she breathed when they were out of earshot.

Tomas nodded.

'I can see why you asked her to be your agent,' my daughter continued.

His laugh surprised both of us, and the serious expression transformed back into the one I'd been used to. Older, a few more lines but no less handsome for that. Perhaps even more so. 'I wish I could claim that honour.'

'I don't understand. I thought Gabby *was* your agent.' Sash looked at me for confirmation and we both looked back at Tomas.

'She is, and for that I am enormously grateful but her taking that position was most certainly nothing to do with me. Having taken over the running of the vineyard—'

'Gabby runs the vineyard?'

'Not now. She used to, once it was obvious that it was not my forte. Now it's run by my godson, Benoit.' He peered over the heads of the assembled guests, taller than many of them. 'He should be here anytime.' Turning back to us, he continued. 'Once Gabby took over the vinery, she told me to go and paint. I already felt a bit of a failure, so to me, this didn't seem the best idea.'

'Why not?' Sasha asked, forgetting for a moment that she'd yet to forgive him.

'Honestly?' he asked her.

Caught up in the story, she nodded, urging him on.

'At the time, it just felt like something else I could fail at.'

'But Gabby believed in you.'

He smiled down at my daughter. 'She did. I'm extremely lucky in that respect. My sister has always had more confidence in my abilities than I have.'

'And now?'

'Now?'

Sasha indicated the swanky surroundings, the rich and beautiful drifting around, admiring the artwork. You could almost smell the wealth.

'Now I feel very fortunate to be in this position but there are still days when I feel like I'll never sell another painting.'

'Imposter syndrome.'

'Exactly,' he replied, his focus on her entirely.

'Well, I don't think you need...' Her words tailed off as her jaw dropped open. Suddenly, she snapped it shut and took a step closer so that we were now in a little huddle. 'Is that Timothée Chalamet?' Her voice was an almost inaudible squeak of excitement.

'Possibly, I—' Tomas began to turn his head and received a punch on the biceps.

'Don't look!' Sash whispered sharply.

Tomas scratched his jaw, attempting to cover the smile that was threatening to break on his face. His eyes cut to me and I gave the tiniest shake of my head. If he laughed, I was lost. Why is everything funnier when you're supposed to be on your best behaviour? At least we weren't in church. Not that that hadn't happened before.

'It's a little difficult to answer the question without looking,' he replied.

'To my left,' she whispered and Tomas shifted his weight in order to change position as naturally as possible whilst getting a good viewing angle.

'Ah. Yes, it is. He did say he might attend if he was able. I believe he's shooting a film here at the moment.'

As he spoke, the A-lister raised his gaze, saw Tomas and waved. Excusing himself from the couple he'd been talking to, he headed our way.

'OhmyGod. He's coming over!' Sash's voice was practically now only audible to dogs.

'Tomas! Good to see you, man.' The two men embraced with the requisite back slapping.

'And you, Timothée.'

Sash turned to me, eyes as wide as the plates the canapés were being circulated on.

'How's the filming?'

'Great, thanks. And thanks again for the invitation. You know I love your work. Anything left?' He laughed, self-deprecating.

'One or two,' Tomas teased, the banter appearing natural.

I wondered if he may have just gone up a notch or two in Sash's opinion.

'Timothée, may I introduce a couple of special guests here tonight.'

Sash looked like she might pass out. The actor had been one of her favourites, and her biggest crush for years.

'Kitty Collins, a very dear friend from university days.'

'Good to meet you,' he said, leaning in for the traditional 'la bise' greeting of kissing both cheeks.

'And you,' I replied.

'And this is Sasha, Kitty's daughter.'

'Pleasure,' Timothée said, hitting Sash with a smile that I was pretty sure she'd remember for a lifetime.

'Hi,' she replied, nearly dying when she too received a kiss on both cheeks.

'British?' he asked her.

'Yep!' she replied. Her exquisitely applied make-up hid the flush on her cheeks but I saw a brief reddening of her décolletage that told me she was already berating herself for not parrying back with something she considered far more clever and suave.

'Great accent,' he continued.

'Kitty and Sasha have just moved to Paris.'

'Oh, wow.' Timothée's eyes flicked to me but quickly settled back on Sash. 'That's so cool. I love Paris. Always have.'

'Me too,' Sash replied, her colour settling a little more now.

'And this guy captures it like no one else. I always end up buying at least one painting even when I tell myself I have enough art.'

'Can one ever have enough art?' Sash asked.

He regarded her for a moment. 'That is a very good point. Probably not. Thanks for reminding me.'

'You're welcome.' She flashed the wide smile she'd always been a little self-conscious of. It was something she'd inherited from me. I hoped in time she'd see it as beautiful as it truly was. Tomas had once told me that my smile was the reason he'd first fallen in love with me.

A tall, very slim, ridiculously chic woman appeared at Timothée's shoulder, from the body language, I assumed an assistant rather than a girlfriend. He sensed her and turned.

'Hey.'

She gave us all a brief, very tight smile. It was hard to tell her age, or her expression. Nothing really moved on her face. It was oddly captivating and I unnecessarily adjusted my bracelet in order to drag my eyes away.

'I'm going to go and take a look at the exhibition. See if there's anything good left to buy,' he said, giving Tomas a gentle slap on the upper arm as he did so.

'Probably not.'

Timothée laughed and raised a hand as we smiled our goodbyes. He began to turn then looked back at us and leant in towards me.

'OK, so we all need to be so careful about what and who we say stuff to these days in case it gets taken the wrong way or out of context but,' his gaze flicked to Sasha and lingered for a few moments, 'can I just say that your daughter has a beautiful smile.'

'Thank you. I think so too,' I said, turning towards my beautiful daughter, who looked like she might float up to the ceiling like a helium balloon let loose by a toddler.

'Thank you,' she repeated and then casually turned back to us, careful not to look gauche in staring after him.

For a moment, we stood in silence. Not awkward like before. An unspoken agreement between Tomas and me told us to remain silent.

'Oh my Goddddd!' Sash squeaked out in a high-C whisper. 'That was...' She was practically vibrating on the spot.

'Cool?' I offered.

'Soooo cool!' Sash continued. 'No one is ever going to believe I met him!'

I could see the cogs in Tomas's mind whirring.

'How long have you known him?'

'Quite a few years now. He bought a painting from my first-ever exhibition. How Gabby got him to attend, I have no idea. I know better than to question the expertise and talent of my sister. As I said, I am just thankful. I'd probably still be painting in a shed at the end of her garden if she hadn't – how do you say – put a rocket up my arse.'

Champagne sprayed out of my mouth and as I clamped my lips together, it quickly changed direction and exited via my nose instead. Automatically, I shifted towards Tomas, his large bulk hiding my faux pas from the rest of the room. My daughter, however, was already well into the process of disowning me.

'Mum!'

Had I even done my job right if I didn't mortify my offspring from time to time?

Tomas, laughing himself now, handed me a perfectly pressed linen handkerchief and I mopped up as gracefully as I could, although that ship had long sailed and was likely shipwrecked by now.

'My fault.' Tomas placed his hand on his chest, that sexy grin completely transforming his features.

I shook my head, still finding it more amusing than my daughter. We locked eyes and he gave a tiny wink. The little shit! How many times had he pulled the same trick back then? Waiting until Gabby or I had a mouthful to say something funny, or outrageous, just to get us to cough and splutter our drinks. Of course, back then, it wasn't champagne dripping off our chins. The two of them may have come from a wealthy family but they never acted in the superior manner of their mother. Perhaps they were more like their father. It had been hard to tell as I'd only met him that once and he'd barely spoken, or had had a chance to speak.

Gabby once told me that he preferred a quiet life and therefore found it easier to give his wife free rein than argue. He'd offer his opinion but more often than not, it had been either overruled or disregarded entirely. It had maddened Gabby but I'd seen that day how perhaps Tomas took after his father more than any of us had realised. I wondered how much of that aspect had changed over the years.

'Definitely your fault!' I couldn't stop the smile.

26

Sash was currently gazing out across the crowd, her back slightly towards us, clearly pretending she was nothing to do with me. Tomas's gaze shifted to Sash then back to me and he pulled a face, his just-generous-enough mouth turning down before tipping back into a grin. I mirrored his expression and mouthed the word 'Oops' at him.

'Sorry,' he mouthed back.

For a moment, we both just stood there, eyes taking in perhaps the changes, but also all that was familiar.

'Kitty—'

'*Bonsoir*! *Bonsoir*! I'm so sorry I am late.' The young man burst the fragile bubble between us as he rushed towards us, firing rapid French at Tomas, clasping him by the upper arms and dropping two kisses before they hugged warmly.

'*Pardon*,' he added as he pulled away.

'*Pas probleme*,' I replied.

Whoever this handsome, ebullient man was, it was clear Tomas was thrilled to see him. His whole being had lit up, eyes sparkling with pleasure as he received the new guest.

'Is Aunt Gabby here?'

'But of course.'

'Ah, *oui*.' He laughed then took in Sasha who had now either forgiven or forgotten that her mother was an embarrassment and had turned back to join us. It wasn't hard to see why.

'Benoit, this is Kitty Collins, and her daughter, Sasha. They've very recently moved to Paris.' There was a flicker of recognition as Tomas said my name but it was quickly smothered. So, he knew.

'Kitty, Sasha, this is my godson, Benoit. As I mentioned, he now, very efficiently and successfully, runs the vineyard.' We greeted each other as Gabby once more approached us.

'Benoit, *mon chéri*. I see you have met our friends,' she said as she kissed his cheeks.

'Just now, yes.' Benoit's gaze, and smile, returned to Sasha. 'Are you enjoying the exhibition?'

'Yes, thank you. Your godfather is very talented.'

Benoit pulled an unimpressed face and pushed out his bottom lip. 'He has his moments.' He leant a little closer to Sash. 'Although I'm not entirely convinced these aren't all paint by numbers.' He grinned and she returned it. 'Now, I see you have an empty glass. Would you allow me to get you another champagne?'

'Perhaps some food would be a good idea too, Benoit. The poor girl hasn't had a chance to eat yet,' Gabby instructed.

'Oh, yes, that would be great.' Sash looked up at him. 'If you don't mind.'

'*Pas de tout*. I'm also famished. Let's go and see what we can find.'

'Your English is excellent,' Sash began as they walked away, her hand resting on Benoit's proffered arm.

'Thank you. I actually studied...' The rest was lost to me but I knew I'd be getting a full run-down later.

'Everything OK?' Tomas asked his sister.

'*Parfait*. But you really ought to mingle a little more, Tomas. We've spoken about this.'

Colour crept up my chest. 'Sorry, that's my fault. We've been hogging him all evening. I didn't even think. Sorry,' I said again. 'I'll let you go mingle.' I wiggled my fingers to signal said mingling.

Tomas caught my hand and wrapped his own around it. 'And, as I say to my dear sister each time, I am an artist, not a salesman. People will buy if they want to. I would rather they choose of their own accord and not because they feel obligated while they're talking to me in front of a piece.'

The thought that people could feel obligated to buy a six-figure piece of art flittered through my mind. I'd occasionally bought a pack of tea towels at the door for the same reason but that was hardly the same thing.

'Plus,' he turned his eyes to me and my gaze met his automatically, 'I'm looking after our VIP.'

'You do remember the A-list actor that was here a while ago?' I asked him.

'Mmhmm.'

'OK. That is a VIP.'

Tomas's gaze remained steady. 'I beg to differ.'

'He wanted *Summer's Bliss* too, by the way,' Gabby put in. 'Sorry to interrupt,' she added, looking anything but sorry.

'What did you tell him?' her brother asked.

'I said I wasn't sure if it had already been sold.' Her voice had dropped. 'I know you didn't want Frank to have it but—'

Tomas shook his head. 'It's not for sale,' he reiterated.

Gabby stared at him for a moment, before giving a quick nod. 'OK. I'll find the curator and ask her to place a notice.' She flashed me a smile then turned on her five-inch spiked heel and strutted across to where the chic woman who'd approached Timothée earlier was standing looking – well, chic.

'You really should go and mingle.'

Tomas was still holding my hand and although I knew I shouldn't, I couldn't help but revel in the feel of it once more. It had always felt so right. Warm, even on the coldest of days, and as though it was made for mine as his large hand wrapped around my far smaller one. The perfect fit. It had felt right and, as unfashionable as it was to say now, safe. But then, once again, perhaps it was merely the champagne talking, and acting, for both of us.

'I hate mingling.'

'Even so.'

'Even so. I hate mingling and would much rather stay here and talk to you.'

He was close now and I looked up, fell once more into those midnight-blue eyes. What I fully intended to reply with was, *It's probably best I leave you to chat with the other guests*, but what actually came out was: 'OK.'

'Let's go and get some food.'

27

'Where do you think you're going?'

We both stopped dead, like naughty children caught in the act.

Gabby was mock-glaring at us, one dark, perfect, laminated (if I wasn't mistaken) brow raised in question. I definitely needed to ask her where she got them done.

'Where do you get your brows done?'

Not now, you chump!

'What?'

'Your eyebrows are the stuff of dreams. This,' I rolled my eyes up as though to look at my own brows, 'is the first time I've had my brows done in yonks! And that was at Sasha's insistence. Mostly, I just ping out the odd grey or rampant – or grey and rampant – ones when I spot them in the mirror along with those super-long hairs that seem to sprout on your face literally overnight. Although I bet you don't get those. I'm not sure they'd dare!'

By this point, both Gabby and Tomas were staring at me.

'Sorry. I had the thought and it...' I made a rolling sort of gesture with my hand, 'all sort of tumbled out. I only meant to make a mental note to ask you where you go but I'm not sure there's much space up there at the moment.'

They were still staring at me.

'Sorry,' I said again. And then I burped. If Sasha were here, she'd have filed familial divorce papers by now.

'Sorry. Again,' I mumbled, my hand in front of my mouth.

Still silence. Then Gabby snorted. Proper snorted, her eyes crinkling with laughter and filling with joyful tears.

'I knew she was still in there somewhere!' she cried, her words full of delight. 'I told you!' she said as she pulled me into the tightest hug I'd ever had in my life. I was pretty sure I turned blue for a few seconds before she stood me back. 'Welcome back! I'm so happy to see you again!'

'Where did I go?'

'Oh, *ma chérie*, I don't know but you're here now! Or at least back on the right path.'

'Oh. That's...' I looked at Tomas, who was grinning. 'Good to know. I think.'

'Right,' Gabby said, appearing to regain her composure. 'We'll come back to this later. In the meantime, as much as I would love to let you young lovers sneak off for a romantic meal and stroll along the Seine at midnight, I need my brother to come and be charming.' She threw him a look. 'It's a long shot, I know, but do try, because I have my eye on some to-die-for shoes at Christian Dior and therefore need as much commission as possible.'

'He was always charming,' I said, then frowned at the fact words kept falling out of my mouth. Usually, I just stood there and nodded in agreement, smiled, or filled an awkward silence with something inane, depending on what the situation called for, and then went home. Admittedly, I didn't normally drink champagne. At least rarely more than a glass. But it wasn't just that. I knew it wasn't just that. There was something else. Was it my friends? Was it the clothes Gabby had lent me? Was it Paris? Was it Tomas?

'Once upon a time, he was,' Gabby said, prodding me from my ponderings. 'But he turned rather moody and grumpy once you left.'

'That's not true.' Tomas frowned at his sister. 'It's not true,' he repeated, looking at me this time.

She gave a 'poof' of disbelief. 'Come on. I'm not doing all the work. *Allez!*'

'It'd be very rude to leave our guest.' Tomas was stalling. Clearly mingling really wasn't his thing these days.

'I'll look after Kitty,' she said, tucking her arm around mine. 'Now, go!'

Tomas hesitated, glanced at me, which was no help as I was trying not to laugh at him being bossed around by his younger sister, the situation different, decades passed, but still so very familiar.

'I thought you'd be on my side.'

Gabrielle huffed. 'For goodness' sake, Tomas! Don't be obtuse.'

We looked at each other.

'You have a hell of a lot more making up to do before Kitty's on your side. Also.' She tapped the side of her nose. 'Girlfriends stick together.' She gave me a squeeze. 'At least the good ones do. Now go!'

Shoving his hands in his pockets, he finally obeyed and wandered off to be charming.

'*Ooh la la!*' Gabby shook her head. '*Mon frère! Alors*, I have someone very interesting for you to meet. Come with me.'

We began crossing the gallery, arms still linked, me still getting used to the stilettos Gabby had lent me. Thankfully, not as high as hers but certainly more so than the shoes I'd fallen into the habit of wearing at home.

'I noticed Benoit and Sasha appear to be getting along very well.' She gestured with her chin towards a corner where Sash was leaning against a wall, her head tilted up as she laughed at whatever Tomas's godson was saying. 'He's one of the good ones.' Gabby read my mind, just as she always had done.

'Good to know. Not that she's mentioned any interest in relationships at the moment. She came out of a long-term one a little over a year ago,' I filled in my friend. 'It was unexpected on her side and left her rather bruised but thankfully, she had her work to throw herself into and, although I would never say it to her, I think he did her a favour.'

'You didn't like him.' No question, just a statement.

'It wasn't that I didn't like him, as such.'

'He wasn't right for her.'

'He wasn't. And I didn't think he treated her in the way she deserved to be.'

'Like a princess.'

'In the good way, yeah.'

'Absolutely. None of us need rescuing these days but that doesn't mean we don't want, or deserve, to be treated like the queens that we are.'

'Exactly.'

'So, let's leave them to it for the moment. I have the most interesting lady I want you to meet. I was chatting to her about the fact we studied fashion together. She used to work at Christian Dior's atelier.'

'Wow!'

'I know. And she ended up marrying one of the clients who used to accompany his mother.'

'Really?'

'Yes, isn't that romantic?'

'Wait, that's her?' I faltered in my step as I saw the diamond-draped lady from earlier.

'*Oui*. What's the matter?'

'I don't think this is a good idea. I'm fairly sure I don't have anything to say that would be of interest to someone like that.'

'Someone like that?'

'Come on, Gabs. The only reason I even look like I fit in here is because I've borrowed your clothes.' There was certainly nothing in my wardrobe that had been fit for an event this chic. With a sartorial sixth sense, Gabby had arrived at the apartment earlier with a suit carrier slung over her shoulder and a Chanel overnight bag hanging on her arm.

'Just in case!' she'd said, gesturing to the items. Putting them on, although they were far removed from my usual style, had caused the years to float away once more, and we were back to those young women, swapping clothes and gossiping about the upcoming evening.

'*Oui*, that is true,' she replied.

'Ouch.' I knew it was true but some attempt at padding around her answer might have been nice.

She tilted her head. 'I was just agreeing with you.'

'You didn't have to!'

'But it is true, *ma chérie*. You said as much yourself. It's no big deal. You always had a great eye, and now it's time to focus it back on you after so long of looking after everyone else. But that can wait for a moment. Now,' she continued leading me, still somewhat reluctantly on my part, towards the other guest, 'smile, Kitty! She won't eat you. Oh, *mon dieu*, what is that?' she asked as she glanced at me, laughter in her voice.

'You said smile. I'm smiling!'

'Are you sure?'

I blew her a raspberry just before we got into earshot.

'That's better. *Alors*...'

Dior lady stood, her hands outstretched to take mine. 'Now you must be Kitty. Gabrielle has told me all about you and your adventures together in Paris. I am Reine Dubaire.'

'*Bonsoir*, Madame Dubaire.' I caught myself just before I curtseyed. She gave off that sort of vibe.

'No, no, no. You must call me Reine. Now.' She glanced over at a waiter and he immediately turned towards us, as though she'd sent out a tractor beam from her striking blue eyes. 'Here we are.' She lifted the glasses off the tray, handing one to each of us. 'Tell me all about your studies in Paris. I want to hear it all!'

'I'd much rather hear about your time in the atelier.'

'Then we shall both get our wish.' She patted the space next to her on the sofa and I took my place.

'I shall leave you two to get to know one another.'

'Thank you, Gabby.' Reine looked at me. 'I think that will be lovely.'

She was right, but it was more than just lovely; it was wonderful. Two hours later, we were still sitting on the sofa, having done a round of the gallery again, Reine asking my opinion on the paintings as we stopped at each one, studying them, appreciating them. She noticed things I didn't and the more we talked, the more I appreciated them.

'Tomas has a very distinct brushwork, so long as you know what you're looking for.'

'He does?'

'Yes. But what I love the most about his paintings is that they are real. There is so much heart in them.' She placed a beringed hand to her chest as she said this. 'I'm not a fan of modern art so much. Perhaps that is old-fashioned?'

'No, I don't think so. Art, like fashion, books, any creative pursuit is entirely subjective. We like what we like.'

'That is true. And what is it you like, my dear?'

'Honestly? I'm not even sure I know any more.'

'Then,' she said, 'we must do something about that.'

By the end of the evening, Reine and I were firm friends and I had had one of the most interesting conversations of my life. Reine's tales of her time in the atelier of one of the world's most recognised couture houses had me asking question after question, apologising each time for doing so. That was until Reine told me that if I apologised one more time, she wasn't going to say another word. That did the trick.

'Never apologise for being interested in someone, my dear,' she said, her accent a heady mix of her native Provence and the place she had called home now for many decades – Paris. 'It is what everyone wishes for, even if they profess differently.'

'I suppose that is true.'

'There's no "suppose" about it. I grew up very poor and was lucky enough to be taught a skill which I used to get myself a life that I wouldn't have had without it. Not to mention that without that skill, I wouldn't have met the love of my life. Nearly sixty years ago, I was walking down the aisle in a Christian Dior dress that I'd helped create. Had anyone told that little girl in the tiny village in Provence that one day, she would be doing so, she'd have run to her mother and asked her to make the strange person telling tales to go away! And yet I did and here I am now. Privileged enough to meet people like you and Tomas and Gabrielle. Life has been good enough to afford me that.

'But I knew what I wanted, and that helped. I knew I wanted to leave the confines of the village. The glossy magazines I managed to get hold of second or third hand showed me there was so much more out there to see. I set my heart on Paris without ever seeing it. And I was determined to work in one of the best ateliers in Paris. I'd have accepted Chanel at a push.' She wrinkled her nose a little and I laughed at the thought of Reine turning up nose up at Coco Chanel and what the lady herself might have thought of that.

'I'd always loved Dior. So beautiful. So feminine. Just perfection in style and design, and of course, workmanship.' She winked at me and for a moment, I got a glance of the young woman that she had been, marching into that famous address on Avenue Montaigne and advising them to take her on.

'I was a pushy little *vache*, now I look back on it,' she said, amusement in her voice. 'But the world is a tough place. Some people get things handed on a plate. Others don't and those are the ones who need to work the hardest, but they're also the ones, like me, that can be the proudest of themselves.' She took my hand and put it to my chest. 'Remember what it was you wanted when you first came to Paris and then decide, in here,' she indicated where my hand lay over my heart, 'if it's still the same thing.'

'Oh, Reine, I'm far too old to follow those dreams now.'

She tutted at me. 'Rubbish. One is never too old, merely too timid.'

'Wow!' I said, surprise mixing with my laughter.

These women were brutal tonight – but that didn't mean they were wrong.

28

I was waiting outside the restaurant, happily people-watching, when a sleek, black car pulled up to the kerb. The late-April sunshine glinted off its black paintwork. After a moment, a uniformed man with at least twenty years on me exited from the driver's seat and turned sedately to the back door, which he proceeded to open. From the dark interior, Reine emerged like the queen her name suggested, the chauffeur extending his arm for steadying assistance as she did so. Her right hand, beringed with diamonds that flashed in the late-winter sun, lay lightly on his arm until she was out of the car. A few words were exchanged, the man nodded, Reine smiled and he turned back towards the driver's door. I took a few steps towards the road and Reine noticed, her hand lifted in a wave as the smile broke on her face. I quickened my pace.

'Kitty, darling.' She stopped and kissed both cheeks. 'How are you? I do hope you haven't been waiting too long?'

'No, not at all. I've been enjoying watching the world go by anyway.'

'An excellent pursuit. Gabby is not here yet?'

'No, she's running a few minutes late but said she should be here soon.'

'Ah, *bon*. Let's go inside and wait in the warm. Have you been here before?'

'No. This sort of place was rather out of my budget when I was here as a student! I remember seeing it back then though and watching all the glamorous people come and go. There used to be a café over there,' I pointed across the street, 'and I'd sit in there and study and people-watch.' The café had gone now, replaced by a vape shop. 'So much has changed since I was here years ago.'

'And yet so much is the same.'

'*Exactement!*' I said, laughing.

'Come on, let's go and get some lunch. I'm famished.'

Inside, the décor was as opulent as I'd imagined it to be when I'd watched those patrons disappear inside from my position in the slightly shabby café opposite decades ago. But it also felt understated. Expensive but without that air of intimidation some establishments seem to enjoy cultivating.

'Reine! Kitty!' Gabby's voice called across the marble atrium as she rushed in through the door, nodding a wide smile at the doorman as she did so then hurrying over and embracing us both. 'I'm so sorry I'm late. I was talking to Ashok on a video call and neither of us wanted to hang up.' She put a hand to her face. 'I feel like I am a teenager again.' She put a hand to her cheek, laughing.

'From what I've heard, it's mutual.' Whenever I spoke to Ashok, a good proportion of the conversation was him gushing about Gabby. And I couldn't have been happier.

'I hope so,' my friend returned, a flash of insecurity dulling the sparkle in her eyes for the briefest moment.

'Definitely!' I reassured her. 'Shall we go in?'

I'd chosen to wear one of the skirts I'd got when shopping

with Gabby recently and it was amazing how much it had boosted my confidence, walking in here. I'd thought about what Reine had said at the gallery, about what I wanted from life now. Most of that was still a bit blurry but something I had decided was that I wanted my love of getting dressed back. I no longer wanted to pull on just what was comfortable or easy. I'd always loved making conscious decisions about what I wore. Somewhere along the line, that had fallen away but I knew now that was step one of finding 'me' again. I'd also been to the place Gabby had recommended for my brows and those too were now looking, if not quite as fabulous as hers due to some ill-advised over-plucking years ago, then certainly well on the way.

Today, I'd chosen a midi denim skirt which I'd paired with a white, cashmere boatneck jumper, the slouchiness of which made it sit to the side, shoulder on show. I'd debated about the wisdom of wearing white to dinner and settled that by resolving to not order anything tomatoey. After years of wearing leggings and t-shirts – Gabby had had to sit down for a moment after this revelation – I was still a work in progress. But that was the key word: progress.

The off-the-shoulder thing was taking a little getting used to. Underwear had been another dilemma. I was still far from rediscovering the air of nonchalance I'd had about that aspect of my dress when I was in my twenties so going braless, especially under a white top, wasn't an option I was prepared for yet. If at all. Instead, I'd compromised with a thin, silk chemise underneath, the ribbon strap of it showing as the jumper slouched.

Gabby ran her eyes over my outfit. 'You look fabulous, *ma chérie*.'

'Thanks to her,' I noted to Reine.

'*Pas de tout!*' Gabby waved her hand. 'I merely went along for the company. All the choices were yours.'

'I love this outfit,' Reine said as I sat down beside her in the curved corner banquette. 'Do shuffle up. My hearing isn't always what it once was and it's far easier to gossip about people when your companions are closer.'

She flashed a wicked grin as Gabby and I duly shuffled along the gold velvet.

'Is this new?' She touched the soft cashmere.

'It's all new, if I'm honest,' I replied, fiddling with the shoulder again.

'It will look even better if you stop fussing with it,' Reine teased and Gabby grinned.

I dropped my hand.

'Gabby showed me some photos of you all, back in the day, didn't you?'

Gabby nodded as she ordered us champagne.

'Oh, crikey.' I pulled a face.

'Not at all. The woman in those photos, where is she now?'

I huffed out some air. 'Buried under a lot of years, motherhood and, I suppose, the mundanities of life. Or perhaps she was just replaced with reality.'

'We make our own reality, Kitty.'

I wasn't sure if I agreed with that but I was unwilling to challenge such a new friend. Gabby merely gave me a flick of her eyebrows, waiting to see what I'd say. I stayed silent.

'You disagree.' Reine was smiling, her words phrased not as a question, but a statement.

'It's not that I disagree as such...'

Reine gave a delicate head tilt, encouraging me to go on.

'I suppose I'd like to believe that we make our own fate but I'm not sure that I can. When I was here before, I was having the best time with big plans and then I got my heart broken and it all fell to pieces.'

'Perhaps those weren't the best plans for you?'

I gave a shrug and what felt like a sad smile. 'I'd have liked to have been given the chance to decide for myself.'

'I can understand that. So do you feel your life has been wasted?'

'No! Not at all. And if things had gone differently, I wouldn't have Sash.' I shrugged. 'I suppose I feel like now that she's grown, I'm not sure what my role is any more. Especially now I'm divorced.'

'You don't have to be "somebody's something" to have a role, *ma chérie*! I do understand, though. When I lost my husband several years ago, there was a time I didn't know what to do with myself. We'd always done everything together – because we wanted to, you understand. But one day, I was lying in bed long past the time we'd normally have been up and about and I just thought, what am I doing? Why am I wasting the day, my life, like this? And I thought how upset my darling husband would be to have seen me like that. And you are decades younger than me! You have all this time now, for yourself! This is a time for you to have the starring role in your own life!' She threw out her arms like a diva and laughed.

'Bravo!' Gabby agreed, giving a few small, elegant claps.

'Oh dear! I'm not so sure I'd pass that particular audition.' I might be getting my style back but the confidence still had a way to go.

'Nonsense. What other possible reason could have brought you back to Paris? It is fate!'

'I thought you said that we make our own fate.' I looked at her in the same way I used to look at Sash when she was telling a fib. 'You can't have it both ways, Reine.'

Her sky-blue eyes danced with joy and amusement.

'Oh, but when one gets to my age, I can have it any way I want and people are too scared to challenge it in case they upset me.'

I thought of some of the older people I knew from the street we'd lived in and how some had changed over the years, losing the confidence they had once had, and becoming as invisible as I myself had felt. I compared them with this vivacious woman who refused to be ignored or judged or condescended to. How I wish she could give lessons to some of the lovely neighbours who were now a paler version of the characters they'd once been when we'd first moved to the road.

We'd been new parents without a clue and several of them had been so kind and helpful, without making us feel like we were failing, or reassuring us that we weren't and that every parent had the same thoughts and insecurities.

Gabby turned to her clutch bag and slid out her phone, glancing at the screen.

'Do you mind if I take this? It's a possible commission for Tomas he's interested in.'

'Go, go!' we both said together, and Gabby placed her phone to her ear as she strode confidently across the restaurant to somewhere more private to continue the call. From our position, we watched the admiring glances cast her way from both men and women as she did so.

'She's a wonderful woman. I hope that things with Ashok work out.'

'She is. I missed her so much. I hadn't realised quite how much until now, now that she's back in my life again. As for Ashok, he's absolutely smitten so...' I held up my crossed fingers.

'And he's worthy of her?'

'The most worthy man I know.'

'*Bon.* Now, where were we?'

'You telling me to be the star of my own show.'

'Ah, yes.'

'So how do *you* do it?'

'Do what?'

'Stay like this.' I waved up and down and saw that she comprehended.

'Without wanting to be crass, I'm afraid money helps. People are less inclined to ignore the power that can wield, as unfair as that is.'

'Yes, the same as it ever was. Although it's hard to tell who has money and who doesn't these days. Jeans with more holes than denim cost four figures, yet when I was growing up, they wouldn't even have been seen as good enough for gardening in!'

'I quite agree. I see some of the magazines and *ooh la la*. I think perhaps I am a little too old-fashioned.' There was a flash of that wicked grin again. 'But then I realise that no. I am not. I just have impeccable taste!' She chinked her glass against mine. 'As do you. So now, what are you going to do about using it?'

'I think it might take a little while. As much as I love it, this new look is still taking some getting used to.' I held back the urge to fiddle with my neckline again. 'My style got a bit lost over the years and I felt rather a frump when I got here. In the rut I lived in back in England, I hadn't noticed.'

Reine remained silent.

'The thing I love about Paris,' I continued, 'is that everyone makes an effort. That seems to have been lost in many places and I think I got lost along with it. Pull on the sweatshirt and leggings and call it done was the easy option and it soon just became the norm. Even though I'm not really a fan of either! I always loved choosing my clothes, doing my make-up and hair, even if that meant *not* doing my make-up and hair. It was all a conscious choice. Until it wasn't and what with a new baby—'

'And a new marriage.'

'And a new marriage to contend with, I lost the interest and the will. Or perhaps it was the other way around. And then I came back to Paris and met Gabby and you and I... I felt worse than invisible. I felt visible here but for all the wrong reasons.'

'You are most certainly not invisible, my dear, and for all the right reasons. Clothes may maketh the woman but there has to be a good framework there to start with.'

'A framework? You mean figure?'

'No, not at all. Figures change and how sad to pin everything on that. I know women, and men, who have done that. They lived on their looks and looks fade – even ones as fabulous as mine.' She pulled a shocked face, laughter dancing in her eyes. 'You can still make the most of what you have and have "tweakments" I believe is the latest phrase.' She rolled her eyes at the wording. 'But trying to hold on to what you had when you were twenty...' She shook her head. 'It can't be done. Not well, anyway.'

I couldn't disagree with her. 'But if people choose to do that, then that's their choice.'

'*Absolutement*,' she agreed. 'But wouldn't it be wonderful if people, women especially, could be appreciated for themselves, whatever their age? This is the framework I'm talking about. Intelligence, a sense of humour, that little *je ne sais quoi*. All the things that you, *ma chérie*, have, how do you say it? In spades.'

Once Gabby had returned, we ordered our main course. I inhaled the smell of the sizzling butter the lemon sole I'd chosen had been sauteed in as it was placed in front of me. A bite of the asparagus was so fresh, it tasted like it was cut moments before.

'Probably so,' Reine said in reply when I mentioned it, spearing another on her fork. 'They have their own kitchen garden here and grow as much as they can. *C'est bon, non?*'

'Oh, very *bon* indeed!' I chuckled, and Gabby sniggered, then we both stopped as I caught Reine's puzzled expression.

'Sorry,' I said. 'Not used to drinking at lunchtime.'

And then her face crinkled, and she burst out laughing, her beringed hand at her chest. 'Oh, Kitty. I have to tell you that coming back to Paris is going to be the best decision you ever made.'

'Are you sure?'

'Definitely! Don't you agree?' she asked, turning to Gabby.

'That's what I keep saying,' my friend said as she nodded to the waiter who had approached in anticipation of a top-up for our glasses.

Reine acknowledged the waiter then took a thoughtful sip.

'Very *bon* indeed!' she repeated and burst out laughing all over again.

29

Sash was out with Benoit – again. Since the night of Tomas's exhibition, I'd barely seen her. And I'd certainly not seen her as happy in a long while. He was good for her and it made me happy to see them together. Between that and the continuing increase in subscribers, something that had begun to speed up with her Paris move and spiked massively with the exclusive content she'd been granted at the exhibition, thanks to Tomas, Sash was living a life she appeared to love and that brought me more joy than anything.

Tomas and Gabby had been away much of the last month with the new exhibition but we'd had video calls from New York, Dubai and various other cities. Sasha had even been guest of honour again at the London showing when she'd been home to visit Hugh – with Benoit, of course, who'd received paternal approval, despite his connection to Tomas. Quite the achievement!

This morning, I'd decided to have a scrub of the apartment. With careful financial management, a bit of luck in the sale of the house and some other investments paying off, money, thankfully, hadn't been too much of a worry but I'd never been the spendthrift type and having recently invested in the best part of a new wardrobe, even with the deals and discounts Gabby had swung for me, it had been an outlay I hadn't exactly budgeted for.

When I'd told Gabs that I had no intention of hiring a cleaner, she'd been horrified but I remained firm. It was an area I could save money, and although I wasn't about to claim that cleaning a loo was my favourite occupation, there was a sense of satisfaction I got when the house was clean and I could sit down with a cup of tea and smell the fresh scent of the essential oils in the cleaner I used, and take pleasure in the shiny, clear surfaces. Even if it didn't last for long where my child was involved. But at least I didn't have a man using the bathroom!

I'd thought, and at least hoped, that Sash's tendency to the scattergun approach with her possessions would improve as she got older but it seemed I was wrong. If anything, she only acquired more stuff. Unfortunately, both these habits were inherited from her father and he'd not improved in this aspect the whole time I'd known him, so I wasn't holding out much hope for our daughter.

I was loaded up with yet another armful of her gubbins when the doorbell to the apartment rang. I shuffled the stuff to balance on one arm and opened the door with the other.

'*Bonjour.*' Tomas was standing there looking, as always, impeccable. I was looking quite the opposite in a pair of well-worn joggers which, when Gabby had held them up in horror during her recent rummage of my wardrobe, had required her to then sit down and call on Sash for a reviving cup of tea. I'd told her to stop being such a drama queen but was glad to see that my introduction to the 'cup of tea helps any situation' habit had survived the years and separation. Today, those were paired with a faded t-shirt that

I'd splashed bleach on years ago while scrubbing the loo (another reason I was glad there was no longer a man in my life – or at least my bathroom!), and had been then relegated to becoming My Cleaning T-Shirt. My hair, in need of a wash, was shoved up in a clip with an old bandanna, long discarded by Sash, to keep my now slightly overlong fringe from my eyes. So of course that would be the perfect time for my long-time ex to ring the doorbell.

'Hi. Oh, I, er, I mean *bonjour*.'

His smile, initially hesitant, widened.

'I'm interrupting.'

'Yes. But that's OK.'

Oh! That's new... I pondered, momentarily. Usually, I ended up giving people the impression that I had been doing nothing at all of importance and had, in fact, been waiting in all day in the hope that they might call. *Interesting...*

'These are for you.' Across his arm lay a large, beautifully hand-tied bunch of blousy pink peonies.

'Would you like to come in?' I stepped back out of the doorway and Tomas entered.

'Please. Allow me,' he said as I made to close the door behind him, still juggling Sasha's junk.

'Thanks. Give me a minute to just drop this in my daughter's bombsite.'

Ooh! Again, no request of 'can you give me a minute?' Just telling him. What was happening?

'Can I help at all?'

'No.' I turned, laughing as I did so. 'You might have broken my heart all those years ago but even I'm not cruel enough to subject you to this disaster zone.'

I carried on my way, not missing the shadow that flicked across his eyes as I joked. Dumping her stuff on the – unmade –

bed, I blinkered my eyes to the rest of the mess and closed the door behind me.

'So, to what do I owe the pleasure?'

'I wanted to see you.' He handed me the flowers.

'These are stunning, Tomas. Peonies are my favourite.' I held them up, inhaling their heady scent.

'I know. You always said you liked "proper flowers", not... what was the phrase? "Namby-pamby" ones.'

Laughter bubbled up. 'That's true. I don't remember saying it but it sounds like me.'

'I remember.'

And he had. He'd remembered important things like my favourite flower as well as silly, throwaway comments that had long slipped my mind.

'I'd better get these in some water,' I said, a convenient excuse to pull myself away from Tomas before I did something I might not regret. Like grab a handful of that expensive shirt fabric and yank him towards me. 'How was Berlin? Did the exhibition go well?'

'Yes, thanks. But I missed home.'

I looked up from where I was filling the vase.

'I missed you.' His voice was soft.

I'd missed him too. Far more than I'd expected. Far more than I'd wanted to. But the truth was I'd waited for and enjoyed his calls, just as I'd done all those years ago. We always had something to talk about. Big things and small. But in the back of my mind, I always felt the need to remind myself that I wasn't that girl any more and I couldn't get sucked into the vortex of Tomas's love – if that's what it was – again. I'd been there before and I never wanted to experience heartache like that again.

'Lots of sales then?' I held up my crossed fingers and tapped my head. 'Touch wood.'

A smile I remembered from a long ago, a different life, shone on Tomas's face.

'I wondered if you still did that. I'm glad to see not everything has changed.'

I gave a shrug. Very Gallic! 'Some things are ingrained a little deeper, I suppose.'

He nodded but remained silent. I waited another moment then picked my cloth back up, squirted the cleaning solution on the island and began polishing.

'You are busy.'

'Yes, but I can talk at the same time.'

He nodded again and I wondered where the once confident man I had dated had gone. Perhaps he had been swallowed up entirely by his parents' expectations and only the shell was left.

'Are you free for lunch?'

'Today?' I asked as I rubbed at a coffee stain.

'*Oui*. I mean, yes.'

'My French is a little rusty but I still remember the basics.'

'I know. You had such fluency. I am sure it will return quickly the longer you are here.'

'I hope so.'

'How... how long are you here?' he asked, a hesitancy in his voice as he shifted his weight.

'The lease on this place is six months. After that, we'll see. I don't have any plans.'

'That sounds unlike you.'

I shook my head as I tidied the cleaning supplies back into the basket I'd assigned them. 'Not really. Not now. Although you're right that I used to plan everything when I was here before but I've found life tends to do its own thing, however many charts and spreadsheets you make. It took me decades but I've decided to just go with the flow now, as they say. See what life brings and all that.'

'It brought you India, finally. I was glad to hear that.'

'Thanks. Yes, it was amazing. And India brought me a good friend. So I'm pretty pleased with how it's going at the moment.'

'And that, in turn, brought you back to Paris.'

'It did.'

He stepped towards me. 'I am "pretty pleased" about that.'

I had no intention of falling for Tomas Bertholle again but God, he was beautiful. In a different way from how he had been but if anything, it had only made him more handsome. He'd lost that perfection of youth, replaced instead with smile lines around his eyes that showed paler in his tan when he was serious and a kindness that hadn't shown as obviously before.

'Are you?'

Another step. 'Very. Please let me take you to lunch.'

I made him wait but I saw from those smile lines he could still see straight through me.

'OK.'

He stepped back as though to open the door.

'Tomas! I have to change,' I said, catching his arm.

'Why?'

'Did you go blind? Look at me!'

'You look beautiful.'

I opened my mouth. Closed it again. Then opened it once more but my brain still couldn't decide on which words to form.

'Even when you are pretending to be a fish.'

I grabbed a duster from the basket and flicked him with it. The laugh that followed hurtled me back through the years and twisted itself with the man standing in front of me now. My mind tumbled images and words and promises together until it was all one big, jumbled mess. A mess I wasn't about to even begin thinking about tidying today. If ever.

'I'm going to change. Take a seat. I won't be long.'

'I have heard that one before.' He grinned as he took a pew on the squashy armchair and picked up the book I'd left there earlier. 'Is this good?'

'I'm enjoying it,' I called out as I disappeared behind the bedroom door.

Five minutes later, I'd had a quick wash, changed, twisted my hair up and applied a quick base and slick of lipstick. Seeing Tomas's double take when I reappeared in the allotted few minutes I'd promised was a joy.

'Now who's pretending to be a fish? Shall we go?'

He hurriedly placed the book back on the coffee table and made quick, long-legged strides across the room in order to beat me to the door, opening it for me.

'After you.'

'*Merci.*'

30

Thankfully, Tomas hadn't chosen one of our old haunts, something I'd wondered about as we descended the winding wooden staircase of the apartment building. Instead, his car was parked outside and pressing a button on the fob in his hand, he unlocked it and opened the passenger door.

'It's such a shame there are no cafés in the city,' I said as I stepped towards him.

He gave me a look.

'You are still a smart arse, I see.'

'Some things are worth keeping.'

'*C'est vrai.*'

He offered his hand as I made to get into the car and I knew it wasn't for show. Tomas had always done this. For all their faults and judgements, his parents had at least instilled some manners into their son. His aftershave had earthy, deep-scented notes but it was only when I got close the fragrance teased my senses. He closed the door and I was ensconced in the cabin of the car, its tan leather seats releasing their own luxurious scent to the mix.

Moments later, Tomas slid behind the wheel and pulled out

onto the cobbled street, before joining a larger road, and pointed the car away from the city centre.

'So where are we going?'

'To a vineyard.'

My head snapped around.

'Not that vineyard,' he answered without looking at me.

'So where?'

'Somewhere different.'

'Oh?'

'A new start.'

He flicked his gaze to me before returning it to the road and we both dropped back into silence.

Paris fell away as we drove on, the urban views gradually morphing into those with a little greenery until that became the overriding prospect.

'We really aren't going to that vineyard, are we?' I said eventually, if only to break the silence and faintest hint of tension.

He shook his head and I studied the silver at his temples. It suited him. Git. The hair that was once collar length and out of a Timotei advert (if that reference didn't date me, I didn't know what would!) was now short and neat. The dark tresses I'd once dragged my fingers through were now cropped tidily, flecks of grey only enhancing the blue eyes. He was, as Sasha would have said had she not taken against him immediately, the very epitome of a Silver Fox.

'You're staring,' he said without turning his head.

'No. I'm studying. It's different.' Oddly, I wasn't thrown by the fact that he'd caught me. Between Reine and the City of Light, something was happening to me, and I was glad of it. Perhaps she was right when she had told me I just needed to bloom again. Perhaps this was the first hint that warmth was hitting my petals and tempting them to think about tentatively beginning to unfurl. But I knew that this time around, Tomas wasn't the sun that I revolved around.

'Still staring.'

'Still studying.'

'And what do your studies tell you?'

'You're going grey.'

'True.'

'And that you're not vain enough to use hair dye.'

'Can you imagine my sister letting me live that down, even if I wanted to?'

'Nope,' I said with a laugh, knowing that he was exactly right. 'Although I might tell her you have, just to enjoy her reaction.'

'At my expense?'

'Obviously.'

He tilted his head as if in acceptance.

'I'm glad you don't dye it, though. It looks good on you.'

He touched the place where the silver strands lay and shrugged.

I burst out laughing. 'Oh, come on. You were never insecure about your looks. You know it does.'

Tomas slowed for a junction and waited for the short line of cars crossing us to pass. He took the time to turn towards me.

'People change, Kitty.'

'True. But I find it hard to believe you lost all your confidence. Especially now you're the big, successful artist.'

He pulled out onto the road and I noticed his jaw was tight, a muscle flickering under the dark stubble.

'What?'

'Nothing.'

I let out a sigh. 'Tomas, if we're just going to be tiptoeing around and being polite all afternoon, you may as well turn around now. I've done that for the last thirty years with people, and you know what?' I felt my face flushing, surprising both of us with the sudden flash of anger. 'I'm done with it. I'm done with being the person that people want me to be.'

Tomas pulled the car over.

Well, that was a short lunch, I thought to myself, deciding whether I was upset about it or not and finding that, if I was going to be pretending, trying, all afternoon then, as I'd told him, I wasn't upset at all. At least I'd know where we stood.

'Did you ever consider that I never had the confidence you're talking about?'

'Oh, come on.'

'Why do you think that I didn't stand up for you all those years ago? Why do you think I nearly ran our family business into the ground because I was flailing? Why do you think I studied business even though I had absolutely zero interest in it and promptly failed my degree?'

'You failed?'

His face scrunched for a moment. 'That's what you took from all that?'

'No. Sorry. I was just... surprised.' I'd left Paris before the results were received and I'd just assumed both Tomas and Gabby had passed, as I had.

'Yes. I failed. Epically, I think was the term used at the time.'

'I'm... sorry?'

He shook his head. 'Don't be. I'm not. I hated every moment.'

'So why did you study it?'

'Aren't you more interested in why I let my parents treat you as they did?'

'No. It's ancient history. It doesn't matter now.'

'It matters to me.'

I swallowed and looked away, out of the window.

'Kitty?'

'What?' I kept my focus on the trees in my sightline, their fuzzy buds looking like they were stuck on the branches with glue by a child, randomly and at will, waiting until there was enough sun, enough warmth to tempt them to unfurl and burst into magnificent cups of magnolia.

'Kitty, look at me.'

I hesitated but then turned.

'I'm sorry.'

'It doesn't matter, Tomas. Really. Like I said, it's...'

'Ancient history, I know. But I never said it then and I should have done. I should have done so much back then that I didn't.'

'Tomas...'

'No, please.' He laid his hand over mine as they rested on my lap. 'Please let me say this before I explode. I've been keeping all this inside for so long and never thought I'd get the chance to say it. And then you were there. In that hotel.'

'Looking like I'd been in a cage fight.'

His rich, warm laugh broke the tension in the cosy cabin of the car, the tears that had sprung into his eyes while he was talking sparkled now in those deep sea-blue eyes.

'You look like you, how do they say, whooped their arse.'

'Yeah, I gave that bath a good whooping with my face. It didn't know what hit it.'

We were both laughing now, both with tears in our eyes, the emotions of that day, that time, swirling around once more in our hearts.

I slid one hand out from under his and laid it on top.

'Let's just go to lunch for now, shall we? I promise I will listen to you but I think that's all the emotion I can cope with for the moment.'

'I apologise. I had all this planned. I was going to be all super cool about it. Benoit told me—'

'Benoit?'

'Yes.'

'You spoke to him about us?'

'Yes. But don't worry, he's under strict instructions not to discuss it with Sasha.'

I shot him a look.

'Believe me, I know she hates my guts.'

'I'm not sure I'd go that far, but no, she's not your biggest fan.'

'I don't blame her.'

'You and Benoit are close.'

He nodded. 'He's the son I never had.'

There was something in his voice, a tremor. He cleared his throat hurriedly, gave my hand a gentle squeeze and dropped the briefest of butterfly kisses on my temple before turning back to the front.

'Let's go and get some food.'

31

A short time later, Tomas turned off the main road and into the driveway signposted 'Lausenne Vineyards'. Fresh, green leaves had unfurled on the apple trees that lined the driveway and to each side, rows and rows of vines stretched out as far as the eye could see.

'The food here is amazing.'

'I'd have been happy in a café in the city. You didn't have to go to all this trouble.'

'It's no trouble.'

Tomas pulled onto a circular gravel drive, centred by a beautiful statue of a water nymph, swinging her legs on the edge of a large, ornate fountain.

'Is this somewhere you discovered through work? I mean... your original work.'

He smiled at my terminology as he smoothly manoeuvred the car into a parking space near the door.

'Yes. Christophe, the owner, was very supportive during that time. There was no competitive spirit between us. We became firm friends very quickly. He knew I was in the wrong job long before I admitted it. Come on, I'm excited for him to meet you.'

He exited smoothly, his body moving athletically. The long-limbed youth I'd known had matured into a solid, muscular and clearly still very fit, in all senses of the word, man.

Tomas was at my door as I swung my feet out and put his hand down, which I took, smoothing my dress as I stood.

'You really do look beautiful, Kitty.'

'Thank you.' I flashed a brief smile. 'Now, please find me some food; I'm starving.' Compliments, especially from this man, were still something I was struggling to accept.

He took my hand and we walked together across the gravel and up the stone steps into the double-doored entrance.

'Tomas!' A tall, slender, impeccably dressed man in a perfectly cut, stone-coloured suit strode towards us, his arms out. The two men embraced before the man, Christophe I assumed, turned to me. 'And you must be Kitty.'

I held out my hand and he shook it. 'I'd have kissed your hand but I don't look good with a black eye.' He winked at his friend.

'Whereas I absolutely rock that look.'

Tomas burst out laughing. Christophe looked confused.

'I'll explain later. It's not how it sounds.'

'I am glad to hear it! Now, come and sit down.'

* * *

As Tomas had promised, the food was indeed fantastic and as I sat back following the last mouthful of a lighter-than-air lemon and elderflower posset Christophe himself had served, I felt about ready to burst.

'I'm so full!'

'Me too.' Tomas laid his hands across what appeared to be a

washboard-flat stomach. 'Christophe's food is as good as his wine. He has one of the best chefs in the world in that kitchen.'

'And you should know,' his friend said as he approached the table. 'You did your best to steal her enough times.'

Tomas looked suitably chagrined.

'And yet you still speak to him?' I teased, pulling out a chair for him.

Christophe shot Tomas a look. I didn't miss it.

'You don't need his permission to sit down. We're not on a date,' I teased. Drinking in the afternoon wasn't necessarily a good idea. Apparently, I was taking longer than expected to learn that lesson. But then again... Why wasn't it a good idea? It wasn't like I had work to go back to. And even if I had, it wasn't unusual to have had a glass or two of wine at lunch here. I needed to remind myself where I was. Just as I was gently and tentatively reminding myself *who* I was.

'And even if we were, you could still sit down without asking his permission.' I swung my gaze to Tomas in a challenge but there was no return there. Just a look that I couldn't quite work out and the softest upturn at the corner of his mouth.

'Kitty is, as usual, completely correct.'

Christophe folded his lanky frame into the chair in as elegant a manner as one would have expected and a waiter appeared from the side with another glass and another bottle of sparkling wine.

'Now that is excellent news. As you, *mon ami*, are driving, this one is just for me and my new friend.'

'Oh, Christophe, I've had more than enough!' I could feel pink in my cheeks and laughter in my voice.

'Just a small one. Humour me,' he said, dropping the H when he spoke. I noted that neither Gabby nor Tomas had ever done that. Something in my brain scuttled in and opined that their parents probably wouldn't have allowed it. The rest of me couldn't, and couldn't be arsed, to disagree.

'So,' he began, elbows on the table, 'tell me everything.'

'Christophe...' Tomas warned, the glint of humour gone from his face now.

His friend waved him off. 'Kitty doesn't mind giving me the gossip on you, do you?'

And actually, I found that I didn't.

Tomas shook his head, but the square shoulders were no longer being worn as earrings, which I took to be a good sign.

'Just a few questions for now,' I countered. 'Tomas promised me you'd allow him to show me the kitchen garden before the light goes.'

'Oh, did he now?'

Tomas picked up the thread seamlessly. 'You're always bragging about it. Kitty was interested in seeing it. I didn't think you'd mind.' He gave a terribly Gallic shrug to punctuate.

'OK,' Christophe agreed easily. 'The rest of the gossip can wait until next time. But this won't.' And with that, he expertly poured both of us a glass of perfectly sparkling wine and proposed a toast. 'To friends, old and new.'

I held up my glass, shooting Tomas a look as I did so.

'This one is trouble,' I said to him, joy in my voice.

We clinked glasses.

'You are right. Again.'

Christophe let out a raucous laugh and looked thoroughly pleased with the announcement.

32

The bitter winds of winter had given way to a beautifully mild breeze of spring. Shoots of green from the bravest of the bulbs had poked their head through the earth in the Tuileries and tested the air, decided that they would persevere and as the next few weeks passed, colour filled and spilled over from the borders.

I'd adopted the habit of walking there every day, often early but sometimes, as now, again later in the afternoon as the light changed. The mornings could still be chilly but this afternoon, the vintage woollen coat Reine had spotted at one of the flea markets we'd taken to strolling through with Gabby was left open. As I sat on one of the metal chairs that resided in the gardens, everything felt perfectly at peace. I people-watched for a while, attaching imaginary lives to some, admiring the style of others, and smiling at the laughter of lovers as they walked, their footsteps crunching on the gravel, hands clasped or tucked through an arm.

I lowered my gaze and opened the book I had just treated myself to at Smith and Sons, the English bookshop on Rue des Rosiers, not too far from where I was now sitting.

> Emma Woodhouse, handsome, clever, and rich, with a comfortable home and happy disposition, seemed to unite some of the best blessings of existence; and had lived nearly twenty-one years in the world with very little to distress or vex her.

The words sent a wash of comforting familiarity through me. It was so long since I had read them, despite them being such favourites, but for some reason, reading, at least for pleasure, had taken a back seat in life once I'd become a mother. At first, I had thought, perhaps naively, that I'd read when Sasha napped but there always seemed to be something else to catch up on. Occasionally, I'd allow that thing to be sleep. And then, gradually, I'd got out of the habit of reading altogether. Just as I had got out of the habit of walking for pleasure.

It had been Tomas who'd suggested the trip to Smiths when we'd met for coffee one morning.

'My French is still pretty good,' I'd replied, half-teasing, but recognising a tiny spark of defensiveness in my reply.

'I know.' He gave a Gallic shrug as if my reply had little to do with his suggestion.

'I can read books in French.'

His eyes narrowed a little. 'I am aware of that too. Did I suggest otherwise?'

'Only by saying I should shop at an English bookshop.'

He put down his espresso cup, the treacly liquid he preferred still looking as unappealing as it had thirty years ago.

'I didn't say you should only read in English. I asked if you wanted to go. The café there is quite cute. I think Sasha would like it too. It is, what do they call it? "Highly Instagrammable".'

'Oh. I see. Right. Thank you.'

He'd been correct, of course, and Sasha had filmed there as part of a vlog which had been super popular with her viewers.

After disappearing into the world of Hartfield for another half an hour, I checked my watch, packed up my book and wandered through the gardens to meet Tomas for coffee as arranged.

I showed him the book once I'd joined him on the comfy sofa he'd bagged.

'I'm glad you and Sasha enjoyed the café. I watched her vlog. I hope that you don't think me suggesting the place was any sort of criticism of your language skills. You know I don't – and never did – think they were anything less than excellent.'

The unspoken allusion to the fact that his mother had felt otherwise was acknowledged. And accepted.

'I should have stood up for you that day when my mother dismissed them. And you.'

'Tomas...'

After spending time with Christophe, laughing and learning, I was reluctant to spoil the wonderful, joyful day by returning to the conversation Tomas had begun earlier in the day at the vineyard, and he'd been kind enough to allow that. But today, it seemed, he was determined to resurrect the subject.

'Please, Kitty. We need to talk about this.'

'Why, Tomas? It was all a very long time ago and going over old ground now won't change anything.'

'But that day did change everything! Don't you see?'

'I know it did.' I did my best to keep my emotions more level than Tomas was managing. 'But who's to say something else wouldn't have come along that—'

'I say!' Tomas said, the effort of keeping his voice low in deference to our fellow café goers showed in the tense tone. 'Kitty, I never got to apologise to you. And you deserved that, at the very least. You deserved so much more. I wanted to give you so much more and I was a coward. A weak, pathetic coward who bent to the whims of my mother instead of defending the woman I loved.'

'Tomas.'

'I know what you're going to say. That it was all a long time ago, another lifetime.'

He was right.

'But I've spent this lifetime regretting that day.'

'Then I'm truly sorry for that.'

He studied my face. 'You haven't?'

I let out a short laugh. 'I had a baby, Tomas. It felt like I didn't have time to shower for about six months, let alone have any thoughts of regret for what might have been before.'

'No. Of course.' He shook his head. 'And please don't think I am wishing that you regretted becoming a mother to Sasha. Anyone can see the love between you.'

'No. I don't regret that. I could never regret her.' I looked down at my hands, laced tightly now in my lap. 'But no, what I said before... that's not true. Obviously, a new baby took up all of my time and energy but I still thought about you. Missed you. Tomas, how could I not? We made plans, talked about our future and then suddenly, everything changed. My whole life, the life I thought I'd have, changed in an instant. It was hard not to wonder what I'd done wrong...'

'You didn't do anything wrong, Kitty. Please don't ever think that.' His hand covered mine as I looked up, met his eyes, tears in both of ours.

He glanced to the side, towards the window, but his focus looked somewhere far past that. 'You're right. It was stupid of me to bring this up.'

I laid my hand over his. 'I never said that it, or you, were stupid, Tomas. And I never would.'

'Even though I was?' His gaze snapped back to mine and hooked onto it. 'I let you go, Kitty. You were everything I wanted and I let you go.'

I didn't know what to say so I said nothing but my heart squeezed in my chest. Tomas had been everything I wanted too and I'd seen us together forever until that day in the restaurant. But it wasn't that simple. How could I regret losing him when I had gained my daughter instead?

He moved his hand, taking mine within it, and lifted it to his lips. 'I will say this now and then never mention it again.'

My eyes lifted from our hands to meet his gaze.

'I am sorry, Kitty. Sorry that I let someone treat you like that. Sorry that I tainted your memory of Paris for so long, and sorry most of all that, because of my weakness, you and my sister lost so many years of friendship. I was a fool. A weak fool. Luck shone on me when my sister forgave me for taking you from her. I don't expect the same from you. I'm not sure I deserve it and it's as it should be. But please know, if I could go back, if I could do it all again, it would be very different. I know now that, as much as I loved you, I didn't deserve you.'

'Tomas...'

'But,' he swallowed, continuing, 'if and when you're ever ready to give me another chance, I will spend the rest of my days doing my utmost to deserve you this time.'

A tear dislodged and traced its way down my cheek. His other hand lifted, his thumb tenderly sweeping the tear away.

'Mum?' Sash's voice broke the moment.

33

I looked up in time to see the look she shot at Tomas as she came around the café sofa and sat down next to me.

'What's wrong?' Another icy look was directed at Tomas's back as he stood and embraced Benoit.

'Nothing.' I smiled at her, the action genuine. 'We were just talking.'

'And once again, he's upset you.' She lowered her voice. 'Why do you even bother? You moved on! Why are you trying to move back?'

'Sasha.' There was a warning note in my voice. Both Tomas and Benoit had clearly heard the words, just as they were supposed to. At least Tomas was. Sasha clearly had more to say, thought about it and instead clamped her mouth into a tight line.

'Benoit,' I said, standing. 'How lovely to see you.'

'And you, Kitty.' He bent and kissed me. He'd attempted to call me Madame Collins once. I soon put a stop to that. It was respectful that he'd tried but it made me feel about one hundred years old. I was learning to be in charge of my image, my persona, my name, once again and finding I liked making those decisions.

'Can I get you another drink?' He glanced at Sasha, who clearly had no wish to stay but chose to ignore her not-so-subtle signals.

'That would be lovely. A peppermint tea if they have one?'

'I'm sure they do. Sash?'

She stood. 'I'll come with you.'

When they were out of earshot, I pulled a face at Tomas. 'I think your godson is getting his ear chewed.'

Tomas gave a smile. 'I'm not surprised. I think everyone in the café got the message that Sasha didn't want to stay. Everyone but Benoit, it would seem.'

'Oh, he got it. He just chose to ignore it. And good for him.'

Tomas looked surprised.

'Sasha is an only child. We did our best to make sure she wasn't spoiled but it's not always the easiest. Occasionally, she has to be reminded that things don't always revolve around her.'

'Ah. I see.'

'Don't get me wrong. She's a good girl.'

'I can see that. I actually enjoyed my time showing her around the exhibition. She had interesting questions and viewpoints. Even if she does hate me.'

'That's a little strong.'

He gave me a look and I chewed my cheek. 'I have to say, I do rather regret telling her the whole story now. Obviously, I had no idea I'd ever see you again, let alone…'

A flash of hope sparked in his eyes and my heart cracked open, a shaft of a love I had long since buried shone out.

'One very slow step at a time.'

'Whatever you want, Kitty.' His lips brushed the back of my hand once more. With perfect timing, Benoit and Sasha returned from placing their order. Clearly, they were planning to stay.

The door opened and the pleasant breeze of earlier had now

morphed into an unseasonal northerly one, blowing in a couple as they navigated an expensive pram through the doorway. The chill caught everyone in its path. And still it was warmer than the atmosphere that now surrounded our little group. Not the most auspicious start for a second chance at love.

But neither of us had fought for it last time. The truth was that the fault didn't just lie at the feet of Tomas. I didn't fight either. I walked out and left. Maybe things would have been different if I'd stayed. Maybe not. We would never know now. But disapproving family had split us once before. Now I knew that flame in my heart still smouldered, I wasn't about to let that happen again. This time, we would take a chance. Make a chance. If it didn't work out, it would be because of us, not someone else's view or decision. I wasn't about to alienate my daughter but she needed to realise that I wasn't just her mum. I was my own person and this was my time.

We went our separate ways from the café, Benoit and Tomas heading in one direction, Sasha and I in the other. For the first few hundred yards, neither of us spoke.

'Are you serious about him?' There was a tension in her voice that no one other than her parents would have picked up on.

'I'm not anything about him at the moment,' I replied, careful to keep my own tone neutral.

'It didn't look like that to me.'

'Appearances can be deceptive.'

She stopped walking. I carried on.

'Mum!'

'I'm not having this conversation in the middle of the street, Sasha.'

I turned back and carried on walking in the direction of the apartment, catching the huff before Sasha strode on and walked, almost reluctantly, beside me.

'You've changed since we came here, Mum.'

'Good.'

From the corner of my eye, I saw her head snap towards me.

'Does Dad know you're seeing your old flame?'

Laughter bubbled up. So much for not talking about it. The bane of the young and their need for instantaneous everything.

'Sash, me seeing or not seeing Tomas has absolutely nothing to do with your father, and whatever I choose, I don't need anyone's approval.' I stopped and faced her. 'You obviously have questions and I will answer those I wish to when we get home, but right now, I just want to walk through the streets of Paris and not think about anything too much.'

My daughter studied me as if the concept of not thinking about anything was completely anathema to her. Which it probably was. Nobody ever got bored now. They weren't allowed to. They didn't know *how* to and I felt that the world was a poorer place for it. Creativity often came from boredom. Ideas that didn't usually have the space to bloom and grow flourished in those moments. But now any second of time that wasn't specifically employed in the doing of something was filled with endless scrolling. Except here. I loved that people here still sat in cafés and people-watched in real life rather than through a screen.

'Not even Tomas?'

'No, I'm not even thinking about Tomas.' Well, I hadn't been, but now...

* * *

'Am I allowed to ask anything yet?' Sasha spoke after a full five minutes of being back home.

'As I imagine you're going to explode if you don't, then I think you'd probably better.'

'I'm not that interested.' She flicked her eyebrows in a brief raise. 'I'm just concerned.'

'OK. What is it that you're concerned about?'

'You! That he's going to make you fall in love with him all over again and break your heart all over again! This was supposed to be a time to fall back in love with Paris.' She hesitated. 'Not him.'

I patted the sofa and she took a seat next to me.

'First of all, it's lovely that you're concerned but you really don't need to be. That's my job.'

'I love you, Mum. I know you think I'm being a bitch and I'm sure Tomas hates me—'

I stopped her. 'No, Sash. He doesn't. Not at all. He was actually talking about how much he enjoyed your discussion at the gallery, and completely understands why you've taken a dislike to him. In fact, he said the same thing to me about you earlier.'

'What do you mean?'

'That you hate him.'

She remained silent for a few moments. 'I don't hate him. I just don't trust him.'

'I know but, as much as I appreciate you wanting to look out for me, I'm old enough to make my own decisions and I'm choosing to allow Tomas back into my life. Right now, we're just friends reconnecting and seeing where it leads.'

She gave a sniff. 'It's obvious he wants more than friends.'

'Possibly,' I replied in another new move. Ordinarily, I'd have eschewed the idea that anyone could be interested but as more glimpses of the old me peeked through the curtain of years past, I felt comfortable acknowledging the possibility that was true. 'And perhaps I do too.' That part I was a little more unsure about but I wasn't prepared to close myself off to the idea, no matter how much my daughter disapproved. 'Sasha. I know this is all a bit strange for you. Believe me, you're not the only one.'

'I'm just worried about you, Mum. You don't know what men can be like.'

The laugh escaped from my throat. 'I'm well aware I've been out of the dating loop for quite some time, but I'm not entirely naïve.'

She sighed, tilted her head and for a moment, I thought she might pat me! 'Things have changed since you were young... er.' The correction was hurriedly added as my eyebrows rose towards my hairline.

'I'm sure they have but it wasn't all chaperones and virginal wedding days. I'm not that old!' Laughter wound its way through the words.

'I know that. I'm just saying.'

'What are you saying, Sash?' I asked her, my tone gentle.

'I just... don't you think it's a bit soon? After splitting up with Dad?' She seemed to have forgotten that her father had jumped into a relationship within weeks of us separating. Or maybe she hadn't...

'Do *you* think it's too soon?'

She gave a shrug.

'You face tells me you do.'

'As you said, it's not up to me.'

'No, it's not. And you might think I don't value your opinion, but I do.'

'I just... it feels weird.'

'I know. And in your position, I'm sure I'd have felt the same.' My parents had both passed away early within a short period of time and Sash couldn't remember them. Hugh had broken contact with his own family when they'd accused me of getting pregnant to 'catch' him. I'd done my best to reconcile them but Hugh had no interest. They'd apparently never been close anyway and whatever choice he made, they always felt there was a better one he could have opted for.

When Sasha was born, I'd encouraged him to try again, hoping a new, beautiful baby might help thaw the ice. Their reply in a plain card gave no congratulatory wishes and merely advised that they would 'not be changing the will'. Needless to say, neither of us bothered again. I looked at the young woman sitting beside me now and thought again on how much they had missed out on. I only felt sorry that she had never experienced the kind of grandparental love I'd want for her.

'I'm not rushing into anything, love. Your dad and I hadn't been in love for a long time. That's why I wasn't surprised, or hurt, when he found someone new so quickly. Life is short. If you find someone you enjoy spending time with, someone who makes you laugh and smile and who brings you joy, and your heart says, "Let's try", then why not?'

'It didn't say that about Ashok though, did it?'

I shook my head. 'No, it didn't. Not for me.'

'I wish it had.'

'I know you do, darling. But it wasn't meant to be. And if I had, then he and Gabby wouldn't have found each other.'

Her smooth brow wrinkled momentarily – and then returned to perfectly smooth. *Make the most of that!*

'I didn't think you believed in all that fate stuff, Mum.'

'I don't necessarily. I'm not sure what I believe in. Apart from taking it one day at a time, being grateful for each new day and all the joys it brings and being grateful for you being here with me. Even if you do hate my new boyfriend's guts.' Tomas and I weren't there yet but I couldn't resist the tease.

Her own brows flicked up until she caught the twinkle in my eye. 'Mum!'

'Come on!' I said, standing and pulling Sash up. 'Let's go and get an indulgent afternoon pastry at The Metropolitan so you can film it for your socials.'

'Is that the only reason?'

'Of course! I'm doing it to help, obviously.'

'You'll force it down?'

'I will. For the greater good of YouTube.'

Her smile, hesitant until now, spread as we headed back out of the apartment and turned in the direction of our favourite local café.

34

Tomas leant against the counter, chatting away in relaxed but rapid French to the barman as I took a seat at a small table near the door. I watched from the corner of my eye. Bloody hell, he was gorgeous. I knew from Gabs that her brother was insistent upon regular exercise. They disagreed as to whether he took it to the extent of obsession. She on the side of yes, he the opposite, professing it was his way of managing stress.

Gabby, of course, wrinkled her nose at the idea of such a thing as organised exercise and maintained her trim figure by the magic of being a Frenchwoman. Also by managing to refuse returning to the bread plate too often. Like many Europeans, she walked a lot, rather than drove. In a city like Paris, and London for that matter, it was so easy and often far quicker to walk. Like others, at home, I'd fallen into the habit of driving everywhere and it was only now, without a car or the inclination to join the city traffic, that I realised how much I'd missed the walks. When Sasha was little, I'd take her for long walks in the old-fashioned Silver Cross pram that we'd bought for a song from the local ad paper because nobody wanted ones like that any more. But I'd loved it and we'd loved the price even more. The sprung carriage would bounce over bumps and Sasha would gurgle happily before eventually nodding off with the gentle motion. I smiled at the memory as my eyes drifted back to the handsome man now approaching me. What would life have brought if I'd taken the other set of sliding doors? Would I have similar precious memories? Would it have been worse or better? There was no way to answer that. It would have been different. And now it didn't matter. We were here, today. And I wouldn't swap that memory for anything.

He smiled and I felt like melting.

Good God, woman. Pull yourself together. You're too old to melt! My sensible self brought me back to reality.

Tomas took the seat beside me, lifted my hand from the table and kissed the back of it. I melted a little bit more. Sensible Me opened my mouth. Joyful new Inner Me gave her a shove.

Bugger off and leave her alone! She's happy!

Sensible Me gave a sniff and stalked off to a corner.

'What was that for?' I asked, smiling at him purely because I couldn't help it.

He shrugged as the coffees arrived. 'You.'

'Well, thank you.'

'You looked miles away earlier.'

'Did I?'

'Yes. But happy.'

'I was thinking about how much more I walk now, and how the last time I used to do that was when I would take Sash out in her pram for long walks to escape the four walls.'

'It made you feel better?'

'It did,' I agreed. 'There's so much information now about how getting out for a walk is good for you, but there was none of that back then. I wish there had been.'

'But you figured it out for yourself. Like you always did.'

I took a sip of coffee. Hot, black and pleasantly bitter. The milky coffees I'd drifted into drinking over the years were once more a thing of the past. At home, it had seemed pretentious. Or at least I'd been led to believe.

'You're not in Paris now!' my mother had only half-joked when I'd asked for one shortly after I got back. Hugh had made a similar comment. His had been meant as a joke but it had still hit a nerve. I didn't want to be reminded that I wasn't there any more. I didn't want to be there either but my emotions were still raw and confused and it had seemed easier to avoid the triggers – even one as apparently insignificant as coffee. But now I was here and drinking the strong, black nectar. I also knew that, whatever happened, now I always would.

'I suppose I did.' I nodded my head towards the barman. 'Old friend?'

'I've been coming here for so long and Louis has been here all that time. I order my coffee, we moan about the world, discuss which part of us aches today, despair of the younger generation and then I take my coffee and we both get on with our day, feeling the better for it.'

'You make yourself sound about a hundred.'

'Sometimes, I feel it!' He laughed as he set his cup back in the saucer.

'Well, you don't look it.'

'Only ninety-nine, eh?'

I wiggled my head from side to side. 'Perhaps ninety-seven. On a good day.'

His bark of laughter made me smile.

'You always were a harsh critic.'

'Pah! I was no such thing.'

He shook his head. 'I disagree.'

'Which is your prerogative. But you're still wrong.'

He laughed again. 'God, I missed you.'

I looked up and the gaze I'd always found so hypnotic fixed on me now.

'I find that hard to believe.' I wagged my finger at him in fun. 'Don't forget I know your sister and we've caught up on a *lot* of gossip since I've been here. I know all about you living the high life as the eligible bachelor.' There was no judgement in my words. We'd gone our separate ways and made the best of them.

He pulled a face. 'I can't disagree. But that doesn't mean I didn't miss you. Because I did.'

'I'm not one of your dolly birds who's going to fawn over you and agree with everything you say. Absence and time might have made you forget certain things.'

He shook his head, laughing. 'Believe me. I don't expect that. I'd be disappointed if you did and if it was the case, you certainly wouldn't be the Kitty I remember. And,' his tone turned from laughing to sincere, 'I promise, I haven't forgotten a thing.'

'Good,' I said. 'Just so that we know where we stand.'

'We do.'

I flashed him a grin which he returned and I felt the teenage squish in my stomach again. *For goodness' sake! This isn't supposed to happen at my age.*

But why isn't it? Stop putting an age limit on things and just bloody well enjoy it, woman!

'How was your day with Reine yesterday?'

'Amazing, as always. She's such an interesting and caring lady.'

I chose the noun 'lady' purposefully. Reine lived up to the meaning of her name – Queen – each and every time I met her.

'I agree. I'm very fortunate she showed an interest in my paintings so long ago when I had no clue what I was doing. If it hadn't been for her encouragement, I'm not sure I would have continued.'

'Really?'

'Really,' he agreed. 'I mean, she bought some truly terrible artwork in the beginning!' Laughter danced in his eyes.

'I'm sure that's only what you think now, looking back.'

'Oh, no. She agrees!'

Laughter wound through my words. 'She does not!'

'She does!' Tomas insisted. 'Last time I visited her, she was making cocktails and I was looking at a painting on the wall. A *very* early one. She came to stand beside me and we were both studying it in silence for a moment, then Reine said, "It really is a bit shit, isn't it, darling?"'

'She didn't!'

'True story,' he replied with a grin. 'And she was right.'

The day was warm and I shuffled my chair a little so that I could catch the breeze coming through the door.

'Are you OK?'

'Yes, just getting some air.'

'Do you want to move? We could—'

'Tomas, I'm fine. Stop fussing.'

Hugh had been very kind but definitely not a fusser.

Tomas tilted his head to the side. 'I'm too old to change. Get used to it.'

And in that moment, as our eyes met, my mind spun back through time and I remembered how Tomas had indeed always been, not a fusser, but very attentive. And I'd loved it.

'I'd forgotten,' I replied.

'I haven't.'

35

'Did Reine really tell you your painting was shit?' I asked as we walked along the bank of the Seine later, my arm tucked through his, his hand resting on mine. We'd had an easy day, wandering the streets of Paris, stopping for lunch and coffee whenever we felt like it. I couldn't remember being happier.

'She did. I've offered to do another to replace it but she refuses. It says it reminds her of how far I've come. And it certainly keeps me grounded.'

'It's lovely of her to want that reminder.'

'Yes.' He paused. 'Or perhaps it's a way of making sure I don't, what's that phrase you used to use, get too big for my slippers?'

'Boots. And I don't think that's an issue. Unless you've very much changed, being egotistical wasn't one of your faults.'

'Although there were many others,' he grinned good-naturedly.

'Oh, yes. Plenty.' The tease was easy and fun. From the beginning, I'd felt at home with Tomas and Gabrielle. I'd been able to be myself. Or at least who I thought I was at the time. It was strange really that I'd had more idea who I was back then than I'd had in the decades that followed. But being back here now, back with those friends, made it easier to discover who I was now and what I wanted. People pleasing, it appeared, had dropped dramatically down the list. Thank God. 'Also, even with all your apparent success, with your sister as your manager, there's no way on earth she'd have stood for any of that nonsense.'

'Very true.' We stopped and leant on the wall of the Pont Alexandre III, both gazing down at the dark water beneath us, the ripples made by the gentle breeze catching both moon and streetlight, making it dance before us.

'So,' I said, turning and resting my back against the wall as Tomas remained facing it. 'How did that come about? Gabby becoming your manager, I mean.'

His eyes fixed on a point far in the distance – or perhaps in the past – and it was a few moments before he spoke.

'As you know, the grand plan of running the vineyard did not go well. I spent a couple of years travelling, doing an assortment of jobs. Gabby and I had fallen out with our parents and I wanted to take myself away from everything I knew here. Gabby and I stayed in contact, obviously, but she felt the same after our degrees finished. She went off to Milan and I, how do they say, bummed around. Eventually, we reconciled with the family and I took on the position they'd always wanted me to. Even after two years, I couldn't get you out of my head so I threw myself into it. I thought that perhaps it would be a good distraction in that I had to use every atom of concentration to get my head around the business side of things. I'd worked there growing up and had been happy to do the tours, remember the spiel and answer the questions. But running a business? Knowing that people's livelihoods depended on me? I struggled with that pressure every day and night.

'I made a couple of bad decisions then decided to bring in

help. I interviewed a financial advisor who came with good references and promises to help turn things around. By this point, profits were already going down. It's harder than it was in my parents' and grandparents' time anyway. Back then, French wine was, what do they say now? The bomb? Or perhaps that was last week's phrase.'

I smiled and felt relieved when a small smile also flashed on his face, however brief, before it turned serious once more. I could feel the tension in his body build as he'd begun recounting the unhappy time.

'Now there is much competition from all over the world.' He stopped and turned. 'I don't mean to say that is a bad thing.' He shifted and gave a furtive glance to the left, then right. 'Between you and me, one of my favourite sparkling wines is English!'

His expression was so serious, the check around so intense, that for a moment, I had thought there was about to be something of monumental significance to be imparted to me. Something at least worthy of knocking the threat level up a notch or two.

'Oh, Tomas.' I sighed and hugged his arm closer. I doubted the French government were interested – although come to think of it, perhaps it was best *not* to pass this titbit on. Tomas was currently their golden child of the art world. Finding out he was partial to an English tipple might be considered close to high treason over here. 'Your secret is safe with me.'

'As I knew it would be.'

'So, you hired someone? A financial assistant?'

'It's getting cooler. Shall we walk on? Are you warm enough?'

'I am, thank you.'

'Are you sure?'

'I promise. Come.' I gave a gentle tug. 'Which direction?' I looked left and right.

'Would you be free for dinner?'

'I would.'

'I'd like to cook for you, if you'll let me.'

I knew from years past that Tomas had always been a dab hand in the kitchen. Much to his parents' dismay, he'd always been more interested in chatting to the chefs than he was in turning up for board meetings. That really should have been one of the many clues they missed – or rather chose to ignore.

'You don't have to do that, Tomas. We can get something on the way.'

He shook his head. 'I'd like to,' he repeated. 'I'm afraid it won't be anything fancy. As much as I'd like to appear sophisticated, not to mention organised, I didn't plan for this but I... I don't want our time together to end yet.'

'You always did do a mean omelette.'

His face broke into a boyish smile, innocent joy. 'You remember?'

'I do. You ruined me for omelettes entirely.'

The innocence turned mischievous. 'Good.'

'You'd better have eggs.'

'I always have eggs.'

'Good. So.' I followed as he turned, presumably towards his own apartment. 'What happened when the financial assistant arrived?'

'He was a financial director so the first thing that happened was that I gave him a lot of money to come in the first place. But I thought it was an investment in the business.'

'From your tone, I'm guessing that wasn't the case.'

He pushed a hand back through his hair. 'I must have had a sign on my back that read "Gullible Idiot". A few months in and we were at risk of losing everything. It was then that I, by chance, met Christophe at a conference. Gabby had come with me. She'd not long split from her husband and moved back to Paris. I think the trip was partly something to take her mind off the divorce, but I know she was worried about me.' He glanced across at me as we walked. 'I think my little sister felt the need to keep an eye on her big brother.'

A chill that had nothing to do with the cool night air ran through my bones.

'And did she have a reason to?' The words croaked out and I cleared my throat.

Tomas stopped. A small puddle of light from a streetlamp illuminated the side of his face, the sharp plane of his cheekbone highlighted. He turned and I saw the gentle expression in his eyes.

'Not in the way you are thinking.' His voice was soft as his cool hand touched my now hot face as thoughts of what he had been going through, what might have been perhaps, if not for his sister, raced through my mind. 'Not in the way you are worrying about. I am here, now, as you see me.'

I pulled my top lip in with my teeth and nodded.

'Yes.' I touched his hand with my own briefly before he tucked it back through his arm and we returned to our walk, turning down a cobbled street.

'I was depressed, there is no doubt of that. But I think she was more worried that I might have another "brilliant idea" at this conference.'

'I see,' I said, part of me feeling relieved but the other part still lingering on the admittance that Tomas had suffered depression as a result of being pushed into doing something he never wanted to.

'We were lucky in that we fell into conversation with Christophe, who had recently launched his own vineyard and was going,' his eyes caught mine briefly, 'gangbusters with it.'

My laughter burst out. 'Gangbusters?'

'Is that not a relevant term?'

'It is to me. But ask my daughter or Benoit and I'm afraid you may just receive a puzzled look!'

He tilted his head and gave a huff of recognition. 'I receive a lot of those although I've taken it upon myself to fill in some of the many gaps in my godson's knowledge of cultural references.'

'And how's that going?'

'Reluctance initially, as of course, his generation already know everything.'

'This is true.'

We exchanged a grin.

'But actually, it's been fun. Watching films, visiting museums of all types, discussing history, it's been good. Indeed, some of my happiest memories.'

I squeezed his arm in reply.

'And when you met Christophe?'

'Also a happy memory!' He laughed and I was glad to hear it. 'And an enlightening one. You see, he knew of my financial director from a previous hotel he had worked at. It turned out that all the references were fake. I didn't know enough to check up on them.'

'Or perhaps too trusting?'

'Or perhaps too stupid?'

'No.' I tugged at his arm. 'Don't say that, Tomas. We all make mistakes and you were doing your best with, apparently, no help.'

Tomas got the gist of my comment.

'My parents were very much of the sink-or-swim mind. They wanted to retire and so it was my job to take their place.'

'Even if it meant losing everything, including your confidence and happiness?' I heard the anger in my tone and clamped my lips closed to resist saying more.

Tomas made no reply but wrapped an arm around my waist and we walked on. He knew. He understood.

'So what happened, after the conference?' I asked, my tone back to conversational.

'My FD was fired.'

'How did that go down?'

'Ah.' He made a 'pfft' noise. 'With many cries of unfair dismissal and threats of court cases.'

'Oh!'

'Yes. And then, the perfect denouement...' He turned, laughter in his eyes. 'The doors opened and my sister walked in with Christophe. The game was up, as they say.'

'Ooh! It sounds like a film!'

'Perhaps it should be,' he laughed. 'Gabrielle was brilliant. She took a seat, as calm as can be, and announced that we would be filing for damages due to his misrepresentation and the money we had lost as a result. Also, that she would also be reporting him to the police for fraud.'

'Wow.'

'*Oui*. And then she got up, told him he looked pale and offered him a drink.'

I chuckled, able to see this in my mind so clearly. My best friend, cool, calm and lethal.

'The funniest thing was that he took it, which gave the police plenty of time to get there.'

'Do you know what happened to him?'

'We chose not to press charges in the end.'

'Really?'

He shrugged. 'He was, how do you call, a chancer?'

'Still a crime.'

'True. And believe me, we went back and forth about it. But in the end, we decided to ask them to let him off with a warning.

This time. It was the first time he'd done it. He'd been a disgruntled employee at the place where Christophe had worked and felt he could do better with a little blurring of the lines.'

'Lying.'

'That too.'

'And Gabby was OK with this?'

He blew out his lips. 'Ah. *Non*. Not for some time. But eventually, we agreed.' He chuckled. 'It was a long night!'

I knew his sister well. 'I bet. Did your willingness to give someone a second chance work out?'

'He went back to college to study finance and business and passed top of his class. Once he was given the knowledge, he excelled at it, rather than just floundering. I already had the floundering part covered.'

'Stop being so hard on yourself. I'm glad it worked out for him although I'm only sorry your original plan didn't. It was a good and sensible one.'

'I know. But perhaps things were meant to be.'

'What do you mean?'

'It was the last straw for me. I was burned out. Everybody could see and I couldn't do it any more. Gabby had had more control and sense in moments than I had in the whole time I'd been made CEO. She wanted a change from fashion and so proposed that I stepped down and she take over.'

'And you were happy with that?'

'Incredibly! Although not as happy as she was when she fired me in the very next moment.' His laughter drifted about in the still air of the quiet street. 'I did tell her she couldn't fire me as I'd already stepped down.'

'And?'

'Oh, she knew it but couldn't resist the opportunity to fire her big brother. Or at least pretend to.'

'That sounds like Gabby.'

He nodded, smiling as he led us to the door of a beautiful townhouse. I looked for the buzzers, wondering how many apartments were within, but there were none.

'What is it?' he asked, catching my puzzled glance.

'This is still one house?'

'Yes.'

'Yours?'

He lowered his lashes momentarily as he nodded. I knew the price of Paris property. This was literally a fortune!

He turned the key, opened the door and stepped back to allow me to enter first.

'The fake financial director who became an excellent one advised me, once I began to make a little money, to invest it in property. I took his advice.'

'Wait, you still know him?' I asked as Tomas helped me off with my coat. I turned to face him once the sleeves had slipped down my arms and he folded the garment over his arm while opening a huge walnut armoire, the scent of cedar drifting from it as he did so. Carefully, he hung my coat, then his own inside before closing the doors once more.

'Gerard is now the CFO of the family vineyard.'

'Noooooo!' My mouth dropped open. 'Seriously?'

He nodded.

'Gabby took him on?'

'Uh huh.'

'Wow. He must *really* have proved himself.'

'Oh, yes. I think he was too terrified not to! Come through to the kitchen.'

36

There is something innately sexy about watching a man cook for you. I'd discovered this the first time Tomas had made me that first omelette all those years ago. And what a revelation that had been!

'I don't like omelettes,' I'd told him at the time.

'Everybody likes omelettes.'

'Clearly not.'

He'd made me one anyway and annoyingly was right. Apparently, I did like omelettes but only the way he made them, and not the pale, rubbery, unappetising discs I'd known prior. These were rich and creamy, the cheese melting together with orange-yolked eggs, the subtle tang of herbs adding another layer of taste. The fact that there was any taste at all, let alone layers, had been incredible to me.

And now, here we were again. This time in a high-end kitchen in a luxuriously renovated townhouse rather than my tiny studio apartment of years back with Tomas cooking on the two-ring hob that only worked intermittently – usually when the landlord came round.

He turned to the floor-to-ceiling fridge, producing a bunch of fresh salad leaves and a bottle of what appeared to be homemade dressing. Moments later, once the leaves had been gently placed on the plate and a drizzle of dressing artfully poured over them, he slid the folded omelette alongside and served it to me.

'*Bon appetit.*'

'Wow. People pay a lot of money for food that looks like this.'

'Please start,' he said, gesturing to me as I waited for his own supper to be ready.

That first mouthful brought all the memories rushing back and for a moment, we were back there, back before the heartbreak, back in that bubble of happiness, that hot final summer, that time when we thought we knew who we were and where we were going and that no one could change that.

'Good?' he asked as he plated up his own meal.

I flicked my gaze up as I finished my mouthful. 'You already know it is.'

He slid into the seat beside me at the huge marble island, grinning. 'True. But I wanted to make sure.'

'It's delicious, Tomas. Thank you.'

We chatted about everything and nothing as we ate and, once finished, Tomas brewed a cafetière of strong, aromatic coffee and poured us both a glass cupful.

'It's decaf,' he said, handing mine to me.

'I did wonder but it smells so good, it'd have been worth being kept awake all night.'

'I've had enough years of not sleeping properly. I'm all for the taste without the caffeine in the evening these days.'

'Fair enough,' I said, sliding from the bar chair and wandering over to one of the large sash windows. Below us, a cobbled street bore the marks of thousands of footsteps and hooves, worn into the fabric of the place. Looking across, I could see the lights of

Paris twinkling in the evening and there, like a scene from a film, was the stunning Tour Eiffel, its twenty thousand lights switching from static to sparkling as the hour chimed on a clock somewhere else in the house.

'Shame you didn't get a view with the place.'

He came to stand beside me.

'I know. It's a bit shit, *non*?'

'It really is.'

He glanced down, his lips tipped into a smile before disappearing behind his coffee cup.

'How long have you lived here?'

'About five years. I bought it around two years before that but it was…' He grimaced. '*Ooh la la.*'

'That bad, eh?'

'Even Gabby struggled to see the potential and you know how much she loves these old places.'

'She always has had great taste.'

He nodded in agreement. 'I think she was worried it was going to be a money pit.'

'Do you have any photos of what it was like?'

'I do. Would you like to see?'

'Very much so.'

'They're upstairs on the computer in the office. Did you want a tour?'

'I thought you'd never ask!'

We finished our coffees, placed the cups back on the counter and headed out of the kitchen. Opposite was a beautiful dining room, decorated in pale blue with white and subtle gold details. A huge, warm oak table dominated the room, easily seating twelve.

'You like to party, party?' I did a little wiggle to accompany my words. Sasha would have died on the spot.

His arm slid to my waist as he smiled at my antics. 'Not especially. But I do like good food shared with good friends.'

'And you cook?'

He shrugged. 'Sometimes. Sometimes, they are catered.'

'Fancy.'

He shot me an amused look before leading me up another flight of stairs to a large, comfortable sitting room, welcoming with overstuffed sofas and chairs in an array of fabrics of rich jewel tones. It was an opulent contrast to the restrained décor of the dining room below. Two stunning chandeliers hung from the ceiling, but the room was currently lit by several table lamps, the soft light they threw out catching the crystal of the spectacular lights above them.

'Wow.'

'Good wow, or no?'

I looked up at him and saw the hesitation in his eyes. It mattered to him.

'Definitely good wow.'

He released a breath and I couldn't help but chuckle.

'Why were you so worried?'

'Because I think this is probably my favourite room.' His hands settled into his pockets, the confidence of earlier now less obvious, something about his stance, the expression on his face, reminding me of the first time he asked me out. I'd been surprised then at how nervous he'd been as we'd already become good friends. But when I'd said that, Tomas had told me that was exactly why he was so nervous and I understood. But now?

'I was hoping you'd love it too.'

'I do. It's so inviting and luxurious. It would be easy for a room like this to seem intimidating, or overdone.' I rephrased. 'Too formal, I mean.'

He nodded.

'But this, even with those magnificent lights, it's... perfect.'

And then I saw it.

'I hope you don't mind?'

I felt tears prick my eyes as I shook my head, my throat too thick to speak just now. There, above the stunning fireplace, hung *Summer's Bliss*, displayed in a simple soft gold frame, the colour choice reflecting both the sun and the colour of my hair in the painting.

'It's part of why it's my favourite room.'

I nodded, smiled again at that girl in the painting and took his hand.

His smile widened and I followed as we crossed the hall to two other rooms. Originally, they had been one, but as part of the renovations, Tomas had chosen to have it made into two. Not that you'd have known that wasn't the original design. Everything had been specified to the highest level.

'I didn't want to do anything that would take away from the character of the house, or look like it wasn't supposed to be there.'

'I'd say it was a resounding triumph,' I said as he closed the door on the snug. I could imagine him in there, the walls lined with cherry-wood bookshelves and filled with an eclectic mix of classic novels in French, English and Spanish, all the languages he spoke fluently. Alongside them sat contemporary novels, non-fiction books in a range of subjects, a great swathe of history books and an entire case of ones on art and architecture. An original fireplace was settled against one wall. I thought of Tomas on a cold, wet rainy night snuggled up in here, the fire crackling, its golden light highlighting the planes of his face, his expression serious as it always was when he read.

'Again. Perfect.'

We climbed to the top of the house. Only the attic rooms were above us now. Tomas opened a set of antique white panelled double doors and stood back, allowing me to enter first.

The carpet of the bedroom was as deep and thick as soft sand.

'I bet this is a nightmare to hoover,' I said almost automatically.

A faint blush coloured his cheeks. 'I'm afraid I don't know.'

The simple and honest reply highlighted the differences between our lifestyles. Both then and now.

'No, I suppose you don't.' I gave him a look. 'Lucky you. It's a beautiful room though, Tomas.' I stayed at the periphery. It didn't seem quite right to stride into there and nose around. We hadn't even agreed that we were officially dating. Were we? Did people 'officially agree' on that sort of thing these days or was it just accepted? Was it automatically assumed that we were, as the Americans put it, 'exclusive' or was it automatically assumed that we weren't? Did it bother me? Was I getting ahead of myself?

'Am I going to be invited into the conversation?'

'Huh?' My head snapped up and I met his eyes, gold flecks in the deep blue dancing in the low light of the lamps that had illuminated when he flicked the switch at the door.

'You seemed to be having a very in-depth conversation over there. I wondered if I was going to be invited to join at any point?'

'Oh!' I laughed with a hint of embarrassment. 'Sorry. Miles away.'

Fibber.

'Really?'

Bugger. That was the thing with old friends. They knew you too well, even when there had been years in between, changes of all kind. The people that knew you *really* knew you.

'You have very good taste. It's all beautiful, Tomas.'

There was a pause. He knew I'd avoided the question and, thankfully, let it go.

'I can't take the credit for that.'

'I'm sure you had input with the interior designer,' I said, stepping from the room and back into the hallway. He followed me and pulled the doors closed behind us.

'Yes.'

'Then don't be so modest.'

'Would you like a drink?'

I checked my watch. 'I ought to be getting home, but thank you.'

A flicker of disappointment crossed his face and I felt the same but I wasn't ready for the possibility that one drink might lead to another and that to something else. I was feeling freer, more confident, than I had in a long time but I'd also not shown my bits off to anyone other than my husband in a very long while and even the latter had been pretty intermittent over the last few years. The last time Tomas and I had gone to bed, I'd been a lot younger, and a lot perkier than I was now. Thankfully, being less endowed in the boob department meant that I was hardly kicking them along if I didn't wear a bra – which, with the French resistance to such undergarments I was succumbing to more and more, was just as well. But they still weren't exactly standing to attention with the same gusto they had in years gone by and various other bits of me were definitely more southerly located than they had been back then. Tomas, on the other hand, appeared to have aged as well as one of his family vineyard's fine wines.

'You're doing it again.'

'What's that?' I asked as he held my coat up and I slipped my arms into the sleeves.

'Chatting away to yourself.'

'Was I?'

'Mentally,' he said, shrugging on his own impeccably cut overcoat.

'Oh. Well, I have a lot to say,' I joked.

'I'd like to hear it.'

'Another time, perhaps.'

He looked like he was about to reply but then changed his mind.

'Why are you putting your coat on?'

'To walk you home.'

'Don't be silly. It's chilly out there now. Stay here in the warm. I know my way.'

'I know that,' he replied, picking up his keys from the gleaming blue marble bowl on the console table he'd dropped them in when we'd entered the house several hours ago. He looked down at me. Even with the new heeled boots I'd chosen to go with my outfit today, he still had a good seven inches of height on me. 'Kitty, would you allow me to walk you home?'

I looked up into his face and knew it wasn't just the wine that meant I'd find it hard to say no to anything this man asked.

'That would be lovely, thank you.'

37

I pulled the key from my pocket and rested my hand on the handle of the apartment door.

'Thank you for seeing me home.'

'Any time. Could I see you again?'

'When?'

'As soon as possible.'

'Tomas...'

His head dropped and he nodded a couple of times before raising it again and meeting my eyes. 'I know. I'm rushing things.' He shook his head. 'Exactly what Christophe told me not to do.'

'Have you been talking about me?' I asked. There was a flirtatious tease in the words. Paris certainly brought that out in me it seemed. Having put the skill away for quite some time, it was good to know it hadn't rotted away to dust.

Hugh and I had sort of drifted together – in the same way that we had drifted apart now that I thought about it. We'd been happy but passion wasn't a big part of our relationship. Tomas, on the other hand...

'As often as I can.'

I looked up through my eyelashes. 'Well, don't make it a habit. You'll bore people before I even get a chance to meet them.'

His hand lifted, the back of it brushing my jaw with the lightest of touches. 'Never. No one could ever get bored with you, *ma chérie*.'

It sounded like a cheesy line but it wasn't. The look in his eyes, the tone of his voice. I knew Tomas and I knew he meant it. Which is why I kissed him.

It was as though, in that moment, all the years in between shrank away. He responded immediately, his mouth against mine, his breath warm and tasting of the wine we'd drunk. One of his hands snaked under my coat and curled around my waist, pulling me closer while the other cupped the back of my head. His lips moved from my mouth to just beside it as he whispered my name and the featherlight kisses traced their way along my jaw and down my neck. I let out a moan and Tomas pulled me even closer.

'I always loved it when you made that noise.'

I didn't respond. I couldn't. My body had forgotten this. Forgotten how it felt to feel like this. Forgotten that I *could* feel like this. And I was not about to interrupt it with conversation.

'Evening!'

My daughter was less concerned about interruptions.

I pulled away, partly in surprise, partly as though I had been caught doing something I shouldn't have. The look on her face suggested the same. A bubble of annoyance rose to the surface and threatened to burst. I swallowed it back down but curled my hand around Tomas's arm.

'Hi. Been anywhere nice?' I kept the tone light. I was not going to be made to feel like I was having some sort of sordid, illicit affair.

'No, actually. The people I was supposed to meet stood me up and then posted all over their social media about how great this new restaurant we were all supposed to go to together is.' She shot Tomas a look as if it were his fault.

'Oh?' I frowned, holding out my other hand towards her. I knew behind the tough exterior, she was bruised. She hesitated. I waited. Tomas shifted his weight and from the corner of my eye, I saw him taking an intense interest in the light fixture. But he didn't try to leave either. 'Did you call them?'

'Yeah.' She shrugged one shoulder as she fiddled with her key. 'Apparently, they forgot.' Her jaw was set. 'Despite the fact we've been planning it, and the content we were going to make, for weeks now.' She dropped my hand and shoved the key into the lock, turning it with a lot more force than was strictly necessary. 'And here's the best thing!' Sash spun back to us. 'The content they're uploading? Those were my ideas.' She rubbed her hand across her forehead. 'I'd made a big thing on my channel that I was going there. I'm going to look an idiot now.'

I followed Sasha into the apartment, tugging Tomas along with me.

'I'm sure people will understand. They follow you because they enjoy what you do.'

'But I *didn't* do it, Mum.' Her shoulders slumped in defeat. 'And I thought we were friends.'

I pulled her close, my heart squeezing at the sadness in her voice. 'I know, love. I'm so sorry they let you down.'

'Can I ask which restaurant it was?' Tomas's voice was soft and empathetic.

'Giardo's,' Sasha replied before remembering that she hadn't decided to like him yet.

He gave a thoughtful 'hmm'. 'Have you heard anything about "Quatorze"?'

'Only that there's a six-month waiting list to even be considered for a table.'

'Would it be helpful to get a reservation there so you can still get the content you were planning up? Or at least...' He stopped. 'I have to be honest, I enjoy watching various YouTube channels but as to the creation of them, I'm rather ignorant.'

'It's OK,' she said, her immediate upset currently standing in front of her grudge against Tomas. 'The problem is, I won't be able to get the content filmed, edited and up in time for the next video.'

'Sash has a strict schedule for her channel,' I added. 'She's never missed one in eleven years.'

Tomas looked impressed. 'It's hard work to do that. It shows you have a passion for it.'

Now that we'd all entered the apartment, she flopped down on the nearest armchair and put her face in her hands.

'I sometimes think a normal job would be easier.'

'True,' Tomas agreed. 'But not what you want to do, I think?'

She peered up through her fingers at him before dropping them onto her lap. 'No. Not really.'

'So? New plan?' he asked.

'I guess,' she replied, as I moved to the kitchen, careful not to make any sudden movements in case I spooked her. The current atmosphere was so much more pleasant than the eggshells we'd been walking on until now.

'Do you have any other content you could use for the next video and explain that plans changed – perhaps for the better? But your viewers will have to wait a tiny bit longer to see?' He held up his thumb and forefinger to emphasise his words.

Sash pushed herself up a little. 'Better?'

'Perhaps. If you're free tomorrow evening, I can get you a table at Quatorze. Would that help at all?'

She sat bolt upright. 'What? Impossible.'

He raised his brows. 'Ah, nothing is impossible.'

A faint frown creased her forehead as I nudged her shoulder to take the camomile tea I'd made her.

'Oh! Thanks, Mum,' she said, taking it and immediately putting it down on the coffee table in between them. 'Are you serious?'

'Absolutely.'

She scrunched her face, scratched her neck then looked back at him. 'Why are you doing this? I haven't exactly been... welcoming.'

I cleared my throat. Sash chewed her cheek. 'That's an understatement, obviously. I've given you a hard time since I met you. Actually, I've been quite the bitch if I'm honest, which I promise isn't like me.'

Tomas chuckled. 'I think you are being a little hard on yourself. Yes, you have been tough on me. But I can take it. And actually, I think it made me like you more. Your mother always defended those she loved with her whole heart. You knew I hurt her before and don't know me enough to trust I won't do it again.'

She nodded.

'You ask why I would help you. The simple answer is because I care for your mother and she loves you very much. By doing this, I make you happy – I hope. And that in turn makes her happy. I also don't like to see people taking advantage of others, which is what seems to have happened?'

Sash huffed in agreement with the latter then looked over to where I'd taken a seat before turning her gaze back on Tomas.

'Don't hurt her, OK?'

'Sash.' I felt my cheeks flush but their conversation continued without looking at me.

'I don't plan to.'

'Good.'

A pause.

'You really think you can get a table at Quatorze?'

He held up a finger, pulled out his phone and scrolled for a moment before making a choice.

'*Gerard? Bonsoir, c'est Tomas Bertholle... oui, très bon, merci... Est-il possible de parler à Simone, s'il vous plaît?*'

A short but warm conversation followed in rapid French and two minutes later, there was a table booked in Sasha's name. From what I understood, he'd mentioned that she was a dear friend of Tomas's with a fantastic YouTube lifestyle channel.

'*Voila* – 8 p.m. tomorrow night. Simone asked if you'd perhaps be interested in a behind-the-scenes tour of the kitchen while you were there?'

'No! Are you serious? Oh my God!'

Tomas shot a glance at me and I nodded. Despite the seriousness of her expression, this was definitely a good 'Oh my God'.

He continued. 'She also offered an interview, if you wanted, but not tomorrow as she wants you to enjoy your meal.'

'You're serious? Simone Deschamps said that?'

'*Oui.* But she did ask me to emphasise that if you didn't, she wouldn't take the slightest offence.'

'Yes! Yes, yes, yes!' She was laughing now.

'I'm taking it that this is someone you admire?' I asked.

Tomas and Sash turned to me as one, exchanged a look that stopped just short of an eye roll before Sash spoke.

'She's only *the* hottest chef at the moment, hence why you can't get a table in her restaurant for months at a time. At least, most people can't.' She turned her eyes to Tomas briefly with a grin before turning back to me. 'Honestly, Mum. If you did social media, you'd know who she was.'

'I do do social media. I watch your videos.'

'That doesn't really count.'

'Yes, it does. It just means I'm very fussy about how I spend my time.'

She bobbed down and kissed me on the cheek. 'Thank you. But it still doesn't count.'

'Well. That's not changing any time soon. I've no desire for any of the rest any more.'

I'd done the Facebook thing as a playground mum and as a local town resident but all it seemed to be was people sniping, either openly or passive aggressively, at others. It made me feel uncomfortable and often stuck in the middle. I'd finally deleted it before we went to Goa. Ironically, just when I had something to actually share, I had no inclination to do so. And then, when I'd deleted it, nothing happened. The sky didn't fall in or a great chasm open beneath me. So then I deleted Twitter (or X or whatever people were calling it now). After that went Instagram, Threads and BlueSky. The latter I'd never once used and still didn't entirely understand what it was or how it worked. I cared even less. The amount of time I'd regained was phenomenal and I didn't miss any of it a jot.

'Anyway! She's amazing. She used to be a model.'

'Ah. Now you say that, the name does ring a distant bell.'

'Yeah, she was a massive name on the catwalk years and years ago.' She gave a wave to acknowledge the very dim and distant past of the late nineties. Presumably in Sash's eyes, Simone was modelling the latest in whalebone corsets and seen as racy for showing a glimpse of ankle. 'But she trained to be a chef without letting anyone know and had been working under a pseudonym. A couple of years ago, she opened Quatorze under her own name. It's been booked solid ever since.'

'I suppose celebrity helps.'

'Of course,' Tomas spoke now. 'But it will only go so far. Her food is incredible. People here are as obsessed with celebrity as anywhere but they won't pay for bad food, no matter whose name is above the door.'

'And she'll really speak to me?' Sash asked him.

'Of course.'

Her expression, which at first had been stunned excitement, something I recognised from the first time we'd taken her to Disneyland and were confused as to why she'd looked so meh when Winnie the Pooh and Mickey Mouse had waved at her. And now, like then, the astonishment had slid into a smile and moved through into a full-blown ear-to-ear grin.

'I don't know what to say!'

'Thank you, Tomas?' I suggested from my seat on the sofa next to him.

'Thank you, Tomas!' She jumped up with the apparent intention of hugging him and then stopped, an awareness hitting her of her previous, rather more cool, behaviour towards him. 'Umm... can I give you a hug?'

Tomas remained silent, but stood from where he'd been perched and opened his arms enough to signal that all was forgotten. His generous nature, both materially and emotionally, had been one of the many attractions both then and now.

'Thank you so much!' she said again. 'You've saved my life.'

His eyes met mine over the top of my daughter's head. A restaurant reservation wasn't life-saving and he knew it. We both did. Just as we knew having not had it wouldn't have been fatal. But right now, to my daughter, that was how it felt, and with a welcome thaw in the atmosphere between the two of them, neither I nor Tomas were about to disavow her of that belief.

'I need to call Benoit and see if he's free tomorrow evening,' Sash said as they parted. Tomas remained standing.

'If I know my godson, I can guarantee he's free if you tell him where you're taking him.'

'He's been before?'

'To Quatorze? No.'

Sash looked up from the phone. 'Really?'

Tomas gave a small shrug before resting his hands in his pockets.

'But you got the reservation... and so much more, so easily. Don't you, you know, do that all the time for people?'

'*Non*. Not really. Generally, I am happy to wait.' He paused, gave a brief side to side wobble of his head, then continued. 'Well. Wait impatiently, just as everyone else has to.'

'But...' Sash looked back to me then at him again.

'I only use my powers for good.' He winked.

She bit her lip, her smile still peeking through as our gazes met.

'I did tell you he wasn't such a terrible monster.'

She widened her eyes as if to shoosh me then made a choice on the phone still, as always, in her hand.

'*Bonsoir*, beautiful.'

'Hi!' she replied with a brief wave at the screen, her cheeks taking on a faint blush, the smile automatic. Happy memories fluttered through my mind like so many butterflies being released.

'I'm with Mum and Tomas.'

'Ah, *bon*.'

Sash's clear warning to Benoit not to say anything he wouldn't want either of us to hear was both subtle yet obvious.

'Are you OK?' he asked.

'Yeah, better now, thanks. Sorry about the meltdown earlier.'

'Not a problem. I'm glad you called.'

Benoit's words were casual but caring. Unhurried with no

concern as to whether they were overheard by family members. I liked him even more for it.

'I'm still cross, obviously. Well, more upset than cross, I suppose.'

'Understandable.'

'So! Are you free tomorrow night?'

'For you? Of course,' he replied, not taking a beat.

'Fancy coming with me to Quatorze?'

'The restaurant? Seriously?'

'Yes!' Sash bubbled with excitement and laughter. Benoit's soft, deep tones echoed hers.

'How?'

'Your godfather. I met them when I got home and told them what had happened. Next thing I know, we've got a table at Quatorze and not only that, guess what?' She carried on before he had a chance to. 'Simone Deschamps only told him that I can interview her if I want! *If I want*?' She was practically bouncing now.

'That's fantastic, *ma chérie*. She will love you.'

She blew him a kiss. 'I just need to get all my fangirling out of the way and not make an idiot out of myself.'

'You could never.'

'Oh, believe me, I could, but I need to make sure I don't.'

'I'm afraid I have to go,' Tomas whispered. I stood up, and his hand automatically went to mine. 'I'm sorry. I have an early-morning call. Time zones.' He gave the little head wobble he did when things were mildly annoying. I loved that, as much as he had changed, some things had stayed the same.

'It's fine. You only planned to walk me home and then got dragged into my family drama.'

He gave my hand the gentlest of squeezes to signify that wasn't how he saw it, or if he did, he didn't care.

'Sash, Tomas has to go.'

She turned to him, her pretty face aglow with happiness and excitement, so different from the hurt that had smothered it when we'd first seen her this evening.

'I'm sorry to leave, but I hope you have a wonderful evening tomorrow and that it's useful.'

'It will be! You have no idea!' She hugged him again, this time without hesitation, then turned the phone so that Benoit could see us both.

'*Bonsoir*, Kitty,' he said warmly. 'Pap.' He winked, so much like his godfather, then held up his forefinger and thumb in the shape of a circle. 'Glad to hear your old flames are coming in useful.' The tone was teasing. Tomas tilted his head to one side, one eyebrow raised just a smidge, and his godson barked out a laugh.

'Thank you for that,' Tomas replied. 'I will deal with you when I see you.' The words might have formed a threat but there was nothing but warmth in his voice, and love in his eyes for the young man grinning out from the screen.

Sasha was staring at his godfather, agog.

Tomas and I stepped outside the apartment and I closed the door behind me with a soft click.

'Thank you.'

'It really is my pleasure. I'm so sorry she was let down by people she thought were friends. It's the least I could do.'

I leant back against the door. 'You didn't have to do anything, but thank you for caring. It's so you.' I reached up and laid my hand against his cheek for a moment. He tilted his head into it a little more before I let my hand drop.

'I was so pleased she seemed to have made some friends. She was too. I think the idea of living in Paris really appealed to her, but she's also found it more overwhelming than she expected.

And perhaps a bit lonely. Although obviously meeting Benoit has helped with the latter.'

Tomas leant his shoulder against the wall and looked down at me. 'You know he's... how do you say? Smitten? With Sasha.'

'He is?'

'Totally. Quite pathetic, really. You wouldn't catch me falling for a girl that hard.'

'Is that so?'

'Nope.'

'Not even Simone Deschamps?' I teased. His face was close now.

'I wondered when that might come up,' he replied, his voice soft with that hint of gravel that manifested when he was tired, or turned on. Right now, it seemed he was a little of both. 'And considering I'm here with you right now and wouldn't wish to be anywhere else, I think you have your answer.'

I pushed myself away from the wall, grabbed a fistful of hideously expensive cotton shirt and pulled him towards me, and he let me. The thrill of that control, that allowance, sent a shiver through me. Tomas felt it and I felt his smile as his lips met mine. My hands slid up over the defined chest, slipping under his coat and over the bump of toned trapezoid muscle between his neck and square shoulders, all of it reminding me of his strength. The thought ignited a flame down low in a place that hadn't even smouldered in a long time, let alone known flames. My hips pressed into his thigh as he pulled me closer. I heard Sash laugh but it was way in the distance, barely registering. Right now, right in this moment, it was just Tomas and me. And it felt incredible.

'I have to go,' he whispered in my ear before kissing it and making my knees sink. His arms wrapped tighter. 'Believe me, I don't want to.'

'I can tell,' I teased.

His laugh was deep and soft and full of promise.

'I don't want you to go either.'

'Tomorrow.'

'Tomorrow.'

His hands cupped my face, kissed me again softly before sinking back into something far more raw. And then he broke away, shaking his head. 'If I don't go now, I never will.'

I didn't want him to. I knew that now. For all the going slow, not rushing things, right now, I wanted to rush in like the ocean in a storm.

'Tomorrow,' he repeated and I nodded, beyond speech now. And then he was gone, hurrying down the twisting wrought-iron stairs with me looking over the banister like a lovesick teenager. Which perhaps I was. Just in a fifty-year-old's body.

38

Tomorrow turned out to be postponed. The unsociably scheduled meeting that Tomas had spoken about turned into something that could be very interesting, he explained when he called to cancel early the following morning. The potential client was interested in a one-of-a-kind mural on the living area wall of his new plane and was now on the way home from a business trip in Australia and very keen for a face-to-face meeting to discuss the commission in more depth. Tomas was therefore booked on the next flight out to Bahrain. First class, of course. He'd popped round for a quick hello and goodbye.

'You didn't have to come all the way over here.' I wrapped my arms around his waist as he kissed me good morning. 'Although, now I'm glad you did.'

'Of course I did,' he replied. 'Besides,' his voice dropped a little lower, the timbre hitting me in all the right places, 'I don't get to kiss you like that over the phone.'

'If you've come hoping to get more idolatry from my daughter, I'm afraid you're out of luck. Gabby has taken her shopping for an outfit for tonight.'

'I didn't, although I wouldn't turn it down,' he chuckled. 'Mostly, I'm just glad she doesn't hate me quite so much any more.'

'She never hated you.' I traced my finger along the weave of his linen shirt he wore under his jacket. The blue skies of earlier days, dotted with fuzzy-edged blobs of white cloud, was today replaced with a flat greyscale one that was practically colourless as though the continually drizzling rain had rinsed away the hue of the city until all that was left was grey. A living version of the many prints of Paris that hung on so many walls all over the world.

'Are you allowed to say who the commission is for?'

'No. But I will of course tell you once I know. Although then you're sworn to secrecy too.'

I widened my eyes in a tease. 'I've never dated a celebrity before.'

'Are we dating?' He took a step forward.

'Who said I was talking about you?'

'We're not exclusive?' he murmured as his head bent towards my neck.

If this was exclusivity, I'd take it for the rest of my life...

'I might consider it.'

'Anything I can do to persuade you?' His lips were now meandering their way along my collar bone.

So many things...

A noise in the hall made us both start and then we heard the door to the apartment opposite open and close. Tomas checked his watch.

'*Merde*,' he mumbled under his breath.

'You'd better get going. You don't want to miss your flight.'

He gave me a look that no one had given me in a very, very long time. 'I really do.' The corners of his mouth tipped into the sexy smile that, even in the many intervening years, had never entirely extinguished itself from my memory. And there it was. There he was.

'Me too.' I stood from the sofa. 'But one of us has to be sensible.' I held out my hand to pull him up – or at least give the impression of doing so. At nearly twice my bulk and almost a foot taller, physics tended to favour him. 'Come on. Up you get.'

He did as he was bid.

'By the way, assuming you were referring to me, I don't consider myself a celebrity.'

'Says the man who got my daughter not only a seat at one of the world's most exclusive restaurants but also an interview with its *celebrity* owner.'

'That's different.'

'Because she's an old flame?' I teased.

'I forgot how much of a pain in the arse you were.'

'Remembering now, though?'

His arms slid around me. 'Oh, yeah.'

'So this plane you're being commissioned to paint?'

'Umhmm.'

'You're definitely sure it's the inside? They're not just going to hand you a massive spray can of white and tell you to get going?'

He appeared to consider this as he shrugged his coat back on then gave a tiny tilt of his head.

'Well, that'd be fun too.'

The dull weather had encouraged me to light some candles I'd styled in the ornate period fireplace. Before Tomas had arrived, I'd been cocooned in a squishy armchair with a light blanket, and engrossed in a novel, the easy comfort keeping me both emotionally and physically warm. The room was cosy and snug and the soft light of the candles and reading lamp were successfully keeping away the gloom of the day. Tomas looked around.

'I could stay here all day.'

'I'd like that.'

We both appeared to be considering the idea until I placed my hands on Tomas's arms and turned him bodily towards the door. 'But unfortunately, it's not an option.'

'Well, it is,' he replied, looking back over his shoulder as I pushed him towards the door like a small human bulldozer.

'No,' I said with a little puff, 'it's not. God, you're heavy.'

'Only when I need to be.'

I ignored the allusion in his tone and, as much as possible, the images it conjured in my mind.

'Right,' I said, now that we were at the door. 'Got everything? Passport? Phone? Wallet?'

He nodded as he patted a couple of pockets. 'And glasses.' The smile was rueful but the fact he now had to wear glasses to read did nothing to affect the attraction for me. If anything, it only enhanced it.

'Good.'

'I'll call you when I land.'

'Thanks. Just so I know you're safe.'

'And so I can hear your voice.'

I made to give him a gentle bat away and he caught my hand.

'I mean it.'

I met his eyes. 'I know,' I said softly. I still found it hard to believe that was the truth. I knew he meant it.

His phone pinged and he pulled it from his pocket to read the text.

'This painting,' I pondered as he read.

'Yes?'

'How long would it take?'

'It depends on what he wants exactly and the size. I'll know more after this meeting. It'll be a little while yet anyway as there's various tests that have to be done to ensure the paint I use passes a burn test, apparently.'

I pulled a face. 'That sounds ominous.'

'Hopefully, it's never put to that particular test in the real world but rules are rules, I suppose.'

'Says the man who I remember as never being a particular fan of such things.'

'It depends on what they are and who makes them.' He flicked his dark brows, his eyes flashing with mischief as he leant in for another brief kiss before glancing at the plain face of a watch that Sash had reliably informed me cost more than her entire education. 'I'd better get to the airport.' His tone was of one heading to Madame Guillotine rather than the blue skies and opulent surroundings of a five-star luxury Bahraini hotel. Another kiss and then he was gone, jogging down the stairs and back out into the gloom of the day.

39

'She was soooo nice.' Sash hadn't stopped talking since she'd got home. 'Wasn't she?' She turned to Benoit, her face almost glowing with happiness. 'And oh God, Mum, the food! You have to get Tomas to take you there. It's Ah. May. Zing.'

I had no intention of asking Tomas to take me there. Anything that didn't have a price on its menu was far too expensive for my taste. 'And Simone served us every course. It was just...' She took a gulp of the glass of water I'd just handed her. 'Unbelievable. All these people were looking... it was a bit weird to start but she was just so nice and, like, normal, I kind of forgot about all that after a bit.'

'I'm so glad you enjoyed yourself. Did you have a good night, Benoit?'

'I did, thank you. Seeing Sasha this happy meant that whatever we did would have been a good night.'

She stopped scribbling in her notebook for a moment to lean over and kiss his cheek.

'I imagine those other creators will be a little jealous when they see these videos.'

'That's not why I'm doing it.' Sash's head snapped up.

He raised his hands in defence. 'I know. I was just saying.'

'I'm not interested in getting back at them, or one-upmanship, Benoit.'

He shook his head. 'No.'

Sash went back to her notes and Benoit looked over at me, pulling a 'whoops' face. There was a shadow of a smile but I could see his normal confidence had taken a dip. I gave the merest hint of shrug with one shoulder. It was up to them to discover each other's beliefs and quirks and morals. As much as I liked Benoit, I wasn't about to give him an indication to ignore Sash's reply. He was undoubtedly right and those women who'd pretended to befriend my daughter would likely be turning rather 'vert' with envy when she uploaded her content from this and may well regret their unkindness, not to mention their immaturity. Hopefully, they'd learn from it just as Sasha would have.

I fully expected them to contact her after and perhaps try to mend bridges but it was unlikely to work. They'd hurt her badly and at a time when she'd needed friends. I'd been in two minds whether to caution her against them should they try but she pre-empted me.

'It wouldn't surprise me if my "friends" try and contact me once these videos go up, though.'

'And?' I asked, as casually as I could.

'Not interested,' she said. 'It'd be pretty obvious why they'd be getting back in touch, wouldn't it? They can make their own contacts and come up with their own ideas once they've exhausted the ones I gave them.' She tried to shrug it off but her eyes showed the hurt was still there.

Benoit remained silent, clearly thinking twice about any more accidental faux pas.

'Not that I made this contact myself, obviously. I know that was down to Tomas.' She gave a small smile. 'And you.'

'Was that a roundabout way of saying you approve of my boyfriend?'

'Oh my God, that sounds so weird.'

I snorted a laugh. 'Thanks.'

'No, it's just...' She turned to Benoit beside her. 'You know what I mean?'

He looked from one of us to the other, the faintest sheen of panic on his handsome face.

'Don't drag the poor man into it,' I said, unhooking him from the predicament.

'I'm just not used to...' She tailed off.

'Neither am I,' I allowed. 'Let's just stick to calling him Tomas rather than labelling him, shall we?'

'Partner?' she suggested lightly. But this was my daughter. She'd never been a complicated personality, much like her father, which I'd always felt was a real quality. Mystery and many layers might be interesting in books but I'd always found it so exhausting, not to mention occasionally a tad pretentious, in real life. But even when she attempted to hide her real meaning, like now, I was able to employ the magic X-ray specs of motherhood and see through to her true meaning.

'A little too soon for that. Like I said, "Tomas" is fine for now.'

'Ooh, for now...' She threw a glance at Benoit, who seemed relieved to receive a smile and happily returned it.

'When are you going to interview Simone?'

'Oh! The day after tomorrow. She's invited me to her house and said I can film there. Honestly... it's just...' She let out a squeal of excitement in lieu of being able to find the best superlative to express herself well enough. 'Where is Tomas, anyway? I thought he'd be here tonight?'

'On his way to the Middle East for a meeting,' Benoit said, glancing down at his phone then tapping out a message.

'Oh? For how long?'

'I'm not sure, actually. He just said see you soon,' I said.

'Just a few days.' Benoit filled in the informational gap.

'Right. You OK while he's gone, Mum?'

I let out a laugh. 'Absolutely fine, love. I'm not about to mope about the place, wringing my hands just because my *boyfriend*,' I emphasised the word at her teasingly, 'has gone away for a few days. I'm pretty sure I'll survive.'

'Just checking.'

'I'm meeting Gabby and Ashok for dinner tomorrow night and Reine for lunch the next day.'

'Aww, Ashok was at Gabby's when I got there yesterday. They're so sweet. Like, madly in love. I know I was hoping you two would get together in India but I'm kind of glad you didn't now.'

Benoit was looking interested. As this indirectly involved his godfather and a woman who was as good as his godmother, I could understand his curiosity.

'It would have made it a tad awkward.'

'You were...' Benoit began then stumbled.

'No, we weren't,' I clarified for him. 'Sash and I met Ashok on holiday but he and I are, and only ever were, friends.'

'Ah. Does Gabby know this?'

'Yes,' I answered with another chuckle. 'Everyone does,' I added, just to ensure he knew that Tomas was also entirely understanding of the situation.

A brief flush touched high on his cheekbones. 'I apologise if I seemed...' He made a gesture with his hands as his brain scrambled to find the right words.

'It's fine, Benoit. You're clearly extremely close to both Tomas and Gabby. It's natural for you to be concerned with their happiness. As you yourself witnessed, my daughter did the same with your godfather.'

'I didn't want you hurt again, that's all,' she replied.

'I know. And I appreciate that.'

'You were very tough on him,' Benoit added.

She turned to face him. 'Have you any idea how badly he hurt Mum back then?'

He opened his mouth to reply but apparently, it was a rhetorical question.

'She didn't even come back to Paris once in all that time despite her loving the place! Not once. Not even France!'

'Sash, that's in the past and it's not Benoit's job to try and find a defence for his godfather. Neither of you were even born, so let's move on and live in the present, eh?'

She looked from me to Benoit then back again before letting out a slow sigh.

'Yes, of course. Sorry,' she said, her hand tentatively brushing his. His easy nature accepted the apology and lifted it to his lips, placing a soft kiss there as a reply.

'Good. Now,' I said, pushing myself up out of the chair, the novel I'd finished earlier on the coffee table in front of me, 'I am off to bed as it's way past my bedtime.' I placed a hand on Benoit's shoulder and leant down and kissed Sash's cheek. 'Night, darling.'

'Night, Mum. Love you.'

'Love you too.'

I poured a glass of water in the kitchen, picked up the new book I was looking forward to starting and headed through to my bedroom. Within minutes of getting into bed, I was fast asleep, the book still open on the first page.

40

The city was awash with chestnut blossom and swathes of wisteria as spring put on its finest show in the City of Lights. Love was certainly in the air with Ashok practically living in his new Parisian hotel now that he and Gabby were most definitely an item. It brought me joy to see both of my friends, old and new, so happy. A recent visit home to India had confirmed that this was serious. His mum had loved Gabby from the moment she'd met her and the feeling was mutual.

'I think Gabby video calls her more than I do now!' Ashok had laughed, the happiness radiating from him. I couldn't have been more pleased that he had finally found The One he'd been waiting for and I knew Gabby felt the same.

Sasha and Benoit had also been spending more and more time together, with the apartment being entirely mine much of the time now that she had taken to staying over at his place. I was also pleased to meet some of the true friends she had made in the past month as Simone took her under her wing, not to mention being thrilled to see Vikram, Alaria and Mira last weekend as they finally managed to tie up their busy schedules enough to visit for a few days. Between Simone, Benoit and her apparently new friend, Tomas, Sasha had a very full social diary with pages and pages of notes for new content to create and film.

In the meantime, Tomas and I had taken the opportunity to also spend more time together which meant that I wasn't exactly upset my daughter had practically moved in with Benoit when the same could be said of Tomas and me.

* * *

'Was it good?' Reine had asked the day after Tomas had returned from Bahrain.

'What's that?' I asked as I'd taken a sip of the excellent wine she'd ordered for us. Crisp, not too sweet, a hint of apple-y undertones. The waiter placed her terrine in front of her and I nodded my thanks at him as the Coquilles St Jacques I'd ordered was placed before me.

'The sex, darling. You look like you've been thoroughly... is the expression "rogered"?'

Considering he was currently dripping second-hand wine from his nose, eyebrows and chin, the fact that the waiter continued to look as composed as a Grecian carving was quite astonishing. I, conversely, was now the colour of the fully dressed lobster Thermidor his colleague was serving to the neighbouring table.

'Oh! I'm so sorry! I mean, *je suis très désolée! Très, très, très!* Reine, stop laughing and no, that is most definitely *not* the expression! Where on earth did you hear that?'

'Ah. Shame.'

'Reine!'

The waiter checked that I didn't want my starter replaced. I did not. What I actually wanted to do was disappear down a large hole in the ground. Or a small one. I'd make it work. Reine, on the other hand, was unconcerned about the scene I'd caused.

'So you didn't have sex?' she asked. 'The terrine is excellent, by the way.'

'Great. And...' I swallowed before lowering my voice to a whisper. 'Yes, we did, but I don't exactly need everyone in the restaurant to know.'

'Oh, my darling,' she laughed, placing a bejewelled hand on mine. 'Everyone knew that the moment you walked in.'

'What!'

She gave me a mischievous smile, her bright eyes crinkling at the corners.

'What?' I asked again, feeling the smallest upwards tilt of my lips. In the face of Reine's amusement and nonchalance, it was hard to stay quite so mortified.

'You. You have a, a,' she waved her one hand as she popped a point of toast slathered with the pate in her mouth, 'a glow about you.' She leant in. 'From the rogering.'

'Oh my God!' Laughter snorted out of me. 'You are incorrigible! And where on earth did you pick up such terms?'

She merely wobbled her head, amusement dancing in her eyes once more.

'So?'

'So what?'

'Was it?'

'Was it what?'

'*Ooh la la.*' She rolled her eyes. 'Was it good? The sex? Was it as good as before? Aww, my darling friend, you are blushing. Forgive my nosiness,' she said, not actually making an apology for it at all. It was one of the many things I liked about Reine. She was as you found her – only better.

I took another sip of wine and managed to swallow it this time.

'It wasn't good, no.'

'Ah...'

I leant in. 'It was *incroyable*!' I used the French word because, somehow, that had more emphasis. And believe me, the emphasis was needed.

Reine sat back and clapped her hands in delight. 'Champagne!' she called. 'Great sex always deserves champagne!'

Oh, God. Everyone was now staring once more. I shifted in my seat. And then I began to smile. So what? Who cared about them? I didn't know them so what did it matter? What mattered was that I was here with my friend, having a wonderful time. *And* I'd had fantastic, multi-orgasmic sex the night before. Twice. And once this morning.

This was one of the many other things I'd noticed between my life here and my 'old' life in provincial England. The conversation. At least the conversations I had been having as opposed to those I was having now.

Obviously, that was a bit of a sweeping statement but, for me, the topics in Paris were far more interesting than the latest menopausal symptom, which often seemed a large proportion of the fare offered at home. While those did seem to offer a plethora of choice from which to discuss, I wasn't interested in doing so. Yes, it was there and I, like so many others, was just getting on with it, as I had with the monthly joy of periods for so many years before. Gabby and I had touched on the misery and annoyance of it but had then moved onto far more interesting subjects and for that, I was glad.

And now here, with Reine, the conversation had taken an

entirely different turn indeed! True, this particular topic was unlikely to have come up at home. Without putting Hugh down, things had been different with him. But also because I'd found a new level of relaxation out here – or perhaps regained one – that I'd never had at home, leaving me free to talk about whatever I wanted without embarrassment. Well, at least not too often.

41

It was a few days later, during a meal in the restaurant of Ashok's hotel, that the elephant in the room wandered over and plonked its sizeable bottom on the table.

'I have to take a trip to the vineyard at the end of the week,' Benoit said, his attention on Sasha. 'I wondered if you might want to come? You're free to film whatever you want. Or not film anything if you don't want to.'

'That sounds amazing! You sure that will be OK?'

Benoit looked to Tomas and Gabby, who both nodded to confirm their assent.

'Very sure.'

Sash's eyes sparkled with happiness and creative excitement. Ever since she'd begun her sojourn in Paris, her subscription figures had been increasing at a faster rate than before. The vlog at Quatorze had given them another huge boost. Tomorrow was the upload of the interview she'd done with Simone herself and from the comments she'd received when she'd announced it, we all had our fingers quietly crossed for another advance in her numbers.

Creative pursuits, however talented you were, relied a certain amount on luck. In every endeavour, there was an enormous amount of competition and it was serendipity as to whether you were one that got noticed or not. But Sasha was determined to make her channel the best it could be. It wasn't merely about getting freebies – she'd actually been very select about those who approached her. If she didn't believe in the product, or felt it didn't fit her aesthetic or morals, then she had no qualms about turning it down. I admired that about her. But living in Paris, the opportunity to visit a thriving, not to mention beautiful, vineyard and get exclusive behind-the-scenes access certainly fit the bill.

'Why don't we all go?' Gabby asked. 'Make a weekend of it? It'd be lovely to take a trip all together.' Ashok's hand was curled around hers, as it so often was when we saw them now.

'Sounds great to me,' he said.

'I'm available,' Tomas added. 'You're right, it would be great to spend more than a couple of hours together.'

I felt several pairs of eyes fall on me as the only one who hadn't spoken. The vineyard. The family business. My mind sailed back through the years as thoughts tumbled over themselves. This place, its very existence and the pressure that that had wrought on Tomas had been instrumental in our break-up. Just the thought of it left a sourness in my mind.

Since returning to France, I'd paid it no attention other than cursory during the explanation of how Tomas had nearly ruined it and Gabby had stepped in. Other than that, I had pushed it to a far corner of my mind and left it to rot quietly away with time. But now it had been dragged out to look upon once more.

My gaze lifted to Sash. Her initial enthusiasm had stilled a little as she looked at me and joined the dots of my lack of excitement. Her smile was soft, an understanding in her eyes.

'Although I'm not sure if Mum already had something

planned for this weekend? I should have checked the diary,' she said to Benoit. 'Sorry.'

Her comment sounded natural but I was her mum. I knew. She *so* wanted to go. And the truth was I wanted to spend more time with these people. People I loved and trusted. The vineyard and the problems it had brought were a spectre of the past and I no longer wished to give it power. I most certainly wasn't going to let it haunt my daughter.

'Nothing in the diary, Sash.' I took a deep breath while attempting to appear not to. 'You're right, Gabs. It sounds like a fabulous idea.'

Gabby leant over and kissed my cheek, her other hand lying momentarily on mine.

As we turned back to our meals, drinks and conversations, Tomas bent towards me.

'Are you sure you're OK with this?'

'Yes,' I answered, turning to meet his eyes, his face close to mine. 'All of that was a long time ago and you're free of it now.' I squeezed his fingers as he'd laced them through mine. 'That's all that matters. It was a bit of an unexpected flashback. That's all.'

'I am free of it. And you're here. Everything is perfect.' He lifted my hand, kissed the back of it then stole another at my temple before the waiters arrived bearing puddings.

* * *

Benoit's car rolled along in front of us, Ashok and Gabby in the back seat of Tomas's. And here we were. Once more.

The trees that lined the drive were larger now, providing a serene, shady avenue to approach the large house. A curve in the drive and there it was, looking exactly the same as it had done years ago when the three of us, plus Gabby's latest boyfriend, had come down for a weekend to escape the hot, stifling air of a Paris summer. Tomas's parents were away. At the time, it had seemed perfect timing. Afterwards, I'd realised that hadn't been a coincidence. Perhaps he'd already suspected that I wouldn't be approved of.

'Did you know?' I asked, the thoughts in my head tumbling out.

'Hmm?' Tomas replied, his eyes flicking to me momentarily, his whole being relaxed. Ashok and Gabby were deep in conversation behind us, lost in their own very happy world.

'Before? When we came here.' There was no animosity in my tone. That time had passed. Now I was just curious.

Tomas shifted a little in his seat. 'Did I know what?'

'That I wasn't going to be approved of. Is that why you waited until your parents were away to bring me here?'

He shook his head, the corner of his mouth tipped up. 'That wasn't why I wanted my parents out of the way.'

Ridiculously I felt a faint blush warm my cheeks and shook it off.

'You did know, though,' I persisted. 'Didn't you?'

Tomas let out a sigh.

'No,' he said as he slowed to a stop, the tyres crunching on the gravel drive that framed the front of the house. 'I didn't know.' He applied the handbrake and turned to me. 'But I did suspect.'

'Yes.'

Ashok and Gabby exited from the car and closed the back doors. We remained in the front.

'I should have discussed it with you.'

'No,' I said, my hand touching his jaw. 'Because then it would have ended earlier.'

His eyes shone for a moment as emotion pushed up through the years. 'Quite probably and, selfish as that was, I didn't want that. I wanted to hold on to you for as long as possible. I'd hoped that would be forever but life had other ideas.'

'Your mother had other ideas.'

He didn't reply but I knew he'd heard and he knew I was right.

He looked out towards the beautiful house, his mind elsewhere. Or perhaps not. I leant over and kissed his cheek. 'None of it matters now. Come on.'

A smile lit his face – and my heart. 'Would you like a drink?' The blue gaze hooked mine, lighter now in the late-afternoon sun. 'I've heard this place isn't too shabby.' He grinned. 'Is that the right expression?'

'It is right,' I replied.

'Ah!' He seemed pleased. 'Sasha has introduced me to some new YouTube channels and I heard this phrase the other day. I like it.'

'I'm so glad,' I said, laughter in my voice as Benoit opened the door for me and offered his hand.

'Thank you.'

I caught Tomas's eye as he came around from the other side of the car. 'You've done well with him. You should be very proud.'

Tomas looked at his godson as he returned to Sasha, who was busy filming the exterior of the mansion, her expression slightly agog. I knew the feeling. Like mother, like daughter. She'd had a lot more than I had growing up but neither of us had ever known anything like this.

'In everything but blood, he is my son. I would give anything for his parents to still be alive so that they could see what a good man he is. So that he still had them in his life.'

His voice faltered on the last word and I wrapped my arm around his waist, his own arm mirroring the action. 'But I do believe they are looking down and are proud of him.'

'As they should be, with thanks to you.' I kissed his cheek and snuggled into his side, pride and love for the man he now was overwhelming me as I thought about his words.

I wasn't half so sure about the existence of such an afterlife as he was and we'd had long, deep discussions about such things long ago. Clearly, Tomas's opinions on the subject hadn't altered. Mine, however, had wavered a little. Life changes you. The things that happen. The paths that you take, or that appear before you and before others.

When Sash was at primary school, I'd got chatting to a new mum, Amelia, at the nursery. We'd bonded quickly, which was unusual for me since returning from Paris. We shared the same sense of humour and the same wish of having conversations about something other than our children, meeting up often for a cup of tea and playdates. And then one day, she didn't turn up at the gates. She'd not replied to any messages for a few days, which was unusual but I'd not put any stock in it. People led busy lives. A few days later, I met her husband at the gates. I almost didn't recognise him. Amelia was gone.

She'd been on her way home from visiting her parents. They were all supposed to have been going but George, their son, was feeling grouchy and with the threat of chicken pox running amok around the local schools, they'd decided that just Amelia would go. Ten minutes from home, someone coming the other way had felt replying to a text message was a more important task than keeping their eyes on the road. They'd hit Amelia head-on. They'd walked away with barely a scratch. Amelia had been killed instantly.

'You still believe that then?'

'In an afterlife?' Tomas replied. 'I do.' He turned his head. 'Have you changed your mind?'

'I'm not sure,' I answered honestly. 'I like to think now that there's somewhere wonderful and good that those we love go to. Other than that, I'm ..' I shrugged. 'I'm fuzzy on the details.'

'Who says there have to be details?'

He was right. Why did it all have to be explained? Beliefs so rarely fell into the minutely detailed camp and why should they?

'You lost someone?' he asked, perceptive as ever.

'Yes. A close friend. Many years ago now.'

'Time doesn't lessen our love, or how much we miss them.'

'No. You're right, it doesn't. But I like to think she's up there, happy. Although... how can you be happy when you've left your child and the love of your life behind?' I looked back at him. 'It's very complicated.'

'It is.' Then he kissed me and that was blissfully simple. 'I'm sorry about your friend.'

'And I'm sorry about yours, for you and for Benoit. They made an excellent decision making you his godfather.'

'It wasn't thought so at the time, believe me.'

'And yet they stuck to their guns and look...'

Our gazes landed on Sasha and Benoit, his expression one of deep concentration as Sasha showed him something on the camera, her hands moving in explanation as they did so. 'You helped him become who he is today.'

'The man who's very much in love with your daughter.'

I let out a sigh. 'The man my daughter is very much in love with...'

Tomas turned. 'She is?'

'She is.'

He shifted his weight. 'You don't seem pleased.'

'No.' I shook my head. 'It's not that. She's happy and that makes me happy. I just don't... she's never felt like this about anyone. Not this strongly.' I shrugged, feeling the tears spring to my eyes, the surroundings adding to the emotion. 'I don't want her heart broken.'

Tomas held my gaze for a long moment. The words I hadn't added were still there. *Like mine was*. Both of us heard them, even unspoken.

'I can't promise that,' he said. 'All I can say is that ever since Sasha entered his life, Benoit has been the happiest I have ever seen him.'

I untangled myself from him and rummaged in my handbag, still a little larger than Gabby and Reine would have me carry, and unearthed a pocket pack of tissues. Extracting one, I dabbed at my eyes and nose.

'Look OK?' I asked Tomas.

'Perfect.'

It wasn't true but I knew, in that moment, he believed it to be and for once, instead of batting the compliment away, I took it and we crunched forward up the gravel drive to catch up with the others.

42

While the other four took the tour of the vineyard, Benoit doing the honours, Tomas and I headed off to explore the grounds. Stuffy, chilly wine cellars had far less appeal to me, especially on such a glorious day, than the wild meadows I'd been told a couple of the former horse paddocks had now been turned into: one spring, one summer. As we approached, in the peace of the countryside, the sound of buzzing could be heard on the rippling breeze and there, in front of us, was the source. The spring meadow was alive with both colour and insects, feasting on the pollen of those bright flowers. Wild daises, pink campion, a rambling wild rose that now wrapped itself around the dead trunk of an old oak that had once stood there proudly until a bolt of lightning during a raging summer thunderstorm had cleaved it in two. One half had fallen to the ground, small saplings now sprouting from the length of it. The other half had remained standing, its skeletal remains bleached almost white by the sun, providing shelter for wildlife and a natural obelisk for the rose.

'I'm surprised this was left. Your parents weren't especially interested in nature, or ecology, I seem to remember.'

'People change.'

'Yes. I suppose so.'

'When I took over the place, I was keen to reduce the amount of pesticides and so on being used. There was rather a battle about that.' He pulled a face. 'They weren't keen to help me with the business side but still had opinions about how vines should be grown, it seemed. Gabby, being brilliant as always and despite having her own career, set about finding evidence to support the benefits of working more with nature. And, of course, once she took over, the place ran even more smoothly, made more money and we were able to hire more people who had experience in that aspect of the business. It's been totally organic for the last nine years.'

'I didn't know that.'

He shrugged.

The truth was, I hadn't asked. This part of his life connected me, connected us, too much to the past and I wanted to keep looking forward.

'That's great, Tomas. Well done.'

He huffed out a laugh. 'I did very little.'

'You took the first step. That's often the hardest part. And this,' I turned back to the meadow, 'is stunning.'

'I love it here. I'm rather glad you didn't want to go on the tour. Coming here, especially at this time of day, is one of my favourite things to do.'

'You come here often then?'

'Fairly often. I like to keep up with things even if I'm not involved in running them any more. Thank God. And Benoit sometimes likes my opinion on marketing strategies or images. It's easier to do it when you have the place you're marketing as a backdrop. For some reason, he thinks I have a creative eye.'

'I can't think why he would think that.'

'Me neither. Not a creative bone in my body.'

'If Reine were here, I have a feeling she would say something entirely inappropriate right about now.'

Tomas wrapped his arm around me and pulled me close, my back now resting against the wooden bar fence at the edge of the meadow.

'I have a feeling you're right,' he replied, his voice low and husky as he moved to nibble on my ear lobe and I let go of any thought but of the man in front of me as Tomas slid his hand down the outside of my hip and slowly began ruffling up the front wrap of my dress until I could feel the breeze on my bare skin. His hand lingered at my knicker line, two fingers gently brushing up and down against the lacy elastic.

'Kitty?'

I opened my eyes. 'Yes.' I answered the unasked question and the next moment, Tomas had wrapped both arms around me and my legs automatically wrapped around him. One hand deftly freed the belt of my dress as the other supported me and leant me back towards the fence once more.

* * *

'Did you have a nice walk?' Gabby asked when we all reconvened for dinner that night. There was a twinkle in her eye. She knew. I hadn't told her and I certainly knew Tomas wouldn't have but she still knew.

'Really good, thanks,' I replied, the first glass of sparkling wine going straight to my head.

She grinned widely, scarlet lips enhancing the effect, and gave an almost imperceptible raise of her glass towards me, which I just as subtly returned. The last thing I wanted was to be explaining my afternoon exploits to my daughter.

'Are you having a good time, Sash?' I asked, eager to change the focus.

'It's so beautiful. I feel like I'm in a period film! Benoit's been telling me the history of the house. Did you know one of the owners in the eighteenth century used to be a dairymaid? The lord that owned it fell in love with her and married her and no one in their circle would speak to them. I know class was the be all and end all back then but...' She pulled a disapproving face. 'Snobbery is just... ugh!'

'Mmm. Isn't it?' I replied.

'Anyway,' she carried on, apparently unaware of the slight frisson that had just rippled around the room. 'The last laugh was on them as they persevered and she ended up hosting the best house parties and people were dying to get invites from her. She had maharajahs dripping with jewels, the latest poets, explorers. All sorts. Isn't that brilliant?'

'It is. Are you going to mention that in your vlogs?'

'Definitely. I love that she stayed true to herself and their love and still made it.'

Dinner was served and after, we moved to the drawing room. Tomas asked how Sasha was getting on with her filming.

'I've got some great footage of the house and grounds already. Benoit is going to show me the meadows tomorrow. Did you see them this afternoon?'

'Is he now?' I asked, my eyes flicking to his and catching the faintest blush.

Gabby sniggered and quickly turned it into a cough as I swung my eyes to her.

'Perhaps we could all go?' Tomas suggested.

'Yeah. That'd be...' Benoit seemed a little less enthusiastic.

'Oh, yes! That would be lovely. Maybe we could take a picnic?' Sasha had always loved a picnic and suddenly, she was my little girl again, wishing for a picnic even though it was tipping with rain. So we'd had car picnics and carpet picnics with potted plants around us, pretending we were deep in the jungle.

Of course, her favourite part of *Emma* was the picnic scene. The first time she'd turned to her father, aged twelve, when he'd said something a bit thoughtless and announced that it had been 'badly done indeed', I'd hardly been able to control my laughter. Moments later, having given her opinion, she'd stalked off and we'd been free to burst out laughing, the upset forgotten. It might not have been a marriage of passion but it had been one of love and from it had come the one thing I held above all others.

'A picnic sounds perfect,' Tomas stated, casting a glance at his godson. 'I shall arrange it myself.'

I leant over. 'It's OK. She already likes you,' I said in a loud whisper, with slightly tiddly giggles.

Sash gave me a 'haha' look, pushed herself up from the sofa and came across to where Tomas and I were sitting together on a very small two-seater loveseat. It might not actually have been that small but I'd forgotten just how much space Tomas took up. But I loved it. I loved being snuggled against him and thankfully, judging by the genuine hug that Sash now gave him, my daughter now approved too.

'Well, this seems like a very jolly party.'

The clear evening sky had brought a chill. The old house might be beautiful but can't have been efficient at heat retention. To stave off the coolness, a crackling fire had been lit in the ornate fireplace but those few words sent ice down my spine despite the roaring heat that, just moments ago, had been turning us all a little pink.

43

I felt Tomas shift beside me, sensing the stiffening of my body.

'Grandmère!' Benoit jumped up and hastened towards the sound of her voice. Something inside me acknowledged the warmth in his tone. The joy at seeing her. Clearly, he was accepted as family in every way. I was happy for him and for Tomas in that. But as for other feelings? Right now, there were too many racing about to pin any specific one down. That would come, though. I knew.

I could feel Gabby's eyes burning into me but I refused to look up. Not yet.

'Mama.' She rose next and from the corner of my eye, I saw an embrace. The voice was coming nearer now.

'Gabby, darling. And this must be Ashok. How delightful to meet you at last.'

'And you, Madame Bertholle.'

'Ah, tsk. None of that formality here. Please call me Isobel.'

I practically choked. This from the Queen of Formality. But then Ashok was successful, rich and handsome. He would, of course, meet with approval.

It was Tomas's turn to stand. 'Mama.' He embraced her too. 'You're looking very well. Your cold has gone now?'

'It has, thank you.'

And that's when it struck me. I flicked my eyes across to Sash, who was looking at me with a slightly panicked expression. I ticked the corner of my lips up in an effort to let her know I was fine. Although I wasn't fine. Because what I'd realised was that they knew. They all, apart from Sash clearly, knew this woman was going to be here.

'Grandmère, this is Sasha, who I told you about,' Benoit began.

Sash flicked her eyes up to him and then to me.

An almost imperceptible nod gave her the go-ahead to proceed. But if that woman began attacking my daughter the way she'd torn me down back in that restaurant, my God, there'd be hell to pay.

But she didn't. Incredibly, she asked how Sasha was liking her time in Paris, what the journey down here had been like and whether she'd enjoyed the tour. I saw Sasha visibly relax. Apparently, I'd unwittingly set my daughter up to expect the same treatment. I felt a wave of nausea wash over me. Not for the Koh-i-noor would I have done that and yet I had. But then again, I hadn't expected to ever see Madame Bertholle this weekend. Or ever. And nobody had chosen to tell me. That was the worst part. Yes, it had been a long time ago and I'd done my best to push it out of my mind. Tell myself it didn't matter now. But I hadn't expected this, not tonight. In time, perhaps, if our relationship continued to strengthen. But not tonight and without warning. I needed to get out.

'And this is Kitty.' She turned to me before I could make my escape. Tomas's hand went to rest on mine but I moved it away and stood. At least this way, I had the height advantage on her, if nothing else. It was pathetic, I accepted that, but I needed something. Although she probably took it as a sign of respect that I was standing for her.

'Madame Bertholle.'

'It's been a long time.'

'Yes. Hasn't it?' I replied, catching the note of coolness in my voice and feeling it settle all around me. Part of me felt bad for raining on the parade but the other part was still furious that I'd been ambushed.

'You look well,' she continued.

'Thank you.' I made no effort to return the compliment, if that's what it was. One was never sure with this woman. I'd initially thought she was pleased with my appearance years ago when she'd complimented me on my dress. It was only as the dinner progressed that I'd realised it was another dig. That I'd clearly not had anything that would meet her approval in my wardrobe so I'd had to borrow one of her daughter's dresses, which she, of course, had recognised.

'If you'll excuse me, it's rather warm in here. I'm going to get some air.' With that, I left the room.

I stalked out through the flagstoned hall. Perhaps that was terribly rude but I didn't care. She'd hurt me all those years ago and I had thought I was over it, that it didn't matter any more, but actually, it did bloody well matter! Especially as I'd unwittingly made my daughter panic about her own acceptance in the Great Woman's Presence, having relayed her the tale of 'back in the day'.

I stepped out into the cold, clear night. Above me, the deep navy sky was pinpricked with a million stars. As I stared up, thoughts racing, a shooting star sailed across the darkness, its tail burning brightly for just a moment before it flared out and disappeared from view.

'Did you make a wish?'

I whirled around at the deep voice.

'I don't think you want to know what I wished for, Tomas.'

He looked at me for a moment and I glared back.

'No,' he said eventually. 'Probably not.' Silence dropped back between us. 'Are you coming back in?'

'No.'

'It's cold, Kitty. You can't stay out here all night.'

'I can do what I bloody well please, Tomas. And I don't accept you, or anyone else, telling me what's right or wrong, or what I should or shouldn't do any more!'

'Kitty...'

'You knew, didn't you? All of you knew she'd be here.'

He heaved in a deep breath, paused then let it out on a sigh.

'She has an apartment in the house. The whole thing is too much for her now so much of it is only opened for guests.'

'So, it wasn't even that she *might* be here? It was a certainty!'

He opened his mouth as if to contradict then closed it again before speaking. 'Yes.'

I huffed out a laugh entirely devoid of humour. 'And here I was thinking all this was behind us.'

'It *is* behind us, Kitty!'

'You *lied* to me, Tomas! You all lied to me and Benoit lied to my daughter! It might be by omission but it was still deceitful.'

'Leave Benoit out of it. This is between me and you.'

'No, Tomas. It's not. He should have told Sasha that your mother would be here just as you should have told me!'

'If we had, would you have come?'

'Of course I bloody wouldn't!' I snapped back.

He held out his hands as if that were enough reasoning for him to have been correct in his choices.

'But I should have had a choice. As should Sasha.'

'Who also wouldn't have come because of what you'd told her about my mother!'

'I told her the truth, Tomas! That's all!'

'She's changed. You heard what she said about formalities.'

'Yes, to a man whom she couldn't help but approve of.'

'It's not just that.'

'Not *just* that?'

He pushed his fingers back through his hair and let out an exclamation of frustration before blowing out another breath.

'Please. Come back in. Mama is quite upset.'

It was the final straw.

'Oh? Is she? Is she upset, Tomas? I'm so sorry. I tell you what. You go back in and comfort your mama. My daughter and I will be on the next train to Paris anyway so all reasons for her being "upset",' I made the shapes at him, sarcastic in my hurt, 'will be swept away from her.' Anger and snippiness was all I could manage right now. It was either that or let out the wrenching, twisted sob caught in my throat and I was certainly not going to give Tomas, his mother, or any of them the satisfaction of seeing that. It would come, in time, but not yet. Not here.

'Kitty, there's no need to be—'

'Be what, Tomas? Be upset that you lied? Be upset that I was so *stupid* to believe I could trust you for a second time? Be upset that I'm now going to be the one to break my daughter's heart because her boyfriend is also a liar?'

'Kitty.' His tone was a warning.

'You're right, Tomas. He *is* your son in everything but blood.'

I pushed past him, shivering now, although I wasn't sure if it was from the cold or sheer rage. His footsteps were close behind me and I cursed his long legs as he caught up to me just inside the doorway.

'Kitty, wait.'

I spun around. 'Why, Tomas? Why should I wait? Because this time, you bothered to follow me?'

He stopped a little short of me. 'What?'

'I waited for you, Tomas. Do you know that?' Tears thickened my words. 'I waited for you to follow me out at that restaurant or at the very least to come round later that evening. To explain what had happened. To apologise for how your mother treated me. But no. You did nothing. So I went home. And I'm going home now.'

'You said all this was behind us! That none of it mattered now!'

'And I thought that was true. I was convinced it was but you know what? It still hurts, Tomas. I loved you! I loved you more than...' My breath hitched. 'More than anything. And I lost you.' I shook my head. 'No. I didn't lose you. You were taken from me because I wasn't deemed good enough and that judgement, because it stole so much from me, had consequences for the rest of my life! I was always worried I wouldn't be good enough so I bent over backwards to try and please everyone. To make them like me! Because the one person I needed to "like" me when I was young didn't.' I swiped at my tears. 'Saying it out loud now... it seems ridiculous but that's the truth, Tomas. However ridiculous it is.'

Silence, heavy and uncomfortable, settled between us until, eventually, he broke it. 'But you're prepared to break your daughter's heart instead of letting her make her own judgement?'

'No. Instead of letting Benoit break it.'

'She's an adult, Kitty! She'll make mistakes. We all do! Some of us forgive ourselves and forgive others. That's the difference.'

I took a step closer until I was practically touching his chest and glared up at him. 'What the hell is that supposed to mean?'

'It means that yes, my mother was incredibly rude and disrespectful to you that day and I was too weak to stand up for either you or myself. And I should have come after you. Gabby told me to, of course.'

'She always did have more balls than you.'

The briefest flicker of a smile flared and faded, just as the shooting star had earlier.

'True. But you didn't fight either.'

'What? So now it's my fault?' I shook my head. 'You're unbelievable.'

He caught my arm as I moved to stride off. 'That's not what I said. But neither of us fought for "us", did we? And no, I didn't come to you because as I said, I was weak. And because I knew you weren't.' He paused. 'I thought you would come to me.'

'You thought I'd come and crawl back after that?'

'No, no. Of course not! The opposite. I thought you'd come over to yell at me. Justifiably. But I thought it would give me the opportunity of at least trying to explain...'

'And that explanation was?'

He shook his head. 'I didn't have one. I hadn't got that far. The only thing I knew was that I loved you.'

The silence of the house settled around us, interspersed with the odd creak as it made itself comfortable for the night.

'Tomas... what am I doing here?'

'What do you mean?'

'What are we doing? Why are we trying to recapture something that was dead and buried a long time ago?'

'Don't say that.' He stepped closer, the sadness in his voice piercing my already fracturing heart.

'Why not? It's true! It's too late, Tomas.'

'No, it's not. It's never too late. Just because it didn't happen then doesn't mean we can't have something now! You know that!'

'Do I? Or am I just pretending? Pretending to be someone I'm not. The carefree divorcee living life to the full!'

'I thought you were happy here.'

I huffed out a sad laugh. 'So did I.'

'Then why?'

I rounded on him. 'Because you lied. Because you *all* lied.'

'I didn't think you'd give it a chance if I told you and I was right.'

'So you decided to make the decisions for me? Just like your mother did for you in your life?'

He stepped back.

'Low blow, Kitty.'

I squared my shoulders. He was right but I was hurting.

'You blindsided me, Tomas. You should have told me. Perhaps, with all the information, with warning, you might have even convinced me to come. But this way?' I gestured back towards the room. 'Have you any idea how I felt when she walked in?'

The unsure expression on his face told me he hadn't a clue.

'Like I was back in that restaurant, in borrowed clothes, feeling entirely out of place and not good enough. Not good enough for her and not good enough for you.'

'Kitty, you know that's not true,' he said, moving back towards me.

I stepped back. 'Yes! I do. That's the point, Tomas. I do know that. I'm a fifty-year-old woman who now knows her own mind and yet, without even trying, she still made me feel like I wasn't enough.'

'She really has changed, Kitty. If you could—'

Laughter drifted from the other room. My daughter's and another, older one mingled together. I should be happy for her. I knew that. I turned away from him and strode up the corridor back to the drawing room.

Everyone looked up as I opened the door. Sash was perched on a chair close to Madame Bertholle, my daughter holding her phone in front of them as she evidently showed her something, their happy smiles cutting into me.

'I'm sorry, Sash, but we have to go.'

Sash's face paled. 'Why? Is it Dad? Has something happened—'

Benoit's arm went to her shoulder, drawing her in.

'No, no.' I hurried over, wrapping my arm around her waist. Benoit got the message and stepped back. 'Everyone's fine.'

'Then... why?' Sash looked across to Tomas. His hair was slightly askew from where he'd run his hands through it and his brow was furrowed. I knew he was angry with me but I didn't care. Right now, I wanted to be away from him. From all of them.

44

'I think I may be able to answer that.' The upper-class tones cut through the silence. 'Perhaps, if you could stay a little longer, I can explain.'

'I don't think—'

'Mum?' Sash interrupted, looking between us. 'You always say about giving people a chance to explain.'

What a moment for my own altruism to bite me in the arse!

'You have a wise and kind mother, Sasha.'

'I seem to remember you didn't think I was wise enough to be deemed a suitable partner for your son.'

In my peripheral vision, I saw Tomas's head snap towards me.

A flutter of memory crossed her features before they settled back into their usual serene coolness. I was almost ashamed of the pathetic sense of achievement I felt, knowing I'd touched a nerve.

'Would you mind if we both sat?' she asked, indicating the chair opposite the sofa she was sitting on. I hesitated but, after a beat, crossed to the chair she had indicated and perched on it. I had no intention of getting comfortable.

'Thank you.' The smile was brief but gracious.

'Shall we go and—' Ashok, ever the diplomat, began but Madame Bertholle shook her head.

'I would like you all here, if you don't mind.'

It seemed that despite Tomas's reassurance his mother had changed, she was still the one calling the shots and telling people what she wanted them to do. Inner Me rolled her eyes.

Isobel continued. 'I owe Kitty not only an explanation, but also an apology.'

Inner Me fell over. Outer Me was glad she was sitting down.

'Thank you,' she said, once everyone took their seats again. She turned back to face me. 'And thank you, Kitty, for allowing me this chance to speak to you.'

I swallowed and gave a brief nod.

'If I were in your shoes, which, by the way, are beautiful...' She cast an appraising eye over the bargain postbox-red pair of stilettos I'd got in a designer outlet back in the UK but never worn. Until I got to Paris. Until I'd regained the confidence to do so.

'Thank you.'

She flickered a smile and I was surprised to see the insecurity there.

'When we met before, I was unforgivably rude. Which is why, although you have been kind enough to stay and listen, I do not expect forgiveness. However, I do not wish to go to my grave—'

'Mama!' Tomas interceded.

Madame Bertholle waved her hand, amusement softening her features. 'Ah, Tomas.' She leant forward in a conspiratorial manner. 'He does worry so.' There was a pause as she straightened, the ramrod-straight back still in play. I couldn't help but admire that she'd kept her excellent posture. 'And I know I am exceptionally lucky that he does. Lucky that either of my children even speak to me, let alone care, after how I behaved. Neither of them spoke to me for some time after that day. Did you know that?'

I glanced at Tomas but he was looking down at his hands.

'Yes.' My voice came out as a croak and I cleared my throat. 'Tomas told me. I'm sorry for that.'

Madame Bertholle's eyes widened in astonishment. 'Kitty, darling girl.' She shook her head. 'Why should you be sorry? You did nothing but try to please me. You wore my daughter's dress, despite it not being your style. It wasn't even Gabrielle's style but she would also wear it just to please me.' She adjusted her position and a wince of pain marred her expression for a moment.

'Are you all right?' My question was automatic.

'I'm fine. I'm old, that's all.'

'I only hope I look as good as you when I'm older.' Sash, sitting near us both, spoke.

Madame Bertholle smiled and laid her hand, wrinkled, with a light-brown sunspot near the wrist, over the top, contrasting with Sash's pale, youthful one.

'That's very kind of you, Sasha.' She looked back to me. 'Your daughter is a credit to you. Talented, kind and beautiful,' she said as she turned back to Sasha. Her hand lifted to my child's cheek. 'But remember, my dear, looks are not everything. It is what is in the heart that counts. Although, from the short acquaintance I have had with you tonight, and from the many stories I have heard from Benoit, I think your *maman* has already instilled that in you.'

I gave a small tilt of my head as Madame Bertholle focused her attention back on me. 'I tried my best.'

'As you did on that day. And the truth was, you were a delight.'

Inner Me had just staggered to her feet. At this, she went down again, out for the count.

For a moment, I was silent. I could feel everyone's eyes on me and then the laughter burst out. Unexpected and taking us both a little by surprise. 'You could have fooled me!' I said, genuinely amused.

She returned a smile but hers was shaded with embarrassment. 'That was rather the point, I'm afraid.' A deep breath, followed by a sigh. 'I was so arrogant back then. How I had any friends, I don't know. Although perhaps I didn't. And that was all deserved.'

'Madame Bertholle, you really don't have to—'

But she held up her hand. 'I do. For you, for my children,' she glanced at Sasha, 'for your child, and for me.' Her bright eyes hooked onto mine and I saw the pain in them. 'Please.'

I nodded my acceptance.

'I had such great plans for my children. Expectations. But what right did I have to choose what they did with their precious lives? To dictate who they loved and see off anyone I deemed "unworthy"?'

The word stung, even now.

She saw. 'I'm sorry.'

'It's fine. It was a long time ago.' The response, even after all I had said to Tomas, was automatic.

'And yet it still hurts. I know. And I am truly sorry. Tomas has never stopped loving you. Every day he's lived without you was because of me.'

'Maman, this is all irrelevant now.' Tomas stepped forward.

'Is it, my darling?' She turned back to me. 'I separated him from the love of his life and he thinks it's irrelevant.'

'I think what he means is that we have both lived other lives.'

'You did. And I hope you were happy.' She turned to Sasha. 'I can only imagine the joy that this child brought into your life.'

'Most days,' I teased, giving Sasha a wink. Her jaw was tight with anxiety but at this, I saw it relax.

It's OK, it told her. *I'm OK.*

'The sleep deprivation is the worst, *non?*'

'Oh, God... I was so tired, I once left part of a new pushchair I'd just bought in a car park and sparked a bomb scare.'

Madame Bertholle's hand went to her mouth, her eyes round with surprise before crinkling with amusement.

'Oh, *merde!*'

I let out a snort of laughter. Somehow, those words coming from this woman seemed so incongruous. This fierce, arrogant, unforgiveable snob... but she wasn't. Not any more.

'Yes, it was a bit. My husband was furious.'

From the corner of my eye, I saw Tomas shift position.

Madame Bertholle rolled her eyes. 'Men.' It said it all. 'I love my children very much,' she continued. 'I thought, at the time, I was doing the right thing. And although men have no idea about some things, see above,' she pointed her finger in the air as if to highlight our previous conversation, 'sometimes, they do. My husband was very wise in many ways. He told me to let my children be who they wanted to be, do what they wanted to do and love who they wanted to love. But, of course,' she waved a hand, the large diamond ring I remembered admiring glinting in the lamplight, 'I knew better. Or at least, I thought I did. I took my husband for granted.'

She gave a tiny shake of her head and I noticed the tremor in her hand. Without thinking, I leant forward and rested my hand over hers. She raised her eyes, now swimming with tears, and met mine before allowing her gaze to drift to her son.

When she spoke, her voice was barely audible. 'Oh, Tomas. What did I do?'

'Madame, please.' Tears now swam in my own eyes.

'Please call me Isobel.'

'Isobel.' The word felt unfamiliar and not quite right on my tongue but a lot had changed this evening, including the spectre lodged in my mind of the woman in front of me.

'We can't regret the past,' I said. 'There is nothing we can do to change it now. All we can hope to do is learn from it.'

'So wise. You would have got on so well with my husband. He would have loved you. He did, in fact. We had one of the worst rows of our marriage that day after dinner. He saw something in you that I hadn't. That I didn't want to. That you made Tomas happy. I had grand ideas about marrying my son off to the daughter of another vineyard owner. A merging of the two empires!' She gave a grand sweep of her arm then rolled her eyes. 'I can see the ridiculousness of it now. The world doesn't work like that these days and it shouldn't. As it turned out, that daughter is now happily married to another woman so that shows how much I knew. Once again, my husband was wiser than I.

'I lost two years of my children's lives due to my arrogance. I am lucky that they forgave me and if it hadn't been for my husband's secret machinations in mending that breach, it would likely have been a lot longer. I was, of course, far too proud to apologise or even consider that I had done anything wrong. You see,' she swallowed hard and the tears returned to her eyes, 'it was only when I lost my husband that I realised what I'd had. How lucky I had been. I'd been far too arrogant to appreciate him when he was alive and once he was gone...' She shrugged one slim shoulder. 'Well, then it's far too late for all of us, isn't it? God knows what he ever saw in me.' Her gaze dropped to her lap, her thoughts, I guessed, in the past.

'I am sure you are being too hard on yourself. He was, as you said, quite wise. I think perhaps he saw the best qualities in both of us.'

'So kind,' she said. 'Too kind.' She looked up. 'Do you still have to leave?'

Sash was looking at me. As, I now noticed, was everyone else.

Gabby stood. 'We should have told you that Mama would be here.'

I now stood too. 'Yes,' I replied, catching Tomas in my glance as I too stood. 'You should have.' I looked down at their mother and touched her shoulder, feeling the thin, fragile bone beneath the silk blouse. Tomas's concern for his mother, especially with his caring, attentive nature, was entirely understandable. 'But I appreciate why you didn't.'

'I'm so sorry!' Gabby's words bubbled out as she flung her arms around me. 'So very sorry! I thought I was about to lose you for a second time! And this time, I'd lose my goddaughter too.' The last word was almost entirely swallowed by a sob.

'You do realise you're not actually her godmother, don't you?' I replied, half-laughing, half-crying myself now.

'Semantics,' she sniffed into my shoulder.

I gently pulled her back so that I could hold her face. 'Although, if Sash agrees, perhaps we could make that official?'

Gabby's tears burst through again as Sasha, also now in floods, nodded vigorously and flung herself at us.

A few minutes later, when we had all recovered a little, although our make-up was beyond help and we were beyond caring, Benoit returned from a brief disappearance with several bottles of the vineyard's best sparkling wine – champagne in everything but name.

'I think a toast?' he suggested, holding a bottle aloft.

'At least one!' Gabby agreed, her hand still clasped around her 'new' goddaughter's. 'Wait. Where's Tomas?'

In all the commotion, none of us had noticed that he was no longer in the room.

'He'll be in the rose garden,' Isobel said, her eyes finding mine.

45

I remembered the way from earlier. The roses were in bud but it was still a little too early for the flowers to be out. Tomas had promised to bring me back when they were in full bloom. Neither of us had mentioned the fact that, by then, my six-month lease on the apartment would be coming to an end. I couldn't live off my savings indefinitely and I'd have to make a decision about what the next step in life would be.

He didn't turn as I approached. The borders were all artfully uplit but it was the large, bright moon that highlighted his profile against the darkness.

'*Bonsoir.*'

'*Bonsoir,*' he replied, still not turning.

I walked up and took a seat next to him on the acacia wood Lutyens-style bench.

'Thank you for accepting my mother's apology.'

I took a deep breath of the cool night air. 'It took a lot for her to do that. I appreciate that.'

'Even so.'

'I know.'

'I'll drive you to the station. I don't want you in a cab alone at this time of night.' He turned his face towards me, the jaw tight, the eyes sad. 'I know I have absolutely no right to insist, or even ask that, but I'd appreciate it if you would let me.'

'What's that?' In the low light, I could see he was holding something.

He held it up to the bright light of the moon. A torn photograph taped together, the tape now yellowed with age. Two young, laughing faces looked out of it, full of love and hope and expectations.

'You kept this?' I said, taking it off him carefully to look at it.

'All of them.' His voice was quiet.

'Are they all repaired, like this?'

He nodded. 'Stupid, I suppose... but it was all I had left of you. Of us.'

'Oh, Tomas.'

He took the photo carefully back from me. 'And now you're leaving once more. Even I'm not stupid enough to think I'll have a third chance.'

'Tomas?'

His eyes remained focused on the past in his hands. 'Yes?'

'Tomas, look at me.'

He heaved a deep breath, let it out slowly then did as I asked.

'I'm not leaving.'

The brow creased, eyes widened just a little. '*Pardon?*' In confusion, he dropped back into French.

God, that accent, that language, was so ridiculously sexy. Or perhaps it was just him.

'I'm not leaving,' I repeated.

'But you said... you said we should have told you. And you were absolutely right. Of course. I can see that now.'

'Was that when you left?'

He dropped his head. 'I didn't want... didn't need to hear any more.'

I thumped him on the arm. 'You idiot.'

The bark of laughter he emitted startled a nearby owl who flew off with an indignant hoot.

'*Merci pour ça.*'

'You missed the good bit.'

He shifted around, his thigh brushing mine now. 'There was a good bit? I thought... I assumed...'

'Hasn't life taught you anything? You can never assume, Tomas. What's the point of getting older if you never get any wiser?' I teased, knowing he could hear the smile in my voice even if his shadow hid my features from the light of the moon.

'So what else did I miss?' His hand found mine. 'Apart from the fact that you're not leaving?' Excitement and relief tangled themselves within his words.

'Well, your sister is officially going to be Sash's godmother.'

'*Vraiment?*' he asked, emotion sliding him once more back into his native tongue.

'Yes!'

Joyous laughter rang out in the still night. 'She must be overjoyed. She and her ex chose not to have children but she's always been desperate to be an aunt. Obviously, I let her down on that part.'

'You didn't let anyone down, Tomas. That's just how life played out. And this way, she got to choose her own godchild.'

'That is a very good way of looking at it.'

I squeezed his hand. 'It's the only way of looking at it. And you're also missing the best bottles of plonk Benoit could find. Which means you're making me miss them, which is even worse.'

He gave a low chuckle. 'Then we'd better rectify that, sooner rather than later if my sister is celebrating.'

'I hardly think the supply is going to run out!'

'That is a very good point.'

'Although... perhaps best to be safe.' I pushed myself up from the bench, but Tomas's hand stilled me.

'What is it?'

He stood and I tilted my chin up to his face as he looked down at me in the moonlight.

'When you said you're not leaving, did you only mean tonight?'

'Yes, I meant tonight.'

I felt the tension return to his body.

'But I'm open to discussion on the rest.'

And then his arms were under my knees, mine around his neck as he swept me up and spun us both around in the moonlight.

EPILOGUE
TWO MONTHS LATER

The thought of getting married again had never crossed my mind. But then, neither had the possibility of ever seeing Tomas Bertholle again. Coming to Paris was meant to lay ghosts to rest. To make new memories of Paris. And I had most certainly done so. Very happy ones. Happier still because they included the people I'd made those first treasured ones with and now that the painful ones were vanquished, washed away by happy tears and joyful laughter, I could look back on the rest with an easier eye and share them with my daughter.

I watched her now, in her bridesmaid dress of the softest rose pink, made by hand, by Reine.

'Better than Dior!' Sash had exclaimed when she'd spun around at the final fitting.

'She looks so beautiful,' Benoit said as he took the seat next to me. 'I don't know what I did to deserve her.'

'I know the feeling.' I turned to face him. 'Hurt her and I will kill you and make it look like an accident.'

'And I'll help her move the body,' Tomas's deep tones added as his hands rested on my bare shoulders.

Benoit nodded. 'Understood. I'm going to leave now. The conversation has taken rather a dark turn.' His mouth was serious but delight, and love, danced in his eyes. 'Congratulations again,' he said, kissing me on both cheeks before standing and hugging his godfather. 'Congratulations, Paps.' He leant in with a loud whisper. 'Don't mess it up this time.'

'Believe me, I have no intention of doing so.'

'Good. Because I'm pretty sure Sash will help me move a body too.'

'Without a doubt.' They grinned, exchanged another hug and we watched as Benoit strode back towards Sasha, her arm reaching out to slide around his waist as he approached, the love we'd seen in his eyes reflected in hers.

'Thank you for this,' I said.

'Thank you,' he laughed, facing me. 'For marrying me. I know I said about not rushing things and here we are…'

'There was no reason to wait. As your mum said, life is short.'

'Actually, what she said was what the hell was I waiting for?'

'True. She's wiser than she thinks.'

He smiled and took in his mother, who was now sitting with Sash on one side and Benoit on the other, scrolling through the new phone I'd bought her so that she could video call her family. Technology she'd apparently resisted until now.

'You didn't need to go to all this effort.'

'You always wanted a celebration when you got married. Although I think this is going to look incredibly tame compared to Ashok and Gabby's wedding next month!' His eyes were back on me now, soft, smiling, insanely sexy.

'True. But I can't wait!'

'Me neither. Although I'm a little more excited about our honeymoon travelling around India prior to it.'

I leant over, pretending to whisper. 'Me too. But don't tell Gabby!'

He held a finger to his lips.

We sat for a moment, hands clasped together, the diamond ring Isobel had gifted me, a Berthollé family heirloom, catching the light of the low sun.

'You remember that? About us talking about a wedding like this?'

'I remember everything, *ma chérie*. How could I forget?' He caught my chin gently in his hand. 'I never forgot you. I knew from the first moment I saw you that we were meant to be. That somehow, in some way, you'd come back to me.'

'You did?'

'Always. I always believed it. I had to. There was never going to be anyone else. You were meant to be mine.'

I raised an eyebrow.

He wiggled his head. 'You know what I mean.'

I did and he was right. As much as I'd tried, there had always been a hole in my heart that nothing could fill. Not the love of a decent man or the overwhelming love for the child I never even knew I'd wanted. But now, in the lowering sun at the end of a perfect summer's day in a rose garden overflowing with exquisitely scented blooms, that gap, that missing piece in my heart had finally been slotted back into place.

MORE FROM MAXINE MORREY

Maxine Morrey's next uplifting, heartfelt romance is available to order now here:

https://mybook.to/MaxineMorreyNewBackAd

ACKNOWLEDGEMENTS

If you're here, reading this, thank you for choosing to visit Paris with Kitty and Tomas. I very much hope you enjoyed the trip! I love reading the acknowledgements in books – it's always interesting to take a peek behind the scenes, isn't it? So thanks for taking that extra bit of time to peer behind this particular curtain.

In anticipation of this book, Boldwood ran a competition to name the hero of the piece so I'd like to say thank you to Valerie Findlay, the winner of the competition for their suggestion of 'Tomas'. Thanks for taking the time and effort to enter! I very much hope you enjoyed the story.

Writing is a rather solitary occupation, and, although it suits many of us authors quite well, there is no doubt that having pals on your side helps enormously. When those pals are also writers, it's even better because they understand all the bonkers stuff that drives you round the twist or makes you burst into tears – sometimes both. And then they help make it better through kind words, advice, hugs (if you're lucky enough to be able to see them – not often enough in my case) and the simple fact of being there.

With the above in mind, I want to first of all thank Rachel Burton, who has been an absolute stalwart of friendship and support during the creation of this book. Thank you for all the wise (and sometimes hilarious) advice, and apologies for all the messages, screenshots, questions and rants. I don't think I'd have got there without you.

Also big hugs go to Fiona Walker, who makes me laugh so

much and is an absolute joy to know. I'm so grateful we met. Love and hugs to the fabulous Sarah Bennett, who is always so kind and knowledgeable and generous in sharing said knowledge. Can't believe we didn't get around to clinking glasses last time. Looking forward to the next opportunity!

Thanks, of course, as always go to the fantastic team at Boldwood Books, who are now getting too numerous to mention individually! Thank you to editor, Caroline Ridding for stepping in to take the reins of this one. Much appreciated are also the eagle eyes of my copy editor, Cecily Blench and proofreader, Emily Reader. Special love goes to Sarah Ritherdon for obvious reasons.

Lastly, but never least, thank you to James. There's been a lot going on during the writing of this book – a debilitating Crohn's flare, a new puppy (oh my God, how I'd forgotten the energy and time such a tiny creature can suck out of you!), as well as selling our house after nearly a year of trying to keep it looking perfect 'just in case' and moving across the country. It's been a lot – as often seems the way – and being apart for much of it until we could finally relocate was not the easiest. Thank you for helping me through, one day at a time. I love you.

ABOUT THE AUTHOR

Maxine Morrey is a bestselling author whose novel *You've Got This* won Best Romantic Comedy Novel at the RNA Awards 2024. She lives in the West of England and when not wrangling with words can be found reading, creating, and taking walks in nature. Also known to enjoy gazing out of windows.

Download your exclusive bonus content from Maxine Morrey here:

Follow Maxine on social media:

- facebook.com/MaxineMorreyAuthor
- instagram.com/scribbler_maxi
- pinterest.com/ScribblerMaxi

ALSO BY MAXINE MORREY

#No Filter

My Year of Saying No

Winter at Wishington Bay

Things Are Looking Up

Living Your Best Life

You Only Live Once

Just Say Yes

You've Got This

Just Do It

Be Your Best Self

Reach for the Stars

Never Too Late

Boldwood

Boldwood Books is an award-winning fiction publishing company seeking out the best stories from around the world.

Find out more at www.boldwoodbooks.com

Join our reader community for brilliant books, competitions and offers!

Follow us
@BoldwoodBooks
@TheBoldBookClub

Sign up to our weekly deals newsletter

https://bit.ly/BoldwoodBNewsletter

www.ingramcontent.com/pod-product-compliance
Ingram Content Group UK Ltd.
Pitfield, Milton Keynes, MK11 3LW, UK
UKHW041450201125
9091UKWH00040B/563

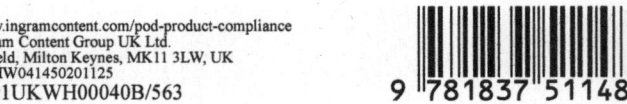